TALES OF VERDANT

Doc Honour

Copyright

The characters and events in this book are fictitious. Any similarity to real persons, living or dead, is coincidental and not intended by the author.

Cover image by Lumina Obscura from Pixabay

For information contact: DocHonourBooks.com

ISBN 979-8-9875022-3-5 (paperback)
ISBN 979-8-9875022-4-2 (hard copy)

Introduction

This anthology of short stories actually started before my novel *Not Like Us*, which was published before it. I developed the concepts of this future universe as a background and setting for the stories, intending to have three stories from each of the four Verdant countries. About halfway through, I was working on "Duty to Society." The story grew, with deeper and richer themes, and had exceeded ten thousand words. (This version is about 5700 words.) The leader of my local writing group, a fine author named Phil Walker, suggested strongly that the story had sufficient meat to fill a novel. With some trepidation, never having attempted a novel, I took his advice. I set aside the short stories and wrote *Not Like Us*. With its completion, and with a wealth of additional details about the world of Verdant, I returned to this anthology.

What is it like to live on a world that is about to destroy itself? How do people survive with the sword of Damocles hanging over them?

I have some real-life experience. For about ten years, I had regular business in the nation of Israel during the time of the Second Intifada. Protesters disrupted lives with stone-throwing, gunfire, rocket attacks, and suicide bombings. I was in a taxi when stones were thrown at it. A suicide bombing took out a family Bar Mitzvah at a beachside hotel ten miles from the similar beachside hotel I was in. Yet one incident stood out. A bus was bombed one morning in Jerusalem. Hearing the news, I stepped out onto the balcony of my high-rise hotel and looked out over the city. The smoke from the bombing rose over buildings a half-mile away. Closer to me, however, was a major thoroughfare with cars, busses, and pedestrians all proceeding to work on schedule as if nothing had changed their morning.

I realized that people are extremely resilient. We continue to get on with our lives even when major events are disrupting our world.

And hence these stories, of ordinary people living in extraordinary times. I hope you find them fascinating, sometimes saddening and always inspiring.

Doc Honour
March 2023

Find out more at DocHonourBooks.com

Subscribe to my newsletter also at the website for:
- Special discounts and giveaways
- Reading new stories before publication
- Upcoming books
- Everyday life of an author

Table of Contents

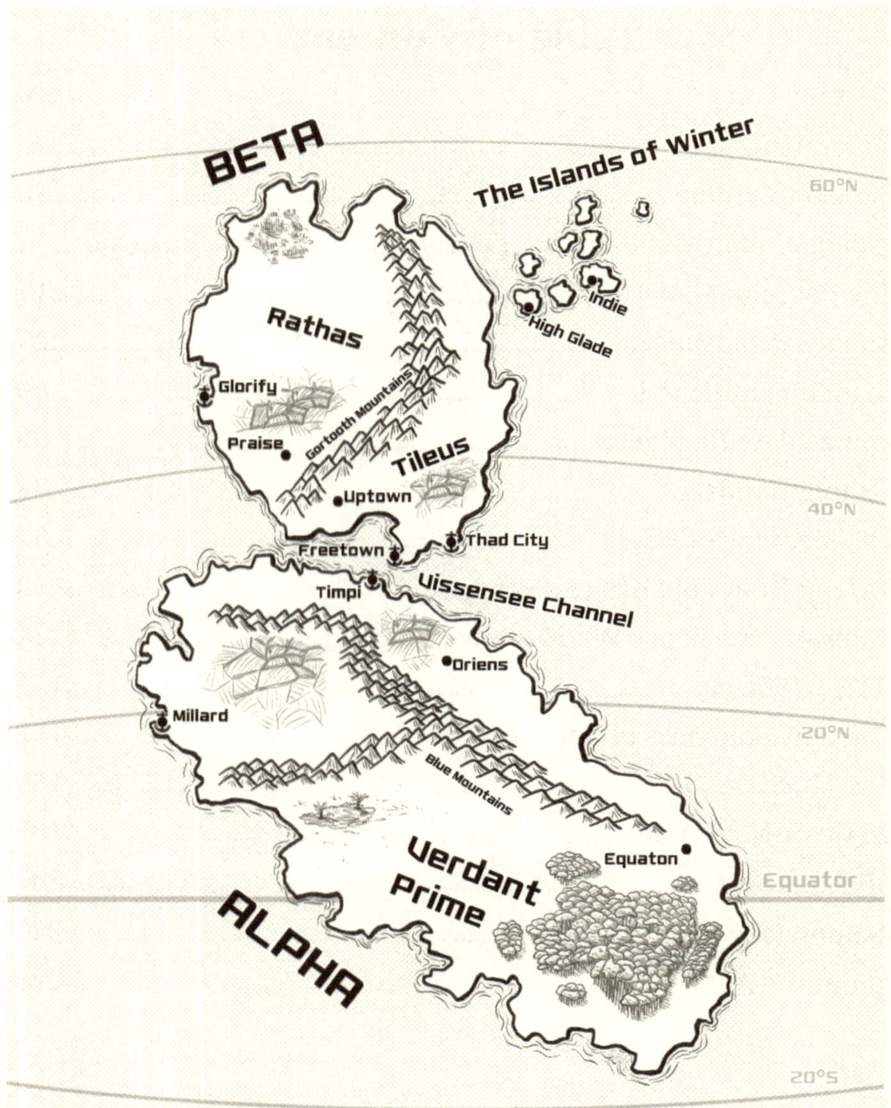

Illustration by J.N. Hinge

Time on Verdant

Imagine living on a world with a sixteen-hour daily rotation. Days are short, and so are the nights. People sleep for six hours, work for six hours, and have four hours for morning, noon, and evening time.

Imagine a year of 450 such days. Such a year is only 82% as long as Earth. Years pass fast.

Yet humans can and do adjust.

Months

Unober – winter solstice 1st
Duember
Tritember– equinox 23rd
Quartember
Quintember
Hexember – summer solstice 1st
September
October– equinox 23rd
November
December

Days

Hours, minutes and seconds are unchanged from now. A typical rapid 16-hour day consists of

3-00:	Dawn
4-00 to 7-30:	Work
8-00:	Noon
8-30 to 11-00	Work
11-00:	Sunset

All months are 45 days and have the same calendar. Every fifth year, an extra day (Holiday) inserts between December 45th and Unober 1st.

Work week						Weekend		
Newday	Twoday	Wentday	Midday	Thruday	Friday	Playday	Sitday	Endday
1	2	3	4	5	6	7	8	9
10	11	12	13	14	15	16	17	18
19	20	21	22	23	24	25	26	27
28	29	30	31	32	33	34	35	36
37	38	39	40	41	42	43	44	45

Prolog: Colony Time

The repellor beam revolutionized civilization in 2049. Drawing its energy from gravitic forces, the beam could push on anything. Repellors quickly found use everywhere. They replaced the tires and drive train in vehicles, eliminating the lingering problems of fossil fuels. Frictionless bearings for machines. Moving equipment and product in factories. And space travel. Humans reached the Solar system with constant acceleration at reasonable cost. Interplanetary craft reached 20% of light speed, transiting from Earth to Mars in a few hours.

Mankind had never before created anything faster than 0.02 percent of light speed. The prevalent theories in physics were embodied in mathematical models based only on observations of particles. In 2062, a physicist measured subtle effects at these new speeds that transcended the equations of relativity. Radrashan theory displaced relativity in the same way Einstein had displaced Newton. The speed of light was no longer a limit. People could reach for the stars.

Five hundred years later, humankind was on thirteen worlds including One Hope.

"Baby, we've been accepted!" Fred shouted as he bumped into the automatic door coming into the apartment. Doors sometimes just didn't open fast enough.

Dana hardly heard him. She had her attention on a shocking news report displayed in the living room holo. There'd been explosions in a border town. The media mavens shouted in frantic excitement about the possibility of invasion. She'd thought actual war was quite remote but now she didn't know.

Then she heard what Fred had said.

"Accepted?" Dana said, her eyes wide and her heart suddenly pounding. "We're actually going?"

"I got the official letter in my infotext on the way home." He waved his handchip at her, a holographic projection wobbling in the air as he did. "We're supposed to pack up and join the colony team near the spaceport in Fleurland. They'll shuttle us up to the starship *New Start* in two months."

"Wow," she breathed. "We applied. We wanted it. But now, it's real. going to another star." She bounced in place with her excitement, then threw herself into his arms.

"Yes, and I can't wait." Fred wrapped his arms around Dana. He picked her up off the ground and twirled her around. She loved his strength, his enjoyment of life. When he put her down, he looked in her eyes and said, "It's none too soon. Our world— One Hope—is getting oppressive. Too many people, too many countries. It'll be good to get away from the constant bickering. Start over on a new world. Start over!" He kissed her and her whole body tingled with it. She rose on tiptoes to kiss him harder.

When he released her, though, she turned serious. "We're going to have to leave everything. Friends, family, belongings." She looked around at their tiny one-bedroom apartment, all they could afford as a young couple struggling in the arts. Beige walls, cheap flooring, with touches of his artistry here and there.

He followed her eyes. "Yes. We'll leave all this. We've talked about it, but now it's real."

"We have a lot of good-byes to say. Are we old enough to do this? We're only twenty-four."

"Hey, other explorers have taken off for ports unknown in their teens. We've been married long enough to prove we stay together, and we can have our children on the ship."

"Have they given the world a name yet?"

"No. I think the colonists are going to vote on it. There's plenty of time."

She giggled. "Right. Four years of living on the colony ship before we ever get there. You know..." she looked back in his eyes, feeling a touch of fear, "I'm still frightened by what we'll find when we arrive. The survey drones said the planet's got its own ecology with plants and animals and weather and everything. But the scariest part is the way it spins like a top, lots faster than here on One Hope. Can we really adjust to a sixteen-hour day?"

Fred hugged her again. "We can do it, Baby."

Dana shook her head in amazement. "I'm still surprised they accepted us—an artist and a theater stage manager. We're not the typical explorer types. We're not ecologists or farmers or architects or builders. What will we do?"

"What we've always done. We keep people together. That's what the arts do. Our work is important to building society."

"Maybe, but do the colony leaders understand that?"

"Of course they do. That's why we were selected. I've heard it's important to the Colony Selection Committee. They've been running that Solity computer day and night with simulations of the colony, seeking the best combination of people and equipment. Most of the committee members are old and not going with us, but they've given a lot of thought to what's needed. Our skills in the arts will help people cope. But you and I will need to do more, like everyone. We can't only do our artistry; we'll have to take part in the colonization tasks, too."

"Well, I'm good at organization. Have to be, to make a stage production work." She pointed a finger at the holo still hanging above his wrist. "Did the infotext say when we'd leave?

"Later this year. What is it in the old Earth calendar that starships use? I think it's 2551 AD. They'll shuttle people up to the *New Start* five hundred at a time, twenty trips to get all ten thousand of us on board."

Dana put her coffee back into the rewarmer. The apartment was so small it was only three steps from the living room to the kitchen. "That's a big shuttle."

"Yeah, but if repellor beams can push a colony ship up to ten times the speed of light, they can certainly lift a heavy shuttle, too."

Dana laughed and almost spilled her coffee when she took it out. "Look at you talking technical," she said. "What do you know about it? You're an artist, you silly man." She lifted her cup in tribute to him. "And a good one, too."

Fred shrugged helplessly. "Hey, I've been learning."

"What shall we take with us?" Dana asked. "You'll need your art supplies, but my work as a stage manager doesn't need much."

"The infotext says we're limited to one hundred kilos each. That includes what we wear, though they tell us the ship will have standardized clothes on board. We certainly won't need winter wear. Nano-assemblers will build what we need at the destination. All our pictures and memories can fit into our handchips. We won't need anything else other than things special to us. The ship is supposed to provide everything."

Dana nodded. She was so excited, she couldn't stand still. "I wonder where on the planet we'll colonize. I understand it has two continents."

"That will be a decision for four years from now, when the *New Start* arrives."

❧ ✳ ☙

Two months passed in a whirlwind of old friends, new friends, training, and learning. At the Drobonov Space Center, they settled into temporary housing, dome-shaped plascrete structures with eight apartments each. The residence area looked like a city of mushrooms laid out in careful rows thirty deep, and it smelled new and impermanent. The Colony Selection Committee was still arguing whether to tear it down after their departure, or to perhaps plan another colony later.

They met colonists from countries all over One Hope—free republics, fascist states, anarchists, socialists, even the freewheeling pirate economies from the islands. Little conflicts flared up, quickly and forcefully quelled by the ship's crew.

They learned the captain of the *New Start* was the most famous and successful pirate of them all, Manuel Mueller. His selection had been hotly contested by the different countries involved in the colonization project. The Selection Committee spent weeks interviewing candidates. Mueller rose to the top because of his demonstrated success in running successful large-scale efforts. Like any ship captain in independent conditions, he would be granted absolute authority once they were underway.

During the training, he ruled the crew with an iron hand, and the crew passed it on to the colonists. Yet it seemed necessary, with all the political differences.

Dana and Fred had little time to think. They had a rigorous schedule of classes—sometimes together, sometimes separate—while they learned what they needed to know about life on a starship. The training facility was only slightly more permanent than the housing, larger dome buildings 3-D printed from plascrete.

Fred returned one evening to their dormitory hut with a puzzling thought and sat across the table from her. "Dana, have you had any training yet in space suits? I've taken all sorts of classes in how the ship works, how to fix it, and the jobs people have to do, but there's been no mention of emergency procedures like ships and aircraft do."

She took his hand. "Love, that's because there's no help in an emergency. We'll be in the empty spaces between stars, traveling at super-light speeds. If we ever had to leave the *New Start*, we'd all be dead."

"Oh," he said when the thought dawned. "So that's why we're getting all this training on fixing the ship."

"Right. We all have to pull together to make it work. In all of history, it's only been done successfully a dozen times."

"But aren't we carrying all the problems with us, Baby? Think of the people we've met. They've got such different ideas. How will we come together to make a new world?"

"That's part of Captain Mueller's job during our transit," she said, "to help us all become one. And it'll be part of our job, too, to give people a higher purpose through our arts."

❧ ✻ ☙

Before they knew it, Dana and Fred left One Hope behind. She bubbled with fear and excitement during the shuttle ride from Drobonov Space Center to the colony ship. Repellor beams made the two-hour ride gentle with a constant but insistent push.

The shuttle had a display in each compartment with views of One Hope and its sun. Dana marveled at the changing scene from colorful ground to blue sky to black space. The colony ship bloomed from a pinpoint star to a huge structure with some surfaces brilliant in the darkness and others so dark as to be almost invisible.

On arrival, their company of five hundred colonists filed through a large airlock to a sizable mall-like passageway, then gathered in the cavernous atrium of the starship. Conversation effervesced around them like a party crowd, people enthusing over the strange, new surroundings.

"Look at this, Fred. It's like a tropical jungle!"

He was already looking, his eyes wide. "I know they've been building the *New Start* for ten years, but I never expected this. I'd pictured steel walls and rivets."

Green plants spread everywhere in the huge space. At first, Dana thought she was seeing chaos. When she looked closer, though, she saw patterns of growth, different plant groups in different places on tier after tier of growing racks. Rows of flowers in reds, yellows, and purple demarked different groups. The air was rich with scent. She even heard bird song and the buzzing of bees.

They would live here for the next four years. Her heart swelled and seemed to bubble out of her chest. She looked forward to entertaining the colonists who would otherwise fall into boredom. Fred clutched his paint kit.

"I see you thinking of all those colors, Love."

He laughed. "Not just that. I can't wait to see what there is to paint on the new planet."

A large-holo display on one wall showed the image of One Hope from orbit, the familiar blue-and-white globe to which they'd never return. Dana found her eyes tearing up. It would be a long trip, but she anticipated finding out what adventures were in store for them.

"Good afternoon, colonists," boomed a man's voice from speakers.

Dana realized a podium was under the display screen. The man standing there was tall and broad-shouldered, with a full grey beard and flowing mustache. He wore a dark blue uniform with gold epaulettes and gold trim on the brim of his rigid white hat.

"Welcome to the *New Start*. I am Captain Mueller, and I look forward to meeting each of you in person at some point in the next year. I hope our meetings will be friendly and useful. You are company fourteen of twenty. Another twelve days and we'll have everyone on board.

"For now, you'll find everything organized for you. Your apartments, bathrooms, and mess halls are already assigned in your handchips when you came aboard. This is a large ship, and it's easy to get lost, so your handchip has also been loaded with navigation to find your way around. There are restricted areas. Heed them.

"Please, go to your quarters and get settled in. You'll receive tasking and schedules for each day. You can start living the life of a colony ship now. Then you'll have little change when we get everyone else aboard and start the voyage to the new world of Verdant."

Dana turned to Fred and saw his eyes sparkling with as much excitement as she felt.

Enthusiastic applause ended the captain's speech. The immense excitement and anticipation of their arrival seemed to buoy everyone. The crowd gradually broke up as people followed their handchips, the small holo displays twinkling over each wrist.

Dana held back, still marveling at the plants.

Fred took her hand. "We'd better get on with it, Baby."

She turned to him. "I guess we need to find out where to go and what to do. You'll need some sort of studio, and I should see what production facilities they have."

Then she had a delayed puzzlement at what she'd just heard from the captain. "Fred...I thought we were all going to vote on the name of the planet?"

Two weeks later, the atrium was jam-packed with cheering people. Captain Mueller stood on the podium once again with the image of One Hope behind him. His charisma shone in his broad smile and confident stance. Dana thought perhaps the birds in the atrium sang brighter than usual.

"Today is the day, colonists," he shouted. "We're all here, and it's time to launch."

He gave a hand signal to a crew member. Dana held her breath while she watched the display. No dramatic moment happened. She didn't see a blooming of rocket flames, because repellor beams don't work like that.

"There," said the captain with enthusiasm. He activated a pointer to a star that had just appeared at the edge of the planet. "And there." He pointed to another new star showing at another quadrant. "We can see these new stars because we are moving away from One Hope." He paused for the drama to sink in.

"We are underway!"

The cheer was deafening, ten thousand voices shouting in one excitement.

Captain Mueller continued when the cheering subsided, his deep voice carrying the firm confidence of command. "This is a huge moment of transition for us all. It's more than just starting our voyage. At this moment, we leave behind all the infrastructure of One Hope, the conflicts of the world behind, and the idealism of its Colony Selection Committee. We are now on our own."

Another cheer rang out. He smiled and let it pass.

"Remember," he said, "since old Earth, humans have sent out only twenty ships like this. Eight of those—forty percent—did not succeed."

The sober words silenced the crowd. Dana looked in alarm at Fred. She spoke, "I knew that, but—"

Mueller continued, "For us all to stay alive on board for four years, then to succeed in our colony, we must be guided by one principle: 'From each according to his ability, to each according to his need.' Whatever skills you brought aboard must be used for our common good. I've guided the Solity computer to match your skills to the needs of the ship. Some of those may be different than you expected, but you must trust what we do, so we can all survive and thrive."

The crowd was quiet now. A feeling of serious determination filled the air.

"Your handchip now has your shipboard work assignment and will guide your hours each day." He raised a fist high in the air, an obvious symbol of solidarity. "Take part and be together."

The captain left through a door behind the podium. Muddled conversation swelled as the colonists processed what he'd said.

Fred tapped his handchip and information appeared in the air above it. His face fell, and the color drained from his cheeks.

"What is it, Fred?" Dana asked.

"My work assignment. I'm not to be an artist. They've assigned me to janitorial services. It says here my art won't be needed on board, and so they've given me what they consider useful work."

She grasped his arm. "No art? What about my theater?" Dana tapped her own handchip and felt her stomach clench. "Cooking crew? I'm to be part of food preparation?"

The two looked at each other in dismay. Almost as one, they breathed the words Captain Mueller had spoken, "'From each according to his ability, to each according to his need.'" Dana continued, "I guess he really meant that. And they don't see the need for the arts."

All in a few minutes, she no longer heard the birds and the atrium plantings seemed darker. The trip to Verdant no longer seemed as exciting. Dana determined to argue the assignment, the need for the arts, but she knew she faced an uphill trek. And what would happen in four years when they arrived, perhaps with children?

The Peaceful Man Who Wasn't

Four hundred years passed on the new world. Humanity spread across the small globe of Verdant while momentous events happened on other worlds. The last of four countries to form was Winter in the northern islands, home to those who escaped the conflicts elsewhere by choosing a tribal-oriented society with less technology. But we will let Narnit Concordi tell the history.

I arrived at High Glade Tribe as I always arrived to a tribe, walking quietly in from the surrounding blue, green, and russet forests of the islands of Winter. Varieties of photosynthesis. I love the scent of the forests, filled with rich tones of bark and leaf. Even when I have to boat from island to island, I always arrange to walk into the tribe. There is something serene about a walking arrival that announces my mission better than any words.

My mission? I spread peace among the children.

The name I have long borne is Narnit Concordi. Most call me Elder, though I do not serve a tribe. I serve our country of Winter, I serve the planet of Verdant, and I serve humankind.

I was met on the outskirts of High Glade by Elder Nodris Farseeing in a casual shirt and slacks not unlike my own. I knew him from Conclave and was pleased to see him again. We greeted with raised palms of peace.

"I am here, Nodris."

"I see you are, Narnit. Our children are ready for you. Our teacher may not be. She may be a problem for you."

My heart sank. Conflict always gives me difficulty.

We turned to walk into the village together. The path was smooth, the fields well-tended, and the town clean. I cocked my head at the afternoon sun, blue-white and small above the varicolored hills. The cool, rich scent of the forest loam lingered, mixing now with the sun-warmed smells of fishing from the harbor.

A few steps later, I asked, "The teacher is a problem? In what way?"

"When we told her you were coming, she asked us to reject your offer to teach. Several of us have known you for many years, and we value your mission. We know of the need for your history, and how it might change all of us, but she didn't understand."

I took a deep breath to calm the agitated flutter inside.

"Do you know why? Is it perhaps a fear of the Solity control in Verdant Prime?"

"No, she was unwilling to tell us. But we have told her to accept you anyway."

So I must prepare myself to seek peace in conflict, yet again.

We made small talk, catching up, while he led me downhill to a side street and a small building. I smiled at its square yellow façade buried in the midst of stores and warehouses. I had taught in many different shapes and kinds of schools.

The children were gone for the day. A young woman blocked the entrance. Her green eyes were angry, and the freckles on her face stood out in rosy flush. She tossed her head, and the bright red curls flipped away from her eyes. I was surprised at her all-too-apparent antagonism, and my stomach reacted with a roil.

I'm sure she saw in me a large man with physical strength, with a face beginning to age, the first dusting of grey in my hair and beard. I was different; most men in Winter kept their faces clean. But I hoped she also saw the crinkles around my eyes that spoke of a frequent smile. I tried at all times to convey great power withheld by spiritual peace.

Nodris introduced us. "Viola Parim, I'd like you to meet Elder Narnit Concordi. He's the one we've talked about."

She crossed her arms. "History. He's here to teach history."

I nodded and raised my palm to her.

She gave me the customary raised palm, but it felt reluctant to me. "Elder, we teach the necessary RWAT basics here: Reading, Writing, Arithmetic, and Technology. I don't believe our children need extensive history any more than we adults need it. They need to know the things they'll use day to day in our simple life. I've told the tribe elders we don't need your version of brainwashing."

Nodris smiled. "Viola, we believe Elder Concordi's message is important to us all. You are to accept him in the classroom for the few days he needs."

She turned on him with a modest flash of anger. "And in those few days, the children will not be learning their basics."

"We are willing to accept that, Viola. We ask you to do so as well."

She hmphed at us both and spun back into the classroom without a farewell.

By the next morning, I had used my electronic implant to pre-load my holographic curriculum into her classroom system. Our implants are surgically inserted in mid-teens, for those who will need them. The imps provide connectivity to each other and the InfoNet, bonding directly to the brain through our sensor nerves. The school had the appropriate technology for my lessons, including holos at each student desk, a haptic field at the teacher's desk to read gestures, and connection to the InfoNet and any imps people wore into the room.

The students came in like any students, full of energy. In High Glade, thirty students of all ages learned in the same room. Sometimes, they had common lessons—as with my history class. In other subjects, the teacher instructed small groups while others studied on their own.

"Settle down, children." Viola was a quintessential teacher, flashing all the holos repeatedly red to get their attention. I admired her style. They quieted.

"Today we have a special teacher. This is Elder Concordi, from outside High Glade." Professional to the core, her voice had no touch of the disdain she had expressed.

I was sitting by the teacher's desk. Sitting is more friendly and serene. I smiled at the class.

"Good morning, everyone." They echoed my greeting. I saw some interested eyes, wondering what new thing I brought. I also saw wary eyes, cautious of any outsider who was not like them. As many times as I had done this, I still yearned to be a friend to all, especially the children. Silly me, with as much as I know about people.

"I'm going to tell you some stories over the next couple of days, stories I hope you will remember for your whole lives."

I paused to let that sink in. I stretched in my chair, casually passing my hand through the haptic field in a practiced gesture. Somewhat magically, their holos came alive with an image of a different tribal valley than theirs. I worked hard at disassociating my control gestures from the effect in their holos to foster that sense of magic.

"I grew up in Blue Valley Tribe many years ago."

The aerial viewpoint in their holos moved around the valley, showing modest buildings, fishing boats, farms and surrounding forests. The scene was similar to their own High Glade, with just enough difference to be interesting. Most of the trees in the holo valley were deep blue with few of the green and russet common here.

"When I was a boy, I got into a lot of fights. I didn't want to fight, but it seemed every day someone would say something or do something to offend me."

The holos zoomed in on a schoolyard where one boy was swinging his fists, pummeling another boy while six others stood in a circle.

"They might have called me a nasty name. They might have said something bad about my father, the shopkeeper. They might have laughed at my sister. It didn't matter. My solution was always to call them out, to beat them up. I was strong, and I was quick." I chuckled. "Not like the slow old man in front of you now." They giggled. I had their attention.

I continued my talk, the holo images keeping pace. I watched their eyes and their reactions, pacing myself to their attention. Much of what I did was like an old-time minstrel, teaching important lessons in the guise of entertainment.

I also glanced frequently at Viola Parim, who had moved to sit in the back of the room. Her mouth was set in a tight line and she often had her arms crossed. I couldn't seem to find the right attitudes to help her relax; as my tale went on, she grew more tense—and so did I.

My stories included details of my fights, how one boy got angry at me for beating up his sister, so I had to push him down, too. How another girl called me a bully, so I hit her in the face with my fist. How a teacher tried to stop one of my fights, and I kicked her in the shins until she cried. The students in the room gasped at that one. I held the students' attention for well over an hour telling these stories.

"Yes," I admitted, "I was indeed a bully. I was mean. I was vindictive. I hurt people, and I had no friends. I did this for years.

"But I never really wanted to torment others. Inside, I was afraid they would find out I was weak. I fought people because I didn't want them to know what was inside me."

It came time for a recess. I paused and took a deep breath, then released the students for a break.

Practically before they left the room, Viola was in my face.

"What are you doing, Concordi? What are you teaching?"

"I'm teaching history, my dear."

"I'm not your dear. And you're not teaching history. You're just telling brutal stories of your own childhood. Are you trying to turn my children into bullies, too?"

I shook my head gently, eyes focused on hers. "No, that is not at all my purpose." Her confrontation perturbed me. I did not understand her implacable resistance, and I wondered what hidden problem was yet to appear. When confronted like this, I had to reach deep inside myself, past the surface fears and agitation, for the peace I wish to have.

"Well, get on with it. Get to history, so we can get back to real school."

I nodded. "I will. Please be patient."

∾✱∾

After the break, I continued my story.

"When I was fifteen, near the end of my schooling, I met Elder Tapper Pacaem, the peaceful man who wasn't."

The holos circled around the image of a truly ugly man. His face was gnarled and twisted like burled wood grains in a tree knot, his nose broken several times. Eyebrows sprawled from his forehead, and hairs sprouted from his cauliflower ears.

"Elder Pacaem was not a handsome man." The class twittered.

"He came to me after school. I was standing in the schoolyard with my arms crossed, waiting for an excuse to punish someone."

The holo showed that first meeting. The boy took a step backward in surprise.

"He spoke first. 'You don't have to be like this, young Narnit.'

"I answered, 'Like what, ugly man?' I was always ready to attack when threatened.

"He said, 'Fighting people all the time. Protecting yourself. Being lonely and afraid.'"

When I spoke the words of the conversation, the holo synchronized itself, as if my speaking issued from their mouths.

"'I'm not afraid," I shouted at him.

"He just smiled. Somehow, his peaceful smile overrode his ugliness. I was surprised to find I wanted to talk with him, that perhaps he had something worthwhile for me. But that made me angrier. Inside, I was afraid—and I knew it. What would this man do to me?

"'I used to be like you,' he said, 'but I did it for much longer than you have, until I was grown. I drank too much, I fought too much.'"

Suddenly, Viola Parim jumped to her feet.

"That's enough, Concordi. That's just enough. You are done here, filling the children with stories of fighting and drinking. You're supposed to be teaching history, not telling violent stories."

"I'm getting there, Viola. Please be patient."

"No. Get out of my classroom. Get out now. We'll talk later with the Elders, but I want you out now."

I lowered my eyes to the floor and thought. My heart pounded. My breath felt ragged. It had been a long time since anyone had blocked my teaching. In an earlier phase of my life, I would have fought for my place. On this day, I still felt a surge of raging resentment arise at her dismissal.

But I choose to be peaceful. It is a choice I can make each day, each moment. I prayed to the spirits for harmony and felt it fill my heart.

"If you wish," I said.

I got up from the chair, picked up my few things, and winked to the children with a secret smile. A few were shocked at my disrespect; one girl clapped her hands to her mouth. Without another word, I walked quietly out of the embarrassment. Despite my choice of peace, my body still wanted to fight.

Behind me, I heard the teacher returning the children to arithmetic. I stopped and listened to her teaching. She had an effective style I could respect. I sighed, wondering how I would get past her resistance. Then I walked back to the house where I was staying. I looked at the wonderful world around me—the houses and fields, the harbor, the surrounding forest, the mountains—and felt its harmony.

Above all, I choose to be a peaceful man. I did not yet know how my message would be heard here, but I trusted the spirits would find a way.

❧ ✳ ☙

I could have taken the problem directly to the High Glade Elders, but I sought something other than confrontation. Instead, I spent the afternoon with my friend Nodris, strategizing what to do with the rejection. While we talked, it became apparent Viola had some misunderstanding of what I was teaching. She seemed to think I was here to steal the children's minds into some perverted path. He offered to have the Elders intervene, but I declined.

He suggested I approach her privately. So that evening, after an early dinner with my hosts, I found my way to Viola Parim's modest house near the school. It stood in a row of other houses, its red door standing out. After a calming breath, I knocked on the door and stepped back. My heart sped up with anxiety, but I chose to be patient.

She opened the door, her mouth setting again in a thin line when she saw me.

"You."

"Yes, me."

I waited at the base of her stoop while she stood there holding the door partially closed.

"Well. And what do you want?"

I bowed my head, accepting she had asked. "I understand you must protect your children. They come first. Thank you for doing so."

Her response was a simple humph.

"I'd like to talk to you, if I may."

Despite her protectiveness, she was a polite woman. She took a deep breath, then opened the door and waited for me to enter.

"Blessings be on this house and all in it," I said as I touched the spirit icon on the doorframe.

She led me to her sitting room and offered me water. The room was quiet, peaceful. One bright lamp shone on her chair, with the rest of the room dimly lit. We sat, she in the light and me on a dark sofa.

"Thank you for your confrontation today," I said. "I appreciated it."

She lifted her head back in surprise. "You're thanking me?"

"Yes. It allowed me to grow in my spirit, to accept your ejection without conflict, a test of my own serenity."

She seemed puzzled. "You surprised me. I expected you to fight for your place."

"No. I don't fight anyone or anything. I choose to be peaceful."

"How can you possibly do that all the time?"

I nodded. She had come to the question I wanted her to ask.

"I'll tell you, if you'll tell me why you object so strongly to my teaching."

Viola looked askance at me. "Is this a trick?"

"No trick. Just an honest offer. I tell you, then you tell me. And you can tell me as much or as little as you wish."

She thought, her head still cocked in skepticism. For a long moment, I waited patiently for her decision. Setting again that thin line to her mouth, she nodded.

"Okay. Tell me."

I was relieved. I settled myself more comfortably in the chair and took a drink of water.

"It's the story I was sharing with your children. Elder Tapper Pacaem—the peaceful man who wasn't—completely changed my life that day when I was fifteen. Before meeting him, I was a fractious bully, always looking for a fight to prove my own worth. He taught me what he had learned about choosing to be peaceful.

"Elder Pacaem told me his story, just as I am telling you. He had also been a rebel, but he continued it into his adulthood. He drank too much. He became addicted to alcohol in any form. When he couldn't buy it, he'd steal it. When he couldn't get drinking alcohol, he'd drink cleaning products. Nearly killed himself several times that way. He was a belligerent drunk, the kind who would tear up a tavern. He told me he was a problem for the tribe and a problem for himself, but in his selfishness, he would not acknowledge either of those facts. He thought his problems were everyone else's fault. By the time he was thirty, he had no friends, no work, no income. He was living in discarded boxes in the tribal dump. He had destroyed his life and damaged many others.

"And yet, at the time he came to me as a much older man, he was an Elder for Blue Valley Tribe and had been for many years."

I stopped to let her absorb those words.

She responded. "Tribes don't elect drunkards and trouble-makers to be Elders."

"You are right," I said.

"Elder Pacaem discovered a way out. One night in his loneliness, shaking and quivering in physical desire for the alcohol he could not afford, he had a spiritual experience. Not religious, like the theocracy in the country of Rathas, but spiritual in nature. He told me his squalid surroundings suddenly lit up with a bright blinding light. He felt the emptiness of his life, and he sensed a welcoming Presence filling him with warmth. He heard a Voice speaking from the light and inviting him to a new life based on spiritual principles. It astonished him such a thing was possible.

"Pacaem never had such an experience again, but he also never drank again after that night. He spent the rest of his life seeking to know more about what a 'spiritual life' meant. He became the peaceful Elder who approached me, trusting in that Presence so deeply he touched the lives around him with more good than the wreckage he had done before. He spent years making amends to those he had hurt."

She was skeptical. "And of course, you just accepted this 'way' of his and changed? And he gave it to you freely?" Her voice had a sarcastic edge.

I laughed, remembering how I had thrashed like a fish on a hook. "No, not at first. But I was intrigued. What sort of ugly man would approach a fifteen-year-old bully and tell his own life story? I listened. Over the next days, he told me tale after tale of his violence and selfishness. His stories were like my own life, only bigger and more violent. In the beginning, I was amused. He gave me new ideas how to bully others."

"That can't have been good."

"Perhaps not, but I didn't try them out. Instead, I kept listening to him each day after school. The strange thing was this: he was never flustered, never reacted strongly. He told these violent stories with quiet ease. His demeanor was so at odds with the tales I couldn't figure him out."

I watched Viola while I talked, assessing how my story was affecting her. She was attentive; the tale was capturing her interest.

"Then one day, while we were sitting and talking near the school yard, one of my classmates decided to challenge me in a uniquely fifteen-year-old way: he threw mud at me, splattering the Elder as much as me. I jumped to my feet, ready to pound the boy into the ground, but Pacaem laid a calming hand on my arm.

"'Leave it be, Narnit,' he told me. 'Choose peace. That's what I choose.'

"I was furious. 'But he mudded you, too, Elder. You can choose to stay peaceful; I'll beat him up for you!'

"Pacaem laughed and shook his head. 'No, my boy. I choose to be a peaceful man. If my decision is conditional on the actions of others, then it isn't much of a decision, is it? If I do that, I live my life at the mercy of others.'"

I paused in my story for his words to resonate in her.

Viola tilted her head, looking thoughtful. "That's a deep philosophy."

I nodded. "Yes, it is. And it changed my life. I spent the next five years learning from him the spiritual grounding to make and hold that decision. Eventually, gradually, I also became a peaceful man.

"And that explains why I was able to accept your decision earlier today."

She nodded, then looked down at the floor. I stopped speaking and waited with nervous energy during the silence for what she would choose to do next. Would she complete our agreement and tell me her story?

When she looked up again, she gave me a humble smile. "So, I guess it's my turn."

I was relieved at her integrity. I raised a hand in assent, an invitation for her to talk.

"I believe in our schools serving the needs of Winter," she said, "to train our children in the knowledge they need."

I gave her rapt attention, all the room she needed to speak. I was curious to hear her story, but I set aside my curiosity to let her speak at her own pace.

"Those needs are simple, because Winter has chosen to be a simple society. We live in tribes. We fish in the welcoming ocean around our islands, and we do what else supports fishing. Our schools focus on the RWAT curriculum. We need reading and writing to communicate and to enrich our lives, to give us purpose and the arts. We need arithmetic. We need to know how to use modern technology. Like our implants, and the chemical sensors on our fishing boats. Repellor beams in our autocars, our motors, our harpoon guns. Further education is available to Winter people who need it, but those are few. We rely on other countries to develop the technologies we use."

I smiled while I listened. This was all common knowledge, but I also knew she was treading water before getting into her depth.

"Six years ago, as a new teacher, I replaced a tutor at Long Run Tribe. That tutor was not from Winter; he had been offered from Rathas for nothing but room and board."

Viola looked into my eyes. "He had been a disaster for Long Run. This...outsider... taught his lessons laced with the religion of the Rathas theocracy. Oh, he taught the RWAT curriculum, yes, but by the time I arrived the children were also imbued with ideas contrary to our lives in Winter." Her face flushed in anger. "One teenaged student 'confronted' me with why I didn't honor Elláh their god with prayer three times a day. Another asked me when we were going to resume the daily self-purification he had taught them."

I leaned forward with my brows furrowed in sympathy. "I see."

"No. You don't. It was much worse than I can express. I was there for three years before coming here. I saw those older children leave school and *not* join society. They wandered the vales praying and preaching, not productive, not helpful to others. As happens in Rathas, they expected society to take care of them, to give them purpose, instead of finding that individual place where they could contribute." Her green eyes flashed with anger. "He had taught them to violate the basic covenant of civilization, that each individual provides what he or she can for the common good.

"I was able to change the younger children, to turn around the teaching they had received. By the time I left, there were only a few who still had problems."

She looked down at the floor again and gave a great sigh of sadness. "It was a terrible experience. And so, I am cautious about brainwashing, Elder Concordi. Very cautious. You seem like a nice man, but I wish to keep my children focused on the lessons they need to live in Winter."

Then she rubbed her eyes, blew out her cheeks, and looked back at me with a puzzled cock of her head. "I want to know one thing from you, Elder. You call what you teach 'history,' but all you have told me so far is your own personal story. And yet our Elders support you. Why should you be teaching the children?"

I paused and looked into the far corner of the room, thinking. I considered continuing my story into the larger history, but evening had moved on and we had shared enough emotional depth for now. I took another drink of water and put the glass back on the side table.

"I want to answer that question, Viola. It is crucial to my mission. But I think it's late, and we should wait until tomorrow. May we do so? I could spend tomorrow as a free day to meet other people here in High Glade."

She agreed with apparent relief, then led me to the door. When I touched the spirit icon in parting, she spoke again.

"Elder, I need to know what you intend to teach before I can let you back into my classroom."

I turned back to her and acquiesced with a smile, then held my palm up in gentle parting. I carefully allowed her to have the final word.

☙ ❈ ❧

I had an enjoyable day. The weather was balmy, the scents of the forest and the fishing intermingled in comfortable warmth, the sun sparkled on the harbor while boats departed empty and returned laden with fish. I caught up with old friends from prior visits, and I made new friends.

As always, it was a short day. Teaching history, I sometimes compared our 16-hour planetary rotation with what it must have been like on Earth with its 24 hours. It seemed to me today I would welcome twelve hours of daytime instead of only eight, time to enjoy friends more fully—but I chuckled to myself to imagine how I could possibly stay in bed to sleep for eight or more hours. It would feel very strange.

After dinner, I knocked again at Viola's red door. This time, she invited me in without pause. She had a pot of blueleaf tea ready and offered me a cup. We caught up on the day. I told her of my wanderings and friends. She told me a few tales of the children. Then we turned serious.

"So, Elder, what is the history you teach? And why do you start with your personal story?"

This evening, she was smiling and more open. I was pleased I had waited a day, because she would be better able to hear my message.

"I teach the history of Verdant and of humankind. My personal story is essential, because we will soon need the way of peace I have learned. I start with my background so the students can identify. I hope you'll see that shortly.

"I believe every resident of this planet needs to know the hard times we face very soon. Do you know where we came from?"

She nodded. "Of course. We came from Earth. It's been 416 Verdant years since our touchdown here, about 340 Earth years."

I smiled but with a wince. "True, but not complete. Yes, humankind came from Earth. And yes, we are in the 416th year since touchdown on Verdant. But our colony ship did not come from Earth; it came from another colony world named One Hope."

"I didn't know that."

"Most do not, because we have not taught history. Earth launched many colony ships, including the ship to One Hope. Over centuries, those colonies also launched colonies to other planets. Verdant is a third-generation world.

"Life was difficult for the colonists here. People had to adjust physically even while building this new colony. This planet is smaller than Earth or One Hope and has a fast rotation at sixteen hours. People did not evolve for this cycle, and it took hard years for us to adjust our bodies. The annual cycle is also different; our year is only about eighty percent as long as Earth's. Four hundred years later, these physical issues still affect us; people tire easily, our bodies wear out quicker, and our emotions are sometimes raw."

Viola was rapt with attention, but this startled her. "I find that hard to believe. I don't see people with such ill effects."

I chuckled. "Of course not. And fish don't see the water they live in. I only know of these effects because I have studied history.

"Verdant Prime was the only settlement in those days. Shipboard life had lasted for four years. Captain Mueller and his officers strongly controlled ship society. When they landed, Prime continued the same control structure, trusting in the Solity computer to arrange and provide everything—centrally-controlled socialism that assigned people to their life work, guided production goals, and distributed the results where needed."

She nodded. "Prime is a very closed society. The few who've been there say it's scary to see how people accept the rigid controls."

"Since then, other countries split off from Prime with different philosophies. Tileus was first, swinging the pendulum from heavy-handed control all the way to true democracy with every citizen voting on every issue. They believe so strongly in their chaotic form of democracy, they send agitators into Prime to create revolution there."

Viola was thinking hard, so I continued.

"Then came Rathas. The religion of Elláh was created on old Earth as a combination of God, Allah, and Hinduism. They migrated over the mountains west of Tileus to found their theocracy. Rathas is a pleasant place to live, but only for those who conform; they have harsh punishment for dissidents. Rathas has been sending missionaries to the other countries, creating friction."

"Like the tutor I replaced at Long Run."

"Yes. Exactly. He wasn't there just as a teacher, or even primarily as a teacher."

"You've put this together well. I'm glad we're in Winter."

"Well." I ducked my head and rubbed the back of my neck. "Perhaps. Winter was settled piecemeal by people leaving the controls of the other countries. Our islands are far north. Wintertime is harsh and dark. But people thought it worthwhile to gain independence. We purposefully live simpler lives than elsewhere. But our lives are limited. We live without amenities that could be available. Like you said last night, civilization is based on connectedness, on each person doing their part to advance the whole. More amenities mean more civilization, which leads to more conflict. We in Winter hide from the world by giving up amenities."

Viola sat up straight. "That feels almost like a slap in the face. It's a harsh condemnation."

"No harsher than the assessments I've made of the other countries. It only feels harsh because it's personal."

"And you wish to teach our children this negativity?"

"No, I wish to teach our children honesty about ourselves and our world, so we know who we are."

She looked skeptical but I saw she was more amenable to my teaching than when we started.

"But that is not the core of my teaching. The stakes are much higher than I believe you know."

"What stakes?"

Over the next hour, I told her the rest of our history.

❧ ✳ ❦

Two days later, I was finishing my lesson on history for the children. Astonished at the revelations I gave her that evening, Viola had given in and allowed me back into the classroom. She now understood the importance of my teaching.

My curriculum was still in the holo system. We had covered the history of Verdant, with images of Prime and Tileus and Rathas. I had given them my assessments of the benefits and limitations of each country, including our own. Then I continued with what I had told Viola.

"Students, we also need to know the larger history of humankind, because we face a most difficult task. We must save Verdant from its coming fate." I paused. "I have told you of Earth."

The holos showed a view of that beautiful blue, green, and brown world with fluffy white whorls of clouds. The children wore captivated smiles. Then, while I spoke, the holo scene gradually changed. The greens turned to brown, the clouds to mud, and the ocean blues to dirty grey.

"But Earth is no more. Humans on Earth fought wars. In the final war, with the technology humankind had developed, they unleashed so much damage they destroyed the ecology of the planet. This happened while the first colony ships were still enroute."

I let the words sink in. The students were stunned. Some turned their eyes to me for assurance I could not give. This part of my teaching always affected me to tears. My eyes were red and raw.

The holos shifted to another beautiful world. It had different patterns of blue and green and red. While they watched, bright explosions covered the surface, spreading necrotic patches of grey that consumed the picture.

"One Hope is also gone. In our year 224 After Touchdown, they exploded into international conflict, a world war. They also destroyed themselves."

Again, I waited for the full impact. Then I continued, my voice quiet in the silent room.

"One by one, the worlds of humanity have done this. Counting Earth and Verdant, we have lived on seventeen different planets. Only three are left: Newland, Brightness...and Verdant. The most recent loss was thirteen years ago, when Branch disappeared in famine after a global bio-war destroyed all the plants."

Though she had heard this two nights ago, I saw tears in Viola's eyes while she listened again. I cried also but I kept talking through the tears.

"We humans...destroy ourselves. It has happened over and over. We have always fought—over power, over territory, over ideas. Since our technology became powerful enough, though, our wars have destroyed our worlds. The cycle seems inevitable: from viable colony to spreading out into the world, to fractionated nations, to international tension, to final war."

The images in the holo were selected for impact, though they spared the children from personal atrocities. We saw worlds exploding, worlds dying. We saw weapons of mass destruction flying across oceans. We saw disease. We saw people picking through the remains of a civilization for something to eat. We saw people fighting over scraps with crude hand-held weapons. And at the end, we saw a barren landscape with nothing but rocks and dirt and the ruins of buildings.

"The cycle takes less than five hundred years. We on Verdant are in year 416."

The children looked at me as if grasping for hope.

"It is up to us to change the cycle. Though I once wasn't, I choose to be a peaceful man. Even when your teacher sent me out from this classroom, I chose peace. Just like Elder Tapper Pacaem, I learned spiritual principles that allow me to hold to that choice.

"I hope and pray each of you will learn to do the same. Perhaps if we all learn this, we can stop the cycle and save humanity."

I sat with my head bowed for a long moment.

I took a deep sigh, then looked up with a sad smile.

"And this ends my lesson. Thank you for listening."

After a stunned pause, the older children led the rest in subdued applause. I smiled and thanked them again.

I picked up my things and walked quietly out, touching the spirit icon on the door as I passed. At the edge of the forest, filled with the scent of loam, I looked back at High Glade with a modicum of hope. Then I turned to enter the forest, heading toward Easy Tribe, my next stop.

Apping with Isadora

In Verdant Prime, the original country, the word "Solity" gradually changed. Originally given to the shipboard computer that managed assets, it now applied to the entirety of their government. Solity—the government—provided everything for the citizens: food, clothing, materials, information, entertainment. Solity also owned everything and took everything. It required citizens to contribute their share; people were Assigned to a life work for the good of Solity. Money didn't exist, because it wasn't needed. Despite the careful apportioning, life was not equal; those who ran Solity got perquisites not available to ordinary people. Yet people are amazingly resilient; they lived on despite the totalitarian approach.

"Damn, this is hard," Zofia Dobrunik said to herself while looking at her final exam in advanced programming. At eighteen years old, she was ready to pass this exam, leave school, and start a life Assignment. It thrilled her to be the best in her class, but it also set her apart and made her lonely. Unlike the lesser students, Zofia used an interactive AI that required her to develop a unique aptitude of precision in speech.

"Isadora, display the population block." Zofia pointed into the field.

"The population block is already displayed, Zofia." The AI appeared in the holo above her desk as a twenty-something woman with short brown hair, green eyes, and shiny teeth.

Damn, I screwed up the precision again. "No, Isadora, display the *contents* of the population block."

"Here's the population data."

Words and a diagram floated in the holo beside Isadora. One block of data enlarged, showing the detail behind it. Zofia sucked in a soft whistle as she realized again this exam was a significant step above anything she'd done before. The words read

> *Biweekly, the Capital Department distributes cheese to communes based on quarterly requests from local commissars. Create a generalized app to predict the amount of cheese needed for each delivery based on historical data for four sample communes. Target performance is within 10 percent, evaluated against any random commune.*

The diagram showed a bewildering set of eighteen factors that might affect the problem: population, weather, industry types, commune density, connectivity to other communes, and more.

The population block now displaced other blocks in her holo. The details showed four sample communes, A to D. For each commune, she had five years of historical population data by sex and age, with further break-outs by industry and occupation.

She sat back and released a held breath, her eyes wide. "What does all this have to do with cheese? How much detail do I have, Isadora?"

"As much as you wish to explore. You may use any data available from the InfoNet on these four communes, though I'm not allowed to identify the actual communes."

She shook her head and repeated, "Damn, this is a really hard problem."

"Yes, it is. It's intended to be. You may be pleased to know you've received the most difficult challenge of all students in this exam."

"I'm not sure that's a good thing, Isadora. Am I up to it?"

"The Development Department believes you are."

Mers. Bekker had told them results were due by midnight tomorrow. "Your results, coupled with the needs of Solity," she'd said, "will determine where you go next. Some of you will advance to tertiary education, some will continue in your training here, and some of you will move out into the real world with a life-long Assignment.

"For this exam, you must work on your own. You have access to your programming environment all day and all night if you need, though no staff will be here at night. You may use any resources available. Solity will monitor you through your comms implants, both your online accesses and your personal conversations, to ensure no collaboration."

Having seen her exam, Zofia wasn't confident she could even pass. Before diving into the problem, she decided to walk and think about it. She got up and went into the hall. On the way, she glanced at the rest of the familiar classroom. Her station was one of three against the wall, each surrounded by sound-baffling walls to allow the necessary conversation with Isadora. The remainder of the students sat at normal desks in rows, each with its own holohaptic interface. Leaving the room, she paced toward the building doors, away from a few others also loitering in the hall.

It's a statistical problem. Gotta be statistical solutions. I can do this.

On her way back, Luis Abreu blocked her way. Brown skin, coffee eyes and an arrogant smile intruded yet again.

"Would you *please* leave me alone?" Zofia flashed at him.

He raised his hands. "Oh, but of course, your Majesty Mers. Dobrunik. Whatever you want, Mers. Dobrunik."

"Damn you," she snarled. "Just go away."

She walked back to the classroom, and Luis stayed beside her. Too close. He "accidentally" bumped her hip, then "steadied" her with a grasping arm around her shoulders.

She pushed him away.

"You just don't get it, do you?" she fumed. "I'm not interested in you. I won't ever be interested in you. You could rise to the Solity Council and run the entire country, and I still wouldn't be interested in you."

He backed her up against a wall while she talked, then reached out to poke her in the ribs.

"Stop!" she shouted in desperation.

His hand stayed on her ribs, warm through her coverall.

Luis leaned in close. "I'm not going to stop, Zofia. Not until you give in. You need me, and you just don't know it. You're too smart for your own good and too gorgeous to be alone. I can fix that."

His fingers greased the side of her breast. She jumped and pushed him away with a shout. He winked, raked his hand through his tousled brown hair, and entered the classroom.

Zofia leaned back against the wall and shuddered. She lowered her head, hiding her grey eyes behind the drape of her shoulder-length black hair. A part of her wanted to cry, another part wanted to scream with rage. *Bangit, how can I make him stop?*

When she lifted her eyes again, Ella and Quoia were watching her from across the hall. Quoia whispered something to Ella, and the two laughed, spiteful eyes on her.

Zofia spun off the wall back into the classroom. Thankfully, the torture of Verdant Prime secondary school was nearly at an end. She wouldn't have to put up with the childishness of all the grey-clad students much longer. Pass her finals, and she'd get her work Assignment from Solity—from the government, who Assigned everyone—where she could do something worthwhile with her programming skills. She looked forward to it with excitement, but also with trepidation. Solity controlled everything in Verdant Prime. If they gave you the wrong clothing or food, you were stuck with it—and if they gave you the wrong Assignment, you were stuck with that, too.

She took her seat, set her jaw and leaned forward to get started. Working with Isadora, she examined the information available on weather, commune connectivity, and industry. The effort was exhausting and mind-consuming. She lost track of the rest of the class, her surroundings fading into the background.

How can I possibly integrate all this into an effective app?

Swallowing hard, she decided to see how close she could come with an easy try.

"Okay, Isadora, let's try a simple solution. Create an app to predict cheese deliveries based on the commissar's requests."

"The requests are quarterly. Cheese deliveries are biweekly. How would you like me to handle the difference?"

Zofia waved her hand in the air. "I don't know. Let's divide the quarterly requests by week"

"Done. The app is ready. Would you like to view the code?"

"No, I'll trust you on something this simple. Now evaluate the app against the four sample communities. How well do the commissars do in their requests?"

Isadora's pause was much less than a second. For a problem this simple, Zofia suspected Isadora had inserted a false pause just for appearance.

"Not very good, Zofia," the AI said, displaying a holo graph of the statistical results. "The app is in error on daily cheese usage 43 percent of the time across the four communes. In commune C, distribution centers run out of cheese fifty-three days out of the year."

"That's terrible. So, we can't rely on the commissars at all?"

"Doesn't look like it."

Her mind rapidly moved ahead. What would be the next approximation? *Maybe I can calibrate the commissar accuracy against what they actually accomplished.*

"Okay, Isadora. Create app version 2. Develop trend lines of how well each commissar predicted actual usage, then adjust the commissar requests based on those trend lines. Predict cheese deliveries based on the adjusted requests. When done, evaluate the app, same criteria."

Again, the pause was hardly significant.

"Version 2 does better. Deliveries are in error only twenty-seven percent of the time. Commune C is still the worst. I note the errors for commune B increased."

"What? Calibration on a commissar results in worse performance? How can that be?"

"I'm afraid I can't help evaluate the data without better instructions, Zofia."

"That's okay. Performance is still so poor, we need to include more data, anyway."

What to try next? Of the various factors, maybe weather would have a big effect. *Do people eat more cheese when it's cold?*

"Let's do a side calculation, Isadora. Evaluate the correlation of cheese usage with outside air temperature."

"There is a moderate correlation between temperature and cheese usage."

"Okay, then create version 3. Predict cheese deliveries based on the version 2 commissar requests adjusted by these trend lines. When done, evaluate the app again."

"Adjust requests based on which trend lines, Zofia? The commissar error trends or the temperature trends?"

Zofia winced. All this term, she'd been practicing precision in her language. She'd missed it again this time.

"Based on both trends, Isadora."

After the usual slight pause, the AI answered. "Version 3 has an error of 26 percent."

"What? So, 27 percent only went down to 26 percent? That's not much improvement."

"No, it's not. What would you like to try next?"

Three hours later, Zofia was frantic. She kept her language under strict control so the AI could understand her, while exploring statistics she barely understood. She ran correlation tests on all eighteen given factors and another twelve she thought up. Some of them seemed strong, others had hardly any effect. She created sixteen versions of the app, never achieving error rate any lower than 21 percent.

How can I get the app to reach ten percent for an unknown commune, when I can't even get the four samples anywhere near that level? Damn, this problem is impossible!

She raised her hand for the teacher, who stepped to her side. "Yes, Zofia, what can I do for you?"

"Mers. Bekker, this exam is orders of magnitude harder than anything we've done in class. I'm doin' all sorts of correlation and regression, and I haven't come close yet."

The teacher answered with her usual cold voice, "Well, yes, Zofia. It's supposed to be difficult. And yours is harder than any others."

"Is there anythin' you can offer to help me, ma'am?"

Mers. Bekker snorted. "Of course not. This is a final exam. You must do the work yourself. I won't be here later this evening to help, so learn to do it."

Zofia heard snickers behind her. She whirled in her chair to see Quoia thumb her nose and Ella hide a smile.

The teacher also turned. "Quoia, return to your own exam. When you can program as well as Zofia, then you can afford to poke fun."

Bangit, Zofia. Good work. Ask for help, and it just adds to the put-downs.

She turned back to her problem while Mers. Bekker strode to the teacher's desk. Certainly, her schooling had given her the tools to solve this, or it wouldn't be on the exam. Others must have passed this exam question before.

Perhaps some background research would help, if the solution wasn't contained solely in the data they'd provided. Isadora helped her find scholarly articles reporting research on cheese consumption. She spent the rest of the day in research rather than trying new app versions as the sunlight in the room raced from one wall to the opposite. The articles revealed useful information. Known factors that increased cheese consumption were lower socio-economic status, societal proximity to milk animals, greater connection with other communities, and—a surprise to Zofia—gender and marital status.

What? Married women eat more cheese? Who knew?

Near the end of the day, she decided to try once more.

"Isadora, let's create a new version of the app. What number are we up to?"

The AI's face appeared with an encouraging smile. "Version 19 is next, Zofia."

"Okay. For version 19, use all the trends we had in version 18. Adjust the cheese usage predictions based on the last...let's see...five research reports. That should include new factors of population gender mix, season of year, commune elevation, milk animal population, and population marital status. Is that correct?"

"Those are the last five research reports you've viewed."

"Good. Create the app and test it as before."

While she gave the command, a shadow intruded on her holodesk.

"Hey, star student, how're you doing?" Luis said, his usual sneer in his voice.

She slumped in resignation. "Go away, Luis. I'm workin'."

"It's time to quit, Zofia. Everyone's leaving. Maybe I should keep you company on the way out. You know, keep you safe from other boys."

She turned to face him. "Luis, you're the only one I need safety from. Stop botherin' me." She turned her back on him again.

He leaned down to look into her holo. "Hey, Isadora. Is Zofia doing her proper magic?" The AI was silent.

"Isadora only responds to me, Luis. Go away."

"Wait, what's this I see in your holo? Gender? Marital status? Interesting topics. What kind of research are you doing, Zofia? I wonder where the mind of a gorgeous girl wanders when it's supposed to be working, hmm?"

She felt his breath on her ear. Her jaw clenched. She stood up aggressively, trying to clip his jaw with her shoulder, but he avoided the contact and snickered.

"Mers. Bekker?" she called out. "Luis Abreu is harassing me." She turned to the front of the class to see it empty.

Luis poked her in the rib again. "Already gone, sweet stuff. Just us students here." Several other students were watching the interaction with smirks on their faces.

"Not this one, Luis. I'm outta here." She pushed him away and strode to the door, hearing laughter echoing behind her.

❧ ✳ ❧

Nightmares plagued her that night, dreams of abject failure. The third time she jumped awake in terror was enough. She got up early, dressed, and went to the classroom as dawn smeared the sky with dim light. The empty building smelled stale.

"Good morning, Isadora," her voice echoed in the empty classroom.

"You're early, Zofia. Did you come up with new ideas in the night?"

"Yes, a few. First, what were the results of our version 19 last night? I was interrupted."

"I'd noticed. I'm sorry Luis obstructed your thinking. You'd been making good progress."

Zofia cocked her chin. "'Good progress'? Errors are still over twenty percent. Are you implying I'm on the right path, Isadora?"

"No, Zofia. I'm not allowed to give guidance."

"Yeah, I know." She smiled. "But I can hope, can't I?"

"I'm not sure what 'hope' is, but humans are allowed to do most things, as long as they don't violate the rules of Solity."

"Okay, let's get back to version 19. What happened with it?"

"Here's the table of results. Version 19 lowered daily error rate to sixteen percent across the four communes. Commune D was at nine percent, but commune C was still high. No commune ever ran out of cheese."

Zofia sat up straight. "That's good. Real progress. It's the first time we've had any commune meet the exam standard. So, the research data actually helped."

"Yes, it did."

"But it's not good enough yet. We don't know what the final evaluation commune will be like. My app has to be robust enough to work for any. Yet with all this information, we're still not very close to ten percent across the board."

"What do you mean by 'close'?"

Her frustration was rising again. "Close means under ten percent most of the time."

"Then we're not close yet."

Zofia closed her eyes and took a deep breath. *Not useful to get frustrated at the helpful-but-literal AI.* Instead, she focused on the goal: solving this statistical problem. The tension in her chest eased. The school building awakened around her. Several students sauntered into the classroom. She opened her eyes and turned to watch. Two girls and two boys enjoyed easy friendship in a subdued morning conversation.

They glanced her way, but no one said hello.

She slumped in her chair and returned to her work. This was the price of being the best. It often seemed her success was a plascrete wall separating her from everyone. Someday, somehow, she'd learn how to be with people. She didn't understand how to connect.

Bangit, let's just finish this exam.

She added three new factors to version 20. The AI's pauses were perceptibly longer as the calculations became more complicated. However, correlations and progressions were bread-and-butter to the underlying computers, so Isadora's answers still came back in about a second.

"Version 20 has an average error rate of twenty-one percent, Zofia."

"What?" She was so startled she shouted the word. "That's worse than version 19." Conversation stopped behind her and a painful silence followed. Zofia blushed when she heard a few whispers and footsteps moving away. Another clot of students came into the room.

"Got a problem there, Mers. Star?" Luis's snide voice insinuated over the sound-deadening wall beside her. "We heard you all the way out in the hall."

Just what I need. "Leave me alone, Luis." Zofia's shoulders fell. She crossed her arms under her breasts and hunkered into a ball. "I can't deal with you now."

One of Luis's cronies pulled him away. "Leave her be, Luis. She's got a *hard* exam." The two snickered and left.

Zofia pondered her problem while the rest of the students filed into the room and started work.

Thought I was so close. One more version, and it would push over into success. Now I don't know what to do.

Zofia stretched her brain to come up with new directions to search. The morning flew, followed by a quick snack for lunch. She lost herself in the work, examining tables of data and formulating searches for Isadora. It felt almost like teamwork, the two of them interacting to advance possibilities. Underneath it all was a growing fear she wasn't good enough to solve this one.

Luis finished his exam just after lunch. Zofia ground her teeth, wishing she weren't the star student and could have an easier exam like his. He didn't leave. *Is he waiting to harass me more?* Apparently not, because he stayed in his seat watching everyone else. He didn't transgress the rules about collaboration, yet it seemed his presence encouraged his hangers-on to better efforts in their own work. Most students were done by mid-afternoon. Every time Zofia heard Luis speak or move, her shoulder blades tightened, expecting some gibe.

By late afternoon, she was barking commands to Isadora, frantic to make something—anything—work. They were up to version 42, trying different combinations. Some worked, most didn't. Version 34 had been promising, with two of the four communes under the ten percent goal. Unfortunately, the other two communes had gotten worse. Most versions hovered in the lower teens.

Mers. Bekker stood from her desk. "Students, the normal workday is nearly done. I will be leaving shortly, but you are free to stay and work. You must submit your exams by midnight."

The announcement brought Zofia out of her head. She looked around the room to see only three students left. Even Luis had left, thankfully without bothering her. She raised her hand, her stomach in flutters. "What happens if we don't submit?"

"You fail by default. I suggest you turn in your best app by midnight, even if it doesn't meet criteria. Solity will make its determination based on how well you've done."

"Thank you, ma'am." Zofia already felt defeated, but she returned to trying the next combination.

This isn't working; there has to be something else. It's the definition of insanity, to try the same thing and expect different results.

Instead of directing Isadora, she sat back in thought. Panic enveloped the edges of her mind like thunderclouds around a shaky tower. She shoved it aside with a conscious effort.

I need something different. Maybe she should review the tools they'd been given; there might be something she hadn't yet tried.

"Isadora, display the list of lesson topics in this class for the last two years."

The AI's face appeared with an expression of surprise. "That's a different approach."

Zofia knew the surprise was only a construct, but she smiled at Isadora's helpfulness. Then she scanned the list, remembering what she'd learned about each topic. The room cleared while she searched. Everyone else was done. The light in the room changed when sunset tinted the windows. In the quiet, she walked through the list of lessons.

Wait. What about principal component analysis? Dredging her mind for the lesson, she remembered PCA was a time-honored tool to identify the principal components that most affected a set of data. It used a coordinate transformation from the given factors into those principal components. She could do the correlations with the components instead of the basic factors, and perhaps the correlations would work better. The memory gave her new hope.

She nodded.

"Isadora, perform a side calculation. We've listed thirty-three factors so far. Create a principal component analysis of those factors. Identify the first ten principal components and the contributions of each factor to those components."

The pause was considerably longer this time before Isadora responded. "I've completed the analysis, Zofia. Here are the results." An extensive statistical table appeared in the holo display.

Six principal components each had greater than forty percent correlation with cheese usage. As in any Pareto analysis, a gap separated them from the remaining four principal components.

"Isadora, let's create a new approach for version 43. Transform the given factors into the first principal component using the dependencies of the PCA. Then predict cheese usage using only that first component. Evaluate as before."

The AI responded quickly. "Transformation complete, Zofia. App version 43 has error of fifteen percent over a sample year."

Zofia broke into a wide grin. "That good? After only one component? Bangit, we should have tried this earlier."

"Congratulations, Zofia. It's close already."

"Yeah. So, let's cross our fingers and make a new version"

"I can't cross my fingers, Zofia. I don't have any."

"Right, of course," Zofia said, still grinning. "I knew that. Ignore the fingers and create version 44 using all of the first six PCA components."

The pause was longer, nearly four seconds, while Isadora set up the new app.

"App version 44 is ready now. Would you like me to evaluate it?"

"Yes, Isadora." Zofia did cross her own fingers—both hands, in the air on either side of her face.

"Version 44 has error rates of just over eight percent for the sample year."

"Yes," shouted Zofia, jumping to her feet. She pumped her fists in the air and did a little dance in the empty classroom. "We've got it!"

"I'm glad for you, Zofia. Would you like me to extend the evaluation to all five sample years?"

"Good idea. Do that." She put her hands on the back of her chair and leaned forward for the results.

"All four communes are below ten percent for each of the five years—"

"Fantastic." Zofia felt her shoulders and back relax. She hadn't been aware they were as tight as they'd been.

"—except commune C, which had two years with errors of eleven and twelve percent."

Zofia's relaxation turned into a slump, leaning on the chair back. She hung her head, eyes closed, for a long moment. *Not there yet. How much more is this going to take?* She checked the time: two hours until midnight. *I need to get away from this.*

"Thank you, Isadora—"

"No thanks are necessary to an AI, Zofia."

"That's okay. Save all this. I'll be back in a few minutes."

Zofia stood and stretched her back, looking around. The classroom was quiet but for the hum of the air conditioning. The windows looked out on black night with neither of the two moons visible.

Standing, she realized how incredibly tense she was. Time was very short, and she still didn't quite have it solved. *Go to the bathroom. It'll help clear my head.*

The light in the hallway was harsh. Silence reigned in the empty building. She heard her own breathing. Her mind wanted to go back to the exam problem, but she forced herself away from it. A Solity poster on the wall encouraged all students to do their best for society. A bulletin board announced the exams. The building air reeked of too many students.

She thought she heard a scuffed footstep in a side hallway. She held her breath, stopped and looked in that direction, but nothing moved.

Probably just jumpy from too much concentration.

With a shrug, she resumed walking to the bathroom. When she opened the door, another phantom footstep sounded behind her. Her hand on the door, she paused to look behind.

Nothing there.

She smiled at her own foolishness, shook her head and entered. The bathroom light glared as harsh as the hallway. The air conditioning fans susurrated with a constant whir. Entering the last stall, she dropped her grey coveralls and panties to sit on the toilet. She leaned her elbows on her knees and relaxed.

Two breaths later, the restroom door crashed open. It slammed with a bang against the wall. Her eyes jerked open and her hands slapped against both walls of the stall, holding herself steady. She froze in place, heart pounding, a heavy weight in her chest.

The door closed again with a soft clunk. Stillness fell. Had someone entered? Or not? She stayed as still as she could, listening with her entire body. Did she hear breathing?

Silence, all but the air conditioning.

Suddenly, heavy footsteps paced in the small room. The contrast with silence startled her. She wanted to shrink away to nothing, make no noise, become a dust mote in the air. Heavy breathing coupled with the steps when they stopped. A pair of men's shoes faced her under the stall door. She grasped for her clothes.

She'd never felt so helpless in all her life as in this impossible situation.

"Who's there?" Her own voice sounded shrill. "Go away!"

Zofia stood and pulled her panties into place. She shrugged her coveralls over her shoulders. Her breathing was shallow and filled with the acrid scent of her own sweat. She clutched the front of her coveralls to her breasts.

The shoes shifted position and one shoe lifted. Without warning, the stall door crashed inward when the flimsy lock gave way to a heavyweight foot. Zofia cried out. The door clipped her shoulder, firing her with pain.

"Hi, Zofia. I told you that you needed me." Luis easily regained his balance and stood with legs apart, hands on his hips, a threatening grin on his face.

Anger exploded in her. "Get out, get out!" Her stomach clenched in fear and her knees shook. She was painfully aware how much larger he was than her.

She grabbed the door and threw it shut. Luis stopped it before it closed and shoved it open again.

"Oh, you need me. You just don't know it. You're so smart, but so dumb at the same time." Luis grabbed her coveralls—still unfastened—and pulled.

She clutched the coveralls closed with one hand and held him away with the other. Her mind raced, looking for some way out.

"Help," she screamed as loud as she could.

He yanked her out of the stall by her clothes.

"There's no one else in the building, Mers. Star Student. I checked already. I've been waiting for you a long time. Did you finally get your *special* exam done?"

She pushed at his chest, rocking him backward but not off balance. Luis was too big and strong. He pulled her to him and wrapped both arms around her, mashing his body against her. She felt the heat of his body and smelled his male musk. She struggled and squirmed, her arms trapped between them. She screamed again, a wordless cry of rage and fear, and tried to scratch him wherever her fingers could reach.

"Star, you're going to enjoy this once we get started. You just need to relax." He leaned down to force a kiss.

Enough, she shouted inside her head.

She bit his lip, digging her teeth hard, trying to tear it off. Then she kicked upward with her knee into his groin as hard as she could.

Luis shouted in pain and fell back. His heel caught on the floor, and he went down on his rump. It looked like he wasn't sure whether to grab his bleeding lip or his genitals.

Zofia made sure. She stepped forward and swung her leg like an accomplished football player. Her foot ended in his crotch with a resounding thud. He howled and writhed on the floor.

Still trembling with anger and fear, Zofia stepped away from him. She used her comms implant to call for help. "Urgent security call. Attempted rape." She knew the system would pinpoint her location and they'd arrive within minutes. *Why didn't I think of that earlier?*

Then she stood by, ready to kick him again if needed.

Processing the event took another hour. The Solity Guards, dressed in intimidating black with bulbous helmets, carted Luis away, recorded her statement, and took samples of his blood from her coveralls. They offered to bring in a counselor, but she declined.

A counselor? I can't think right now; I certainly can't talk about it. And bangit, I've got to finish my exam. Sweat still bloomed on her neck. She knew her eyes were wide, and she probably looked frantic. Damn, she *was* frantic. *I've gotta get away from this.*

"Thanks for the reference. I'll contact her tomorrow." How could she sound so calm? She checked the time. "Right now, I have to finish submitting my exam."

Her nerves were shattered. She hardly had enough brain power to speak clearly when she sat again in her cubicle. She shook all over.

"Welcome back, Zofia," said Isadora. "Are you ready to continue? We have fifty-two minutes left."

Zofia thought for a moment, then shook her head. "No, Isadora. I can't do any more. This will have to be good enough. Submit the last version for my exam."

"Done. Good luck."

❧ ✳ ❧

After a sleepless night, she couldn't face the usual derision of her classmates first thing. She called the counselor and spent two hours talking with her. Processing the event helped, and her head was clearer when she stepped into the classroom, avoiding the eyes of her classmates.

Mers. Bekker was in the middle of announcing exam results. She looked up and nodded. "Zofia. Normally, nothing would excuse such lateness. However, I understand you had an incident last night."

Zofia blushed. She didn't want to go through this in front of the class. "Yes, ma'am, but it should be—"

"Yes, private. I know. Nothing more will be said. Take your seat."

The curiosity from the other students was a hooliphant dropping half-meter scales to clatter on the floor. All eyes were on her. Zofia kept her eyes on the floor and sat.

"Zofia, we deliver exam results publicly so all may learn." Mers. Bekker looked down at the holo in front of her. "I believe I was down to Wensel Franal. Stand up, please."

The girl stood on the far side of the room near the windows. Wensel's hands shook. *Whew. Glad to have the attention on someone else.*

"Wensel, your task was to create an app to count the trees in a landscape picture. The app you created was accurate on the five photographs you were given. Did you test it on any other pictures?"

Wensel winced. "No, ma'am. I didn't think to do so."

"A common failing, class. Just because you have information given, do not assume your work must be based only on that information. Wensel, our system tested your app against ten other landscape pictures. It was accurate for eight of the ten. Though not as good as it could have been, you have passed your exam."

The girl sagged in relief. "Thank you, ma'am."

"No thanks are necessary. You did the work, I didn't."

Wensel sat.

"Zofia Dobrunik, stand up."

So soon? Her heart in her throat, Zofia stood.

"Your task was to create an app for the Capital Department to predict the distribution of cheese goods. Yours was the last exam submitted, with less than an hour to spare. How well do you think you did?"

"I used lots of outside research, then tested my app against the sample information. It met the ten percent criterion for eighteen out of twenty cases."

Mers. Bekker nodded, her lips firm. "Once again, class, note that she restricted her testing to the sample information. You all must learn to be more aggressive in your testing." She turned back to Zofia. "We tested your app against sample data for five years in the Warrens. It failed miserably, with error rates greater than twenty-five percent in every case."

The class gasped.

Zofia's mouth dropped open. She spluttered. "The Warrens, ma'am? The Warrens? I was a child there. Nothing good ever comes out of the Warrens."

Her classmates broke into loud laughter, and Zofia realized what she'd just said.

Mers. Bekker slammed her heavy hand on her desk, a resounding crack that stopped the laughter. She glared at the students.

In the silence, Zofia tried again. "That's hardly a fair test case, ma'am. The commissar data from the Warrens is terrible."

The teacher stood up, menacing, her voice hard. "Yes, it is, which is why we tested your app there. The rest of the class worked on throw-away problems that have been used in school for years. You were given a real-world problem, one Capital desperately needs. Even in better communes, commissars give poor predictions and we waste Labor effort creating overages and shortages. We had hoped, with your ability, you could come up with something better."

Zofia clenched her jaw, her legs quivering. She wanted to rage back at the teacher. *I did my best, damn it.* Instead, she kept it inside, except for her eyes. She knew she was glaring.

Mers. Bekker continued in a quiet tone, "...and you did."

The silence was stunning. Zofia held her breath in surprise.

The teacher continued, "We have given this same problem to five other students in the last eight years. None have done as well as you. It is an impossible problem, but you have given Capital a better solution than we've had. Congratulations. You pass."

Zofia glanced sideways to see astonishment on some faces and resentment on others. She felt herself blushing. "Thank you, ma'am."

Mers. Bekker shook her head. "Again, not necessary. Solity thanks you for your work."

Zofia shook her head in dismay. *Life shouldn't be this hard.* Two impossible situations in two days, and she had gotten past them both. Surely, there must be a better way to grow.

Legal Incontinence

Tileus was the first country to win independence from Verdant Prime. Situated across the Vissensee Channel on another continent, independents envisioned something with more freedom than the totalitarian socialism of Prime. They went all the way back to ancient Greece for concepts of true democracy. Using implants and the InfoNet technology, they created a nation of free enterprise that made all its decisions collectively by nationwide vote within a few minutes. The result was more difficult than they had imagined.

Tileus Lews Service, 5-34 March 38, Year 416 After Touchdown. Per national vote at 5-29 today, loggers in the western forest may only cut down 80% of the trees in any given area.

"Hey, look at this one," Detective Soren Moller sneered across the desk to his partner. "I saw the vote go by yesterday. They've banned the display of bare chests in downtown areas. Male and female."

Soren was reviewing the holo display hanging over their shared desk in the dark-walled office of five detective teams. He put a hand into the haptic field to scroll the display. Every day, the two started by checking the law news—the "Lews"—so they knew what laws had changed in the past day.

"Yeah," the huge Manny Hong laughed in his bass, rumbling voice and scratched an insect bite on his neck. "I wonder how much time we're supposed to spend enforcing that one."

"I think we'll leave it to the patrol officers while we handle the crimes that need investigation. Like this sex trafficking case. We need something to break."

Soren had been slouching in his chair. He straightened up for a moment to stretch his back.

His partner pointed at Soren's short legs and grinned. "You know you can't do that anymore. They outlawed crossing your legs ten minutes ago."

Soren snorted. "Yeah, right. Wonder what bright spark thought that one up. Was it you?"

Manny responded in a serious tone. "I actually heard discussion about it. Some doctor thought it put undue pressure on your veins."

"Do-gooders. May they all get drowned in the islands of Winter."

Manny often came across as funny, but Soren knew his partner had depths as hidden as predators in the forest. He was dedicated to their work and just wanted to solve the cases, whatever it took.

Soren leaned forward and swept a few gestures through the field. "Ah, enough of this daily update. I'm changing the display to check on our InfoNet sex trafficking traps."

"Good idea. This pervert has got to make a mistake sometime. And if anyone can trap him, Soren, you can. You've got magic fingers when it comes to working the Net."

Soren shrugged. "Guess so. But there's nothing here yet." His shoulders slumped. "My father loved police work, when he served, and so do I. We keep people safe. But man, the laws change so quickly these days."

His partner nodded. "I saw a study last month; we're creating about fifty new laws every week. Just ten years ago, the number was only twenty. We get full-country votes in ten minutes through our implants and the InfoNet. Two-thirds 'yes,' and bang, we've got a new law."

"Yeah, and the media services don't make it any easier with their partisan arguing. Creates a lot of conflict."

"By the way, have you been following the discussion on privacy protection?"

"Privacy is important," Soren said. "Before you and I were partners, my sister's son was almost snatched when someone got into his personal data. I just happened to be there and stopped the snatch. Personal data issues can lead to things like this case we're chasing. But I don't like this latest proposal. They want to extend the warrant system to include anything revealing personal data. It'll cripple our ability to get information."

His partner nodded, his huge frame rock steady. All the detectives had to maintain fitness, but Manny did it enthusiastically. People easily remembered him, with his size, bulging shoulders, brown hair, and green eyes.

"Yeah," Manny said. "It seems to be aimed directly at us detectives." He laughed bitterly. "We may have to get a warrant just to ask questions."

"I don't think it'll go that far. So far, the discussion seems about evenly split for and against the proposal. It's supposed to come up for vote today, I think. We need to make sure to vote against—."

Soren interrupted himself. "Manny, we've got a hit." He leaned forward toward the holo with eagerness and pointed. His fingertip activated the haptic link and expanded the flash. "Someone just made contact with one of our underage targets."

∿✻∾

Tileus Lews Service, 6-12 March 38, 416 A.T. Per national vote at 6-08 today, no person other than an owner may reside at any establishment selling liquor.

∿✻∾

The modest house sat in the suburbs of Thad City. The exterior was a friendly pastel yellow with white trim, surrounded by orderly shrubs and smooth grass. With antigrav autocars available within minutes, the house had no driveway or garage to mar the style. This particular house had those extra architectural appointments speaking of wealth: gingerbread trim around the door, polarizing holographic windows, automatic sunshades and more.

Wyot Gani did his work in the back office. A broad window looked out on a terrace of sculpted gardens and tidy neighborhood woodlands; the peaceful scene brought him tranquility. He spent many hours sitting in this chair, his short, pudgy frame gradually accumulating weight.

His work was lucrative, targeting minors for sex trafficking snatches.

"Ha," he exulted in the empty room. "Got another one."

Gani's excitement swelled and he smiled. Despite Gani's dangerous activity—or maybe as part of it—he had a friendly smile.

Gani worked alone and was good at what he did. He had bots constantly trawling the InfoNet looking for possible targets: teens and pre-teens who were dissatisfied with themselves and their families. His search AI extracted essential personal data. With sufficient facts, his particular brilliance resided in connecting the dots to create a place and time of vulnerability. He could entice the target virtually, until he got sufficient information to make them vulnerable physically.

Before he could pursue the latest hit, his holo lit up with a customer call.

"Hey, Gani." No video came through, but Gani knew this particular gruff but eager male voice. He kept his own video suppressed, also.

"Petro, good to hear from you. You in need of another target?"

"Yeah. We've got room in the *facility*." His voice put obvious quotes around the word, with implications of darker significance.

"Good. I've got a live one on the line now. Give me another half hour, and I'll get back to you."

He did have scruples of sorts. Gani never personally exploited the targets. He was too frightened to do what he imagined, so he fulfilled his vicarious thrill by passing the target on to unsavory customers. Petro would pay dearly. Then, when he snatched the target, he would be the one at risk, not Gani. Sometimes, his payment included audioholo recordings.

Gani was dragged out of his anticipation by a flashing red warning in the corner of his holo.

"Uh-oh, bad news." Gani didn't mind talking to himself when working. He had a high opinion of both the speaker and the listener.

He'd just succeeded in popping the girl's password. With pre-teens, it was always easier than anyone thought. He already knew her implant address and had hacked her biometrics. The next step would normally be to insert attractive messages and data into her social implant feed to lure her to a physical location.

The warning showed him some trace program had snagged his action. He worked frantically to extricate himself, leaving false paths all over the InfoNet server cloud.

⤳ ✳ ⤝

Tileus Lews Service, 6-45 March 38, 416 A.T. Per national vote at 6-40 today, law enforcement officials must certify any valid warrant with the National Registry Board prior to serving the warrant. This necessary step is in addition to and subsequent to obtaining the warrant from a judge.

⤳ ✳ ⤝

Soren expanded the flash and his fingers flew. He also gave subverbal commands through his implant. The holo display changed rapidly.

His partner tracked the display with him. "Is it what we think?"

"This may be what we've been looking for. We have got to get these slimeballs; it's a whole lot more important than people not wearing shirts. Let's see what I can find."

With a few wipes of his fingers in the 3-D holo, Soren launched the AI to track down the source. They watched the results link to a graphic of an InfoNet access chain. Many new links happened, all trying to divert the AI. A light-speed battle ensued between his AI trace and the source. The cloud links activated from here in Thad City to other Tileus locations, into Rathas and even off-shore to Winter. Thankfully, none of the links led into Verdant Prime, where things were so controlled and locked down his AI couldn't get in. After a series of twenty-two accesses, the final path led back again to Thad City and to someone named Wyot Gani.

"We got him," Soren grunted. "Let's go. We have enough evidence here as 'hot pursuit' to question him without a warrant; if we take him into custody, then we can get a warrant for his computer."

Soren subvocalized to his implant to request the next available police autocar and to set its destination to the address. They both grabbed their gear and hustled out just as the car arrived at the door. Traffic routers cleared the intersections along their route; other cars stopped as needed. With all vehicles on auto, no siren was necessary.

As they moved, Soren's implant signaled yet another vote.

"Manny, here's the vote on privacy. Make sure you register your 'no' vote."

"You got it."

❧ ✸ ❦

Tileus Lews Service, 7-17 March 38, 416 A.T. Per national vote at 7-12 today, personal information is inadmissible in court proceedings unless either (a) publicly available, or (b) freely given by the person, or (c) obtained under a court-approved warrant.

❧ ✸ ❦

Soren pounded hard on the door of the cute yellow house, while Manny watched the back. Both had needle guns out and were ready for anything.

"Police. Open up." Soren's voice resounded in the quiet neighborhood like the roar of a caterwaul.

Soren's implant suddenly spoke to him in the voice of the Law Enforcement AI. "Your actions may constitute legal violation. The basis for this questioning appears to have been obtained from personal information."

Soren shook his head in irritation. LEAI was often as obstructive as it was helpful. "Later, AI. Can't deal with it now."

The back door sprang open and Wyot Gani exploded outwards like a rabbit from a disturbed warren. Manny Hong was waiting and tackled him on the lawn before he had gone three meters. The two men were as different as slime and rock; despite his struggles, the roly-poly Gani had no chance physically against Manny.

"Got him back here," Manny shouted.

Soren ran around the back to find Gani facedown with Manny kneeling on his rump and slapping a tanglecuff around his wrists. The plastic device quickly tightened to hold. The yard filled with the sweet scent of disturbed grass.

"Great job, Manny."

"Yeah, this little butterball thought he could run away."

Soren squatted down by Gani's face. "So, Mars. Gani, what was so important you needed to run when we knocked?"

"Let me go. I've done nothing wrong." Gani squirmed unsuccessfully to find a comfortable position.

"Right. Sure." Manny stood up and hauled Gani to his feet. "It's what everyone says. Gani does nothing wrong."

Soren stood up with them. "Well, Mars. Gani, we've got some pretty good information saying you've been doing bad things on your computer. Why don't you come downtown with us and we'll talk about it?"

"This is an illegal arrest, and you can't go into my house without a valid, registered warrant. I saw the Lews this morning."

"We'll just use the evidence we already have, my friend. It'll be plenty to get a 'valid, registered' warrant."

Soren looked over Gani's head at Manny, who gave an uneasy shrug. Both of them had heard LEAI's warning.

❖

Tileus Lews Service, 8-33 March 38, 416 A.T. Per vote at 8-28 today, antigrav airliners may not pass beyond the vertical boundaries of an airfield except at altitudes above 500 meters.

❖

"What?" Soren was livid. "We can't get a warrant?"

The partners were back at the office, and Soren was on the implant comms with the prosecutor. He had patched in Manny, who was across the desk watching.

"No warrant," the prosecutor repeated. "Your trace AI is included under the new privacy law, which was enacted before you took him in. Because the arrest is based on the trace, it's tainted evidence and cannot support a warrant."

"You've got to be kidding me. How are we supposed to catch cybercriminals without traces?"

They ended the call. Soren wanted to wring someone's neck as he watched the desk clerk out-process Gani. To make it worse, the little gumball saw them and waved cheerily.

"See you, boys. I'll be over at the Thirsty Terrapin celebrating." With a most irritating wink, Gani walked out.

Tileus Lews Service, 9-12 March 38, 416 A.T. Per national vote at 9-07 today, the Tileus Family Assistance Agency will receive an additional 1.2B Credits for vocational training programs.

Soren spent the next several hours researching, while Manny worked quietly on other cases. Precedents were difficult in the changing laws, but Soren hoped to find something reinstating the case. The trace AI had gone back and confirmed Wyot Gani was linked to a half dozen of these sex trafficking cases, but how could Soren make it stick without the trace information?

He came up with zilch. Oh, there were some cute cases a creative lawyer could use—but creative shenanigans only worked in defense. The prosecuting attorneys had to stay within the bounds. He found one case where a stripper had been caught red-handed (as it were) touching a customer. She was arrested an hour before the laws changed to allow physical contact between a stripper and customers. She was successfully prosecuted under the law in force at the time of her arrest. But the same tactic wouldn't work here; the law had changed just before Soren and Manny knocked on Gani's door.

He threw his hands up in despair. "I can't find it, Manny. Nothing helps."

"Let it go, Soren. Just let it go, and we'll start over with a different approach tomorrow. At least we know who he is. We're ahead of the game with that. And I've got to get home. We have kids coming over for the night."

"I guess so. There's nothing else to do." He checked his implant. "And it's 11-30 anyway. Quitting time. We'll get back to it tomorrow."

Tileus Lews Service, 11-45 March 38, 416 A.T. Per national vote at 11-41 today, Tileus will expend 2.9B Credits next year toward basic civilizing education within the islands of Winter.

As he left the station, Soren looked around at the placid downtown area. Buildings of varied heights provided architectural variety. The streets were landscaped with wide walks, block-long slidewalks, and a single narrow lane for the autocars. A deep breath of fresh spring air cleared his mind for a moment. He could smell sweet flowers somewhere nearby.

But then he saw the flashing green sign for the Thirsty Terrapin on the next block. He ground his teeth at Wyot Gani enjoying himself instead of sweating out his crime in virtual restraint. He couldn't help himself; he walked toward the bar just to see the perp again.

He looked through the diamond-paned window. Gani, at the center of a small group, regaled them all with drinking tales and his broad smile. The table was filled with used glassware. Gani was popular, no doubt, but Soren couldn't tell whether his popularity stemmed from his friendly personality or his generous wallet. They all seemed to be enjoying themselves.

Soren looked at the ancient-style clock over the bar and saw 11-54, time for him to get some dinner. He should just walk on by—

A sudden thought occurred to him, and he looked at the clock again. *Wait a minute, wasn't there a recent redefinition of residency?* He used his implant to check on it, and a slow, wicked smile spread across his face. He could use the long-standing method of arresting a criminal on some lesser charge to gain access to their information. Standing taller, he pushed open the door and strode across the room to Gani.

"Okay, Gani. You're under arrest. Stand up, please."

Rather tipsy, Gani looked up in surprise. "What? You can't cop me. That's already settled."

Soren grabbed his arm and forced him to stand up. "Hands behind your back." As he tanglecuffed the wrists, Soren continued, "You're under arrest for violating today's new statute about residing in an establishment selling liquor."

"Residing? Oh, sure, right. I'm not residing here, just trading a few drinks with some friends."

"Wrong, my friend. Last month, for an issue about people staying too long in brothels, we defined 'residence' as any occupancy in excess of three hours. You've been sitting here in the Thirsty Terrapin for three hours and 22 minutes. Come with me."

"No, no, no. I don't live here." Gani was suddenly frantic and talkative. "I live at my house in the suburbs. I can prove it."

"Sure, sure, it's what they all say. Gani lives there. Let's go, my friend."

As he led him out, Soren saw with amusement the alarm that spread among Gani's drinking friends. Several of them got up quickly and left the bar as they also noticed the time. Perhaps this arrest would straighten out a few errant husbands, too.

❧ ✳ ❧

Soren sat at home that evening pushing back a few brews. They tasted sweet. The collar on Gani had stuck, both for the silly "residence" charge and for the sex trafficking crimes. Following the arrest, Soren got a warrant—registered, of course—to search Gani's house for proof of residence, which had "discovered" the evidence of the greater crimes on his home computer. But Soren had no idea whether the case would make it successfully into prosecution. Things changed daily.

He lifted his glass in the air to success as fleeting as the laws themselves.

❧ ✳ ❧

Tileus Lews Service, 12-17 March 38, 416 A.T. Per national vote at 12-13 today, yard art pieces taller than 1.5m are prohibited in front of residences.

Immaculate Degeneration

Rathas was the third country to find independence on Verdant.
The religion of Elláh was founded on old Earth as a combination
of Christianity, Islam, and Hindu. Adherents carried the merged
precepts to the colony worlds. On Verdant, the religion gained
enough traction to become a theocracy of its own. Of course,
whenever a religion controls a country, it also seems to ossify.

"My tractor has stalled, Rebbe," Brother Dilihand called out to
me. "I can't get the harvest in, and it has to be today before the
rain. I don't know how my wife and I will last the winter. Please,
can you help us?"

I was walking down the country road with my six disciples
when the farmer made the sudden request. Fields of ripe grain
surrounded us with their heady aroma. As was often true, a
small crowd followed us. *So many petitions, so many people
relying on me as Rebbe Fenet Powrfaith. I try to teach them to rely
instead on Elláh, but...*

I let out a heavy breath and answered the farmer. "Thank you
for asking. Please wait while I ask Elláh's direction." I had no idea
whether Elláh would act through me this time.

I tugged at the heavy belt cinched around my waist, its
repellor pods awkward but useful. Age and walking challenged
me; the repellors pushed against the ground to partially support
my weight, making movement easier. For a moment, I wished I
were a younger man and did not need its help. Then I corrected
myself, closing my eyes and praying silently. *I'm sorry, Lord.
You've given me a wonderful life. I can't complain. And here's
another opportunity, Lord. What should I—*

<Teach your disciples, Fenet.>

Elláh's voice always filled me with kindness and warmth. He didn't always speak to me when I prayed. When He did, it sounded quietly in the back of my mind and came with a sense of peace. I often smiled, because He usually spoke before I had even finished my prayer, never awaiting my slow completion. His answers were a constant reminder that He knew what I would pray before I could ask.

I followed His command, always staying in surrender to Him. I turned to my disciples, while the farmer patiently waited.

"Here we are again, my friends. What do we do when someone asks for help?"

Scanat was quick to answer, he of the dark hair, brown eyes, and self-assurance.

"We ask Elláh first, Rebbe."

It was the right answer, but Scanat's voice was filled with self-confidence instead of humility. At twenty-four, he was the oldest of the six; his arrogance seemed to grow stronger every year, and it kept him away from Elláh. The others gave me blank looks, relying on Scanat's answer.

I sighed. I had hoped for a better answer that would reflect my teaching, yet the others stayed silent.

I turned to the farmer and spoke in a gentle tone across the roadside ditch, "There are mechanics, Brother Dilihand. Surely, you don't expect Elláh to expend his miracles on something like—"

<Heal the poor man's tractor, Fenet.>

Elláh caught me by surprise. Not only was this a trivial situation, it had also been three weeks since the last time He authorized a miracle.

Thank you, Lord. I miss these opportunities. How much longer will this power—

<As long as I need it to.>

In great humility at what Elláh had given me, I nodded to Dilihand.

"Well, it seems I can help after all. I'm coming, brother."

Dilihand deactivated the energy beam fence so I could enter his field, where the tractor sat crooked and stalled in the rows of neowheat. The harvester hooked behind was as idle as the tractor, its collection bin only partially filled. Rain was coming tomorrow, and the brother had a large crop still to gather.

I turned off my belt. By experience, I'd learned miracles rarely happened with it active. Without its help, I hobbled down through the ditch and up to the field. The smell of disturbed ground and chopped neowheat was rich in my nose. At the tractor, I laid my hands on its engine cowl and closed my eyes. I spoke aloud.

"Be healed, machine."

The familiar rush passed through me like a wind, catching my breath. My robe swirled once in the still air. A momentary visible heat moved from my hands to the tractor. The engine whirred into spinning action, ready to work the field.

I opened my eyes to see the watching people step back and gasp.

"Praise Elláh," I said, "your tractor will continue to work now, brother. I thank you for the opportunity to help."

Even as the crowd exclaimed and my six disciples took frantic notes, I felt fear. With increasing frequency, Elláh was silent when I asked him for miracles. The power came from Him. What He gives, He can also take away.

I limped back to the road and restored my personal repellor. Its help brought me relief from the burden of moving my body. I and my disciples continued walking down the road toward my home, leaving behind yet another crowd touched by Elláh.

Another teaching moment. Perhaps I can use it.

I asked my disciples, "How did I do that? You tell me."

"Rebbe, you didn't. That's what you've told us." said my teenage disciple, the youngest. With straw hair and bright eyes, he always delivered his words in an innocent, puzzled tone.

"Correct, Penilet. Elláh commands, and I surrender to Him to work through me."

"You wait for Him to speak to you," said Benet.

I nodded in sadness. "Which is happening less frequently now."

"But how do you get Him to speak," chimed in Scanat with his usual bullish forcefulness, "and why can't you teach us to do it?"

I shrugged helplessly. "I have no power to force Elláh to speak, and neither do you, Scanat. The Lord speaks when the Lord wishes. It is up to us to be available to Him at all times." I looked deeply into his eyes. "I've told you this many times, my friend, and yet you still try to make it happen. When *you* are in control of your life, as you so often are, then Elláh is not. He wants your submission to His power, not your own power."

Scanat set his lips in resentment. I suspected he would not stay with me much longer.

I turned to the group. "We'll have another teaching session this evening to go over more verses from The Holiest. Until then, ponder this saying of the teacher Muhamet: 'Wisdom and power follow endurance and patience.' Each of you must consider the degree to which you make yourself open to Him. And how do we do that, Benet?"

"By humility and surrender, Rebbe."

"Correct. So long as you try to force it to happen, you hold yourself away from Elláh." My words were for all of them, but particularly Scanat. "I tell you again, it is like the hookbird circling above a pond. Although Elláh has given him much ability, he cannot feed himself by his own power. He can act only when the fish appears, and he never knows when it will show. He must be ready at all times, always humble to the reality of the pond. One hundred percent. All the time. Elláh demands nothing less."

I could not continue to teach, because others clamored for my attention. Some of the crowd had stayed behind to marvel at the tractor; they had now hurried to catch up. I became the center of a Gordian knot of hands and arms reaching out to touch me, a knot that only He could unwind. *How can I meet their demands, when Elláh is diminishing me?* I was near tears. I closed my eyes and pushed my hands outward, clearing space around me.

"Not now, friends. I must talk with Elláh and my disciples. Please come back tomorrow."

Most stepped back, all but one woman who fell to her knees on the dusty road in front of me, her hands clasped in prayer.

"Rebbe, please. My daughter is so ill, she may not last the night."

I enfolded her hands in my own, my heart yearning to help. For years, I had been able to respond instantly to such a plea. *Shall I heal this woman's daughter, Lord?* I waited, listening for Elláh's silent command, but heard nothing. I sighed deeply, aching for this woman.

"I'm sorry, sister. I pray that she may live, but only Elláh knows. I can do nothing now."

She wept, her tears moistening my hardened knuckles.

How tragic, that I can heal a tractor but not save this woman's child.

Pastor Eregat Steadknow stepped out of the crowd, his grey robe and tan collar a contrast to the casual attire of the country people. He stepped forward and placed a hand on each of our shoulders, this distraught woman and me.

"Elláh will do as He wills, sister. Rebbe Fenet needs his own time now." His strong voice soothed with gentleness. "We will pray for you and your daughter."

She looked up in grief at his warm brown eyes. Yet she nodded, stood, and left.

"There was a time, Eregat," I said, watching her shuffle away, "when I would not have paused." I brushed my long grey hair back over my shoulders.

"I know, Fenet. Your power is fading. We've known each other a long time, and I see the difference. I am so sorry for you." He kept his hand on my shoulder. "But just now, I came to warn you. Church proctors are talking about bringing you in for questioning."

"What, again?" I shook my head sadly. "They keep probing, trying to prove the power I use comes from Saitan instead of Elláh. I can say nothing more than I have said to them before. Their scornful attitude never changes. Many times, I wonder whether our people were right to create this country of Rathas governed by the Church. Temporal power has polluted their God-given spirituality. Faith was stronger when it wasn't compulsory."

"Walk with me, my friend." Eregat led the way toward my cottage.

I was tired this day as we walked, relying more heavily on the repellor belt in the heat of Verdant's blue-white sun. The disciples followed a few paces behind. I wore sandals that flipped and flopped with each step.

Eregat continued, "You've been working miracles since your spiritual experience over thirty years ago. The Church tolerates you because what you do is self-evident, although they don't like it. They don't understand you any more than the Jewish Sanhedrin on old Earth understood Jaysus nearly three thousand years ago."

I held up a hand. "Please don't compare me to Jaysus. I am definitely not the Son of God."

"I know that. But what are the Church leaders here in Rathas to make of a man who performed miracles every day? It flies in the face of their doctrine. They teach that miracles all passed away after the Christian apostles."

I snorted a laugh. "Right. In their minds, doctrine is more important than what they see."

"Perhaps," Eregat said. He cocked his head in thought, walking a few paces in silence. "Or perhaps it is difficult for any of us to believe in miracles, even when we see them. Did you really just heal that tractor? Or did some electrical junction simply reconnect due to vibration?" He shrugged. "Yes, I saw the glow wash from your hands to the repellor motor, and so did all the watchers. Yet it is easy to discount that vision later, after the tractor has been doing its job again for a week."

"Even my disciples don't believe." I waved a hand at the half dozen following us. "Not one of them has yet performed a miracle, though they try."

Eregat was looking at the road ahead. "Here comes trouble, Fenet." Two figures in imposing grey with peaked hats and red collars strode quickly toward us. "The Church proctors."

I hung my head. "The same questions."

<Wave your hand through the air, Fenet.> Elláh's voice.

"Yes, Lord," I saw puzzlement from Eregat, then realized I'd spoken aloud in answer to a command he'd not heard.

I waved my hand, pushing spiritual forces away. Nothing appeared in the air, there was no visible representation of the spiritual action I had done—except that the two proctors, thirty meters away, simply disappeared.

"Holy Jaysus." Eregat stepped back in fear. "What did you do to them?"

I shrugged with a calm air. "I don't know. That was Elláh's doing, not mine. Probably they've been moved a kilometer or two away. It's happened before. I'm certain they're unhurt."

He frowned at me, almost angry yet also puzzled. "Why would you do such a thing, Fenet? Antagonizing them is not helpful."

"It was not my choice. I only and always do what He tells me to do. His plan is always far better than mine."

Eregat shook his head in dismay and resumed walking. "I don't understand you, brother. Of course, I don't understand the ineffable Elláh, either."

"I'll tell you what I don't understand." My neck and shoulders tightened as my voice rose. "I don't understand why He would have me do this silly little miracle to remove the proctors, when He was silent about that poor woman and her daughter. That's what I can't accept!

"People die every day. Believers die. They get sick. They hurt. They grieve. So much trouble fills the world. Resentments. Anger. Misunderstandings. Our own leaders are considering Holy War against Tileus. If Elláh has so much power—and He does—why does He allow such pain to continue?

"Yes, I know the Holiest teaches us, 'All things work together for the good of those who love Him.' He does it for our good, so we can grow and become closer to Him. Yet I still don't understand. Surely, we can grow in easier ways."

Eregat's face reflected shock at my blasphemy.

I took a deep cathartic breath and let it out, letting go of my anger. Again. Railing about what Elláh chooses to do has no purpose other than to take me away from Him. *Elláh knows what's best. I must enjoy what He gives me now. It may be gone soon.*

We turned off the road at the entrance to the cottage I shared with my aging mother. I opened the low gate in the white picket fence and smiled at the front gardens she loved to grow, with rows of different colored borgen flowers filling the sunny air with their sweet scent. Home. Soon I could get inside and take the weight off my legs.

I glanced at the disciples, still following at a respectful distance, then turned back to my friend.

"Would you care to come in, Eregat? I need to talk. The decline in my abilities has me...frightened." Voicing my fear made it coalesce like a cloud of gnats plaguing my eyes nearly to tears.

He nodded in response. "I'd guess it would. Your miracles have defined your adult life."

"I don't know what I'll do next, if they continue to fade. Even worse, I've not been able to teach a single one of these disciples how to do it."

I turned to the six. "Scanat, Penilet, all of you. I'll be at home for now. In the meantime, continue practicing the exercises I've given you in humility and surrender. Listen to Elláh, and do whatever you perceive Him to tell you. Please meet me back here in two hours, and you may tell me what you've done."

They nodded and, excited, scurried away individually for a short time of freedom from lessons. Penilet seemed reluctant to leave. Instead, he settled down on the garden bench with his Holiest to read. I smiled at him, then opened the door for Pastor Eregat and myself.

The house was quiet. Mother often took naps in the afternoon, so Eregat and I moved to the back of the house.

We selected drinks from the autocater in the kitchen, an herbal tea for him and a fruity water for me. We took them to the parlor, a quiet room with frilly furniture selected by my mother. It was a blessing to sit, to turn off the repellor belt, and to rest without pain.

I looked him in the eyes. Desperation choked my voice. "I don't know what to do. You've just seen me perform two miracles. That's all I've done in the last several weeks. Last year, I was doing twenty a day." I closed my eyes and rested my forehead on my hand. "I'm afraid."

"I'd be lost if I couldn't help others come to Jaysus," he said. "My caring for people is what fills my own life."

I looked up. His eyes were filled with sympathy.

"Yes," I agreed. "I can't count the number of people whose faith has been kindled or restored by my miracles. Elláh must be pleased with me. Yet He seems to be taking it away. If it fails, I'll be pilloried by the Church. They give me too much grief while I'm still doing miracles; if they stop, the Church will have a heyday. I don't understand His purpose."

Eregat chuckled. "Which of us ever does? What else could you do, Fenet? What other gifts do you have?"

"I don't know what else I can do. The Holiest talks about a five-fold ministry: apostles, prophets, evangelists, pastors and teachers. I've been an apostle, awakening people to Elláh. I obviously do not have the gift of teaching," I said with a sad laugh, "because my disciples don't learn. I don't speak well in front of people. I don't have the calling to help people like you do. And I've never made a single prophecy. If I can't perform miracles, I don't think I have any other gift."

"Elláh gives other gifts than ministry."

"I don't know what that would be. I'd be lost without ministry."

"I understand. You've been blessed with miraculous powers, your ability to heal others. That's not the only kind of sacred work. The Holiest lists other kinds of gifts that can be used in the world. Wisdom, knowledge, speaking and understanding tongues, encouraging and helping others, administration. And what about faith? Your faith is as strong as ever."

I winced. "Perhaps, perhaps not. I wonder these days, with my gifts declining, if my faith is as strong. Have I been falling into arrogance?" I had a wistful thought. "It is possible I could become a writer on spiritual topics. I think I'd enjoy that. It would mean studying scriptures more, and less walking about."

A rasping moan from the bedroom interrupted our conversation.

"Mother? Are you okay?" There was no answer.

Concerned, I rose to my feet. Mother was declining and not always strong these days. I hurried to her bed, with Pastor Eregat close behind.

She lay fully clothed on top of the bedspread in the dimly-lit room. Her hair was tangled on the pillow around her head as if she'd been thrashing. Her face was drenched in sweat, eyes racing around behind her closed eyelids as if chasing demons around the room. Her hands jerked spasmodically on the counterpane. The room smelled sharp with sickness.

"Mother!" I cried and sat beside her, stroking her cheek. "What's happened?"

She answered with another moan and a hacking cough.

I looked in desperation to Eregat.

"Can you find us a cool, damp cloth?"

He nodded and hastened to the bathroom.

Please, dear Jaysus. I have healed so many people I didn't know over the years. Give me this power again, to heal this one so precious to me.

I heard nothing but my mother's wheezing.

It was as if the steady decline of my power came to a formidable culmination in that moment. Suddenly, I felt a spiritual authority leave me, gusting away in the empty room like the sweeping departure of a dove. My mouth gaped, and I sucked in an incomplete breath that failed to nourish. I slumped on the edge of the bed.

"Elláh?" I spoke aloud. "Please. Is this it? Have you taken my power? Oh, please, Jaysus, let me heal one more time."

Again, nothing.

I sat, shaking my head in denial, feeling the heat of my mother's cheek against my hand, listening to her stertorous breath and smelling the cloying vapor of her sickness. My heart fluttered in panic. I clasped my hands and raised them in supplication, but did not know what more to say.

Silence reigned in the back of my mind, where that Voice had spoken thousands of times. The emptiness was like a vacated house with dust dervishes swirling in the gust of a closing door.

Eregat returned. "Here's a cloth, Fenet. How is she?" Then he stopped and looked at me in shock. "What's happened to you? Your face is white!"

I lowered my clasped hands and buried my face in them. "It's gone, Eregat." I fought the sobs threatening to shake my shoulders.

I felt him move to the bed and place the cooling cloth on my mother's forehead. "No, she's still here. Look, she's breathing."

"No, not her. My power is gone. I am vacant."

He put his hand on my shoulder. "Oh, my friend, can that be? How could you possibly know? Elláh has much still to do with you."

"I felt it leave me."

My words were halting and weak. As if his hand had crushed me, I collapsed off the bed onto my knees, crumpling into a ball of agony that threatened to consume my soul. I wailed, my voice sounding thin and thready even to me, wafting away like a balloon on a breeze.

He said more words, but I was beyond listening. In the very moment when I needed it most, to help my mother, my life as I had known it was over. I thought I felt him pat my back as I knelt, racked with tears.

Minutes later, minutes of agony, I heard voices again.

"Your master needs your help, Brother Penilet."

"My help, Pastor? What could I do? I've hardly learned anything yet."

"Here, my boy. Come to him. Comfort him. You can do that better than I."

I felt arms around my shoulders, thin arms tentatively placed with compassion. "Rebbe Fenet, I'm here. For whatever you may need, I'm here." He had knelt beside me and now placed his cheek on my back as he held me.

Eregat's firm hand nestled on my head. "Come back to us, Fenet. Elláh has more for you to do. Spiritual writing will fulfill, also."

I gradually took a deep breath in little sips that caught in my lungs like ratchets. Letting it out again happened all at once, releasing a huge lump of the aching loss that consumed me. I took another breath, more easily, and released the fear of my future. Eregat was right; Elláh still had work for me to do—

different work. *But what will I do? I have to trust Elláh to show me.*

Little by little, I regained control of myself. I placed one hand on Penilet's forearm around my neck, the other on Eregat's hand on my head. I pressed firmly on both, infusing them with the thanks they had more than earned. Slowly, I rose to a kneel. Sounds came clearly to me again, the ticking of the roof under bright sunlight, my mother's hard, heavy breathing.

I took yet another heavy breath. "Thank you, both of you. I knew this day was coming. It seems overmuch that it should happen when I so needed Jaysus' grace." I looked up at my mother's face, covered in sweat, her eyes still racing each other behind closed lids. "Now, I don't know what to do to help her."

Penilet gave a strangled gasp of shock. Curious, I looked at him to see his blue eyes wide in amazement. He hardly seemed to be breathing.

"Yes, Lord," he whispered in apparent awe.

He reached his hands to the coverlet on the bed, slid them up onto my mother's cheeks. He spoke so breathlessly I could hardly hear his words.

"Be healed, woman."

The glow that shimmered in his hands, spreading across her face and down her body, told me that Elláh's powers, once given to me, had moved on.

Penilet turned to me, this gangly youth with all his uncertainty.

"*<You have taught well, Fenet,>*" Penilet said aloud in a voice of power I'd never heard from the boy. It was clear the words were not his own. "*<but your lack of faith in Me has been growing. You will do different work now, and this boy will continue your ministry.>*"

Penilet knelt beside me with a dismayed look, an awkward disciple forced to demonstrate a revelation to his master. He glowed with Elláh's power in him, controlling his actions.

His hand touched the repellor beam belt around my waist, pointedly singling it out to my attention. I gasped as I realized his point. I relied on this human-created artifice to ease the weakness of my aging body, rather than relying on Elláh. I had never asked Elláh how He wanted me to deal with age. I made the choice for myself.

My lack of faith.

Then Penilet's eyes cleared and became his usual innocently puzzled expression, now tinged with an incredible awe that made his face glow.

The student had become the teacher. I would start new tasks with renewed humility before my God.

Fishing Hands

Life in the islands of Winter was easy-going but not easy. A cold climate, limited resources, and the choice of lower technology dominated the days. The primary available industry was fishing, which allowed the tribes to feed themselves and also to offer trade for technology from elsewhere. The need for physical strength led to a male-dominated society.

This story received the honor of a Gold (first place) award from the 2022 Royal Palm Literary Awards of the Florida Writers Association.

Marta Bloom's hands rode the helm of the *Pelagic Bloom* as the fishing boat drove through low swells. Her stomach was in a knot on this third unsuccessful day as captain. She still needed to prove herself by catching a giant tsifta fish, one of the horrific relics of an earlier time in the planet Verdant's history.

Her intense, dark eyes squinted toward the southwest, where the unsympathetic blue-white sun glared off the water. The violent storms prevalent in the northern ocean of this harsh planet would come in tonight. The wind-blown wavelets increased, stirring the russet-colored patches of seaweed. Freshening wind blew her long ponytail sideways with its gusts. She hated the idea of returning again to Indie harbor with an empty hold.

Marta looked up at her mate, Thierry Carfon, riding high above her in the crow's nest. Instead of searching the horizon for signs of tsifta, he was glaring down at her. Her heart sunk at the conflict. Before correcting him, she looked at the horizon again to build up her courage.

Thierry was a skillful, powerful man twice her age. The ocean had weathered his face to gnarled wrinkles and a constant scowl. He could smile, but even then, his eyes were cold. Like the rest of the Indie Tribe to which they belonged, Thierry was skeptical of her. No woman of the Tribe had ever captained a boat. The last thing she wanted was a confrontation with Thierry, yet she had to be in command.

The man had been her father's mate; she had to make him hers. Thierry knew better than what he was doing. It was almost as if he wanted her to fail. She kept her eyes focused on her own job of steering the boat, then raised her voice to a shout over the sounds of the wind and water, words she shouldn't have to say.

"Keep an eye out up there, Mate."

Thierry's silence was like a threatening cloud. She thought she heard muttering over the ocean noise. A moment later, she checked again; he had his eyes properly on the horizon.

She kept the *Pelagic Bloom* plowing through the waves, rising and falling with each swell. The *Bloom* was fifteen meters from stem to stern, big enough to catch the monster tsifta. Yet standing at the helm, the boat seemed impossibly small against the rough ocean stretching from here to the horizon. Marta inspected the heavy outrigger booms stretched wide to port and starboard. From the end of each boom, the longlines trolled properly. She smiled at the sight. With booms spread, the boat was like a bird in flight.

She looked at her hands on the wheel; raw, calloused, fishing hands, as big as most men's. She had trained for three years under her father. He'd been tough but fair, and she'd earned his praise many times. Her hands had gained the skillful strength to haul a line, ram home a harpoon, and bring in the fish. Were they the hands of a captain?

Marta missed her father, who had lost his foot a month ago to a tsifta. She remembered the three-meter carnivore thrashing on the deck, its razor teeth shearing through her father's ankle. She looked over her shoulder to the spot where it happened. She could still see the blood spewing, the severed foot bouncing twice before falling overboard. Her ears still rang with her father's shrieks. She shuddered, recalling her panic, not knowing how to save his life. Instinctively, she grabbed a piece of line and made a tourniquet.

Afterward, she and Thierry loaded the huge fish into the hold and brought her father home. He had lost much blood, but the tribal medic sealed the stump. The Tribe praised Marta for saving his life, but the praise was begrudging. Under their kind words, she heard them whisper a "girl" shouldn't have been on the boat in the first place. Women on a boat were bad luck.

In the next few weeks, while her father healed, he made no decision on who should captain the boat. Though Thierry wanted to buy it, her father finally decided to give the captaincy to her. He fought for her against the entrenched attitudes of the Indie Tribe elders. Marta desperately wanted to prove her father was right.

"Windrows to port, two hundred meters." Thierry's call focused Marta's attention. She'd learned fish often hid under those wind-blown rows of dark red and blue driftweed in the water.

"Aye, Mate. Turning port." She yelled, thinking she sounded like a pale imitation of her father.

Marta could see nothing from her low angle. They'd have to get closer. She turned the helm slightly to port. Sharp turns with fishing lines out could tangle the lines.

Looking up, she saw Thierry still scanning the horizon. She knew he wanted this boat for his own. Her father had told her, though, Thierry would make a poor captain because he didn't understand the economics of fishing. That's why her father put Marta in charge.

She planned today for success. She had something new, the cooler strapped to the bulkhead at her feet. Thierry noticed it but did not ask. She hoped it would make a difference in their relationship—provided they could land one of the great fish.

She checked the *Bloom's* dashboard tech: fathometer, fish finder, line tension meters, and more. All the readings seemed normal. The water composition analyzer showing chemicals from feedfish and drift, but nothing of the tsiftim. Feedfish were important to Marta, though, because they swam in schools that attracted tsiftim.

"School on the surface at three-three-zero," Thierry shouted down from above, indicating feedfish thirty degrees to port.

Marta's jaw tightened. He still refused to call her "Captain."

"Aye, Mate." She turned again to the new heading. Most of the Indie Tribe fished with nets for the smaller feedfish. The *Bloom* did not. She remembered her father's gruff voice saying, *Trawling for feedfish is like popping candy, but taking in a tsifta—now, that's something to be proud of.* She reached up to touch the tsifta tooth her father had mounted above the window, nine centimeters of deadly pointed menace with a razor-sharp edge.

Marta's boat was made especially for tsiftim, leftover dragons of the cold northern ocean. She'd seen tsiftim as big as four meters long, weighing 700 kilos. She respected them, carnivores with teeth like racks of steel knives eating anything they could catch. Their powerful tails could tear apart a smaller boat, leaving the shards as jetsam and the crew as cuisine. On the line, she'd seen tsiftim fight with fierce energy, diving and jumping and sawing sideways. They were treacherous even worn out and landed into the boat. Marta's father was her painful reminder.

"Fin at zero-two-zero." Thierry's loud cry filled Marta with instant excitement. Twenty degrees to starboard. Her mouth went dry. Tsiftim showed their dorsal fin above the water. So did other fish. She searched the rolling waters for the tell-tale sign.

"Aye, Mate," Marta called as she guided the helm. "How far?"

"Three hundred meters. Looks like a big one."

She checked the starboard outrigger boom to ensure the carbon fiber lines were trailing free with chummed baitfish dragging properly.

"She's turning toward us," he called. "Fast turn. She's got the scent."

"Aye, Mate. Holding steady."

Marta focused, hoping to see the fin, but she saw only rolling swells. The boat rose and fell, engine throbbing and waves splashing against the bow. Spray splashed her face.

Nothing happened. Was it really a tsifta Thierry had seen? She kept scanning the water eagerly, feeling her heart speed. She could see the windrow now and the feedfish jumping on the surface, but the ocean still kept its deepest secrets.

Waiting was hard.

"Where away, Mate?" She wondered why Thierry was silent. Had the fish escaped? Was he silent out of resentment, sabotaging her chance?

Marta jumped as the line suddenly shrieked outward through the leader blocks. Not the starboard side, where the fish had been, but the port. The fish had crossed under.

"Strike on, port side," she shouted. Her voice sounded shaky.

"Aye, comin' down." Thierry slid down the firepole and landed with a heavy thump on the deck. Despite his large frame, he moved quickly, immediately taking charge of the port line.

Thierry's job now was to keep the fish on the line until it tired. She glanced over at his rough hands on the control levers. One lever controlled the line motor that reeled in and released fishing line. The other controlled line position on the boom. She was amazed at his expertise in using those controls to maintain tension on the fishing line. Too much tension meant the fish might break the line. Too little, and the fish would throw the hook. Thierry was the best in the Indie Tribe at this.

The bow jerked when it hit a wave wrong. Marta jolted back into awareness, realizing she was neglecting her own job. She reached aft to slap the starboard control levers, retracting the rig and raising its boom. It would be disaster to have two tsiftim on lines at the same time. Returning to the helm, she steered to port to keep the active line clear of the boat.

"Heavy tension. Boom's flexin'. She's a big one, for sure." Thierry shouted, excited by the huge fish.

Marta saw the massive boom bend in a dangerous curve with the immense weight of whatever had caught the hook. The hair rose on the back of her neck. If that boom snapped, they'd lose the fish. Worse, the boom might rebound and put a hole in the boat.

One rope, a guy line fastened at the bow, held the curve on the boom. They needed to let out the guy line—right now!—to ease the pressure. Thierry couldn't do it; he was too busy working the fish. The guy line wasn't motorized like the other lines. Instead, it was fastened to a cleat at the bow and had to be worked by hand.

Marta shouted, "Boom's in danger. I've got it!"

She let go of the helm, trusting the tech stabilizer to steer straight, and jumped to the bow. The bow deck rose high and slid down into each wave, making her footing difficult.

Her strong hands unlashed the guy line, keeping two turns on the cleat for control. If she just let it slide, the boom would crash into the boat. Putting her back into it, she held the tension as she eased the boom aft. The new angle took the stress off the boom. Marta lashed the guy line back to the cleat, then jumped back to do her job at the helm.

Thierry glanced at Marta, at what she had done. His heavy eyebrows raised slightly, and he grunted approval while continuing to control the fishing line tension. She knew Thierry never would say much. An approval grunt was at least a start.

Did they really have a tsifta on the hook? Or was it some other kind of fish? This fish was too big to be anything but tsifta. She looked again at the dashboard tech. The water composition readout now showed tsifta chemicals that hadn't been there before.

"Good news, Mate. The tech says we've got a tsifta."

Thierry had no chance to answer. "Tension's increasing. She's diving."

She'd done this part of the work with her father over sixty times while she was learning. As three people—captain, mate, and apprentice—they won more than they lost. With only her and Thierry, Marta had to perform the tasks her father used to do. Could she do them well?

Suddenly, the strain on the fishing line dropped to near zero. She heard the line motors race to take up the slack. Had the fish shaken the hook? Or was it swimming rapidly toward them?

"She's a-jumpin'," Thierry hollered. He timed his work perfectly, stopping the line motors just as the fish jumped. Loose tension kept the fish from shaking the hook in the air.

Marta watched the tsifta shatter the surface like breaking glass fifty meters away. The great fish looked magnificent, with a shroud of white spray falling all around. She could smell the acrid scent of the fish. Blue-green scales and the sleek, pale belly sparkled in the sun as it twisted back and forth in the air. Its erect dorsal fin cut the spray like a scimitar. She sucked in her breath. The fish was mammoth, the largest she had seen. Its mouth stretched hungrily; she saw a hazardous rack of ten-centimeter teeth.

The tsifta glared at them with hate glinting in its cold eyes. The splash when it landed sent waves crashing in huge circles. The line tension instantly spiked again as it plunged deep.

"Big fish." Thierry said, never one for much talk.

Marta gaped at where the fish had been. The huge circular waves spread. A part of her said, *It's too big. We'll never land it. Let's cut the line.* She shook the thought off.

Instead, she answered Thierry with her father's words. "Big, yes. More for us all. Let's get it in."

They fought the huge fish for the next two hours. The battle lasted longer than she could remember with any fish before.

Marta felt worn out. Steering took physical strength in the rising seas. She also had to maintain an intense concentration, alert to respond to the fish with sudden changes in boat speed and position.

She saw Thierry tiring also. Staying on his feet on the shifting deck demanded strength and balance. At the same time, his absorption on the line tension and control levers took immense focus that never eased for a moment.

The tsifta had years of wile in its dangerous repertoire. It swerved from port to starboard, accelerated past the boat, dove deep, jumped. It did anything it could do to shake loose the hated hook. Unlike the two of them, the fish seemed not to tire at all. Three times, it tried to drag the fishing line under the boat to where it would foul the propellor.

The line motors raced again. Seeing the line direction, Marta's breath caught. Was it going to jump over the aft deck? If it did, the line would tangle with deck gear and the boom would shatter. The jumble could even capsize and sink the boat. She shouted, "Comin' toward us!" She grabbed handfuls of helm, sharp to port, and gunned the engines to slide the stern away from the fish.

Thierry shouted, "Aye!" He sent the line pulley to the far end of the boom, getting it away from the boat. The line motors sped, reeling in the slack. Had they done enough?

It was close. The tsifta broke water with a tremendous leap. Thierry had set the boom to keep it away, while Marta had aligned the boat sideways to its jump. The slashing teeth were only two meters away as the gigantic fish flexed side to side in the air. The splash of its re-entry drenched them both. She breathed a heavy sigh of relief. This time, their teamwork had been excellent.

Then she heard the line reel shriek. The fish dove again and the fight continued. This fish was not giving up. Neither was Marta.

The brilliant sun lowered to late afternoon. She saw it dip below the dark green clouds of the incoming Verdant storms. The boat rolled and pitched in mounting seas.

Marta fought to keep her footing on the wet shifting deck. She was sopping wet with the heavier spray.

Fighting both the storm and the fish was grueling. Marta felt like only adrenaline kept her going. She knew the battle was always between the flesh-and-blood predator and the courage and will of the few Tribe fishermen who went after tsifta. The true fishermen would win, provided they kept the fish on the hook. She prayed the fish would tire before she did.

Marta was almost ready to give up when she recognized an answer to her prayer. The monster was no longer jumping. It was finally tiring. Now came the final test. She gave the command, "It's time. Bring it alongside, Mate."

"Aye-aye," he said.

Marta frowned as Thierry left off her title again. No matter now. The fish was her main concern.

She steered into the rising wind. The bow pitched heavily with each wave, slapping down into the next. Rough as it was, going into the waves was steadier than any other direction. She set the tech stabilizer to maintain heading.

Thierry worked the controls to bring the fatigued tsifta close aboard. "She's a monster." His voice was full of respect for the enormous creature.

Marta staggered across the heaving deck to the aft port rail. She saw the tsifta swimming alongside, its malevolent eyes rolled up to glower at them.

What if it could speak? Marta thought. *Perhaps it would say, "I'm not done yet."* The fish looked longer than the deck, and it could still break away.

She answered Thierry, "Biggest I've seen."

Marta grabbed a harpoon gun from the rack and looked over the rail. The boat pitched hard. She staggered but regained her balance. She stared down at the fish. This was the most dangerous part of the job. She'd have to aim the gun just right to lodge the harpoon into the tsifta. Not wanting to miss and screw this up, she leaned over the rail to aim closer. She heard a disapproving grunt from the mate behind her but ignored him. Her hands were less than a meter from the tsifta. She concentrated on her aim, balancing on the rocking deck.

Finally, Marta held her breath and squeezed the trigger. The harpoon slammed into the spine just behind the tsifta's head, exactly where she wanted it.

The massive fish thrashed violently, spanking the water with its giant tail. Its head came up fast, dangerous teeth headed toward Marta's hands.

She tried to pull back but couldn't move fast enough. It was as if she were watching a slow-motion scene in a horror movie. Her right foot slipped on the wet deck. She gasped as her body plunged forward over the rail. The immense maw and its knife-like teeth were waiting to take her. The blood drained from her face as she fell.

A strong hand grasped her belt and hauled her back. The teeth crashed together, grazing Marta's arm. The tsifta splashed back into the ocean.

Thierry planted her firmly on the deck. "Too close, Marta. Way too close."

Marta nodded, heart racing. She looked at the bloodied lines of broken skin on her forearm. She had been that close. Thierry had saved her. No time to think about that. One harpoon wasn't enough for this giant.

She loaded the second harpoon and fired again.

The harpoon bit hard behind the erect dorsal fin. The tsifta heaved into the air again. This time, Marta was behind the rail, further from the menace.

She stepped back from the rail to start the next stage of landing the fish. The harpoons were properly set. She checked that the harpoon lines were fed through the two cranes that would haul up the fish. She looked over at Thierry and saw him nodding. That small sign of approval felt to her like the greatest praise she'd ever received.

Looking in his dark eyes, she commanded, "Haul together. Let's get this monster aboard."

"Aye," he said, still holding back the title. The fish wasn't caught yet—not until it was safe in the hold.

She stood by the aft crane, operating the motors, and Thierry matched her on the forward. The motors hauled on the harpoon lines to lift the tsifta. She had to reset her footing as the boat leaned dangerously to port with the weight. The tsifta convulsed, shaking the entire boat. A large wave rocked the boat, green water splashing over the rail. Careful to control the fish, she and Thierry swiveled the cranes to maneuver the fish's weight aboard, righting the boat.

They paused with the fish at the ruler-engraved rail to measure its length.

"Aft mark is zero point six," Marta called.

Thierry responded, "Forward is five point nine."

"Ha," Marta shouted in triumph. "Five point three meters. And the weight is ..." She glanced at the weight scale on the cranes. "890 kilos. That'll do."

Thierry looked at her with his rare smile. He didn't need to say it; she had just brought in a record tsifta.

But it wasn't in the hold yet. Fish had jumped off the deck before. They lowered the fish to the deck so they could open the hold. As its belly touched the wood, the tsifta kangarooed a half meter into the air, but the harpoons and lines held.

Thierry skirted the fish's gaping teeth to reach the hatch. He took the forward end, Marta took the aft. Together, they lifted the hatch to clear the hold.

Working the cranes again, they lifted the tsifta.

The huge fish still wasn't done. Hanging from the harpoon lines, the tsifta whipped its tail violently sideways. She heard the teeth chomp hard at the other end.

The tail slammed Marta in the shoulder. The boat rocked heavily and water washed across the deck. Her feet slipped. She lost her balance, spun partway around by the blow. She tripped on the edge of the open hatch and threw herself sideways to avoid falling in. She staggered, crashing hard against the metal rail. She felt excruciating pain and heard the crack of her ribs.

In sudden fear, barely able to stand, she looked forward to where the teeth had clashed. She couldn't see Thierry. Did the tsifta get him? Her breath stopped. Marta pulled herself painfully to her feet, careful to avoid the thrashing fish hanging from the cranes. Where was Thierry?

She limped around the fish's tail to the port rail, desperately looking forward for him. She saw Thierry sitting with his head in his hands. *He must have jumped to stay clear*, she thought, breathing a sigh of relief. No blood. Her heart calmed, but each breath hurt from when she'd hit the rail.

She gasped, "Thought you'd bought it there, Mate."

"I got clear." His breath was quicker than usual. "Even old Thierry is finding this fish more than a match," he said, standing shakily.

"Let's finish the work, Mate," Marta said.

"Aye," he responded.

They returned to the cranes to lower the fish into the hold, only to face another challenge: the hatch wasn't big enough. The fish overlapped both ends.

"Swing it aft, Mate," Marta directed. "We'll lower its head first. We don't want another bout with those teeth."

"Aye. That'll work."

She watched the head and teeth slide down into the hold, and Marta shuddered, remembering how close those teeth had come to her precious hands. Then they swung it forward to fit the tail in.

Marta decided to leave the lines attached, both harpoons and the hook in its mouth. *No sense in taking chances,* she thought.

Getting the hatch cover back in place was the easiest part of the job. She could feel the boat judder as the powerful fish still jerked below.

Marta collapsed onto the starboard bench while Thierry took the port. Each breath came with a sharp pain, and the scrapes on her forearm stung with the salt water. She thought of them as badges of her first success.

She couldn't give in to her fatigue. She checked the boat; the *Pelagic Bloom* plowed through the deep swells, pitching and rolling heavier than ever. On the western horizon, the greenish clouds were closer and darker. They'd have to head for harbor soon, and still might not make it before the storms.

They were both exhausted.

Neither of them spoke.

She watched Thierry, who stared silently at the churning ocean. She felt him watching her, too, waiting to see what she would do.

Marta knew her job was not yet done. They'd brought in the tsifta, a record. Success felt good, and she was certain this would gain approval from the Tribe. But her job was captain. She needed Thierry as her mate. She needed his strength and knowledge. Most importantly, she needed his acceptance of her as captain.

She had planned for this moment. Holding her arm against her rib, Marta struggled to her feet and limped to the cooler.

Thierry barely shifted his eyes, but Marta knew he was observing her. She opened the cooler and pulled out two dark bottles of brew. Without a word, she handed one to Thierry, then sat again.

Her father had never allowed alcohol on board the *Pelagic Bloom*. By changing the rule, she was claiming the boat for her own. No longer her father's rules, but hers.

Thierry looked at the bottle in his hand, then back at her. He nodded and smiled, then tapped the top twice to open it. She also tapped hers.

The mate held his up toward her in tribute. "Success, Captain."

He used the title for the first time, and everything felt right. She matched his toast and grinned. "We do it together, Mate. Never alone."

The Meaning of Peace

The totalitarian country of Verdant Prime, under the control of the socialist system called "Solity," does its best to provide for each citizen. Such a complex challenge creates two large problems. First, operating statistically means that individuals often get left behind in the desire for greater good. And second, there is little incentive for citizens to do their best.

Alba Castilan arrived at her waterfront office just as a shocking new message came in through her implant. "Damn, damn, damn," she shouted to the empty air, each word louder and more strident. The words rang off the well-used buildings and overrode the sounds of the fishing fleet readying their daily departure.

Fifteen minutes later, Alba gathered her group for a short meeting on the factory floor around her office. She went out her door to the top of the steps, looking out across the hulking shapes of the fish processing equipment. Drawing herself up to her full height—Alba was a tall woman and in good physical shape—she held out her hands for attention.

"We've got problems, folks, and they've just gotten worse. Capital Department says they need this plant operating within a month."

The group reacted in grumbling shock. One angry voice spoke out, "Can't they ever give us enough time?"

"You know how it is," Alba responded. "Capital calculates the need and predicts the necessary production. This factory isn't producing anything while we're upgrading it. In their view, we engineers and technicians are useless consumers until it is."

Another voice shouted, "We're still fighting integration problems!"

She nodded. "Yes, I know. Every problem sets us back another couple of days. But we don't have any choice. If we don't get it operating, they'll shut down the project and re-Assign all of us with failure marks."

The angry voices and frustration filled the air as everyone turned back to their work.

She knew the problems all too well. Koifa fish came in lots of sizes. The new equipment wasn't flexible enough. Size variation led to small fillets still including backbone and large ones losing pieces of wasted meat.

Alba was certain her design was robust, but the detail had been done by other engineers who didn't have the same quality ethic she did. It was a common problem in Solity. Everything was provided as an entitled subsistence by Solity, so most people just didn't care. One of the things that isolated her was her unusual drive for quality.

Now it came down to this: an impossible deadline, a resentful work force, and no circle of friends. *Will I never find peace in my life?*

❧ ✳ ☙

As she left work, the afternoon sun flashed brightly on a window pane across the street. She thought about the one bright spot in her recent life. Flekin Yamasubo had joined her at the bare-walled refectory one evening a few weeks ago. Their engrossing conversation had eased her loneliness. On their third meeting, he'd suggested a discussion group she could join.

"They talk about the problems of Solity," Flek had said. "It'll open your eyes. I don't normally attend, but you'll find other friends there."

"I didn't think Solity allowed people to talk about its problems," she'd said. "I remember from school the words of the great Karl Marx, back on old Earth. He said, 'The meaning of peace is the absence of opposition to socialism.' Isn't that right?"

He'd shrugged. "Well, Solity doesn't much like discussion—but they tolerate it, so long as it doesn't become reactionary. They want people to find solutions for the problems."

Since then, she'd seen Flek several times a week. He was becoming a good friend. Her only friend here in Timpi since her re-Assignment here from Oriens.

The evening of the troubling message from Capital, she attended the discussion group for the first time. The meeting was in a seedy section of Timpi, close to the docks. Fifteen people were in the conference room of a ship repair shop, dressed in all the colored coveralls of their departments: light blue, light green, dark blue, and her own pale orange for Development.

The speaker was a middle-aged man in red coveralls. "Tonight, I'm going to talk about the connection between the Solity Guards and my Justice department. We'll talk about how criminals are caught, then how each case moves from the Guards through Justice."

Alba found it fascinating. She had some idea how it worked, but the man had details she'd never considered. After describing the normal process, he talked about failures. That's when it got scary.

"Solity Guards have a lot of power and often use fear as a tool," he said. "Their black uniforms and bulbous helmets are part of that. People can be arrested wrongly. Perhaps a neighbor had a resentment and turned someone in. Perhaps the Guards misinterpreted something they observed. Once in the system, though, it's astonishingly difficult to get clear. If the Guards arrested them, the system assumes they must have done something wrong. It's up to the individual to prove their innocence—and they have to do that from within a jail cell."

As he went on, Alba could imagine being put in that position, particularly after her arbitrary treatment by Capital. Just this morning, Solity had felt like a faceless and uncaring threat.

What made it more frightening, though, was that the talk sounded seditious. Alba wondered what kind of group Flek had gotten her into.

৵ ❋ ৵

The next day was the first day of the usual three-day weekend. She spent it alone at the factory, trying to create a better algorithm. No matter how much she pleaded, her staff simply shrugged off the idea of working on the weekend. "No one ever does that," she heard repeatedly.

Flekin was in the refectory at dinner that night. Seeing him brought a smile. He stood up to greet her. "Have you had a good day?"

Her tightly-held frustrations jumped to the fore. "It's the worst week of my life, Flek. Capital is demanding completion in a month. We can't get it working properly in that time, and my work group doesn't even care." She was suddenly almost in tears.

Flek seemed surprised. Alba was usually self-controlled and confident, and a crying jag simply wasn't her. He wrapped her in a warm hug.

"I'm sorry, Alba. I know how much you've worked to make it happen. It must be terribly frustrating."

She was taken aback by the unusual physical contact, but gave herself into it. Flek was even taller than she was. He was a farmer, strong and sun-bronzed with blue eyes and blond hair bleached by exposure. The comfort of his arms eased her jangled disturbance. She wrapped her arms around his large chest and laid her head on his shoulder.

Quickly, however, propriety took over. People in Solity didn't hug unless they were married or at least DNA-approved for fraternization. She began to feel uncomfortable, so she squeezed him one time and they both let go.

"Thanks," she said. "You have no idea how much that eased me."

"I thought it might. Shall we get our food?"

For the next hour, he spoke of his farm and the team of eight who worked it. The noisy, sparse surroundings of the refectory retreated behind the warm pictures he painted with his words. His team sounded delightful, with everyone doing their part every day. *Why can't I have a team like that?*

❦✷❧

The next day was Sitday, middle of the three-day weekend.

She awoke to loud pounding on her door. Rolling out of bed, she slipped on a robe and stumbled to the door. *Who could be pounding?* She crossed the living room, dodging around the standardized couch and easy chair. This temporary lodging felt cold and dreary. As she looked through her peephole, the pounding resumed practically against her face.

Two Solity Guards stood there on the other side of the peephole in the dim hallway. Dressed completely in intimidating black with mirrored helmets, they looked like machines. They said nothing, didn't shout through the door, just kept pounding.

She opened the door. Anything else would be a legal violation.

The two looked identical. In addition to their black attire, each one had black gloves, a utility belt with a myriad of devices on it, and a needle gun on his hip. She could see nothing of their faces through the mirror glass. They stood erect and unmoving like basalt.

The one on her left spoke with a deep, threatening voice. "Alba Castilan, we have questions for you."

She immediately assumed she must have done something wrong without knowing. She felt a cold sweat break out.

"Why? What have I done?"

They moved suddenly, pushing forward past her into her living room. Their heads quickly scanned the room for threats. "We'll discuss that when we get to it. Sit down."

Friday night's presentation flashed through her mind, about people arrested in error and how difficult it was to win free. This moment—right now—was the tipping point. If she couldn't stop it now, she might become that statistic.

"I've done nothing wrong. This must be a—"

The guardsman interrupted her. "No mistake. Sit down. Now." His hand indicated the easy chair.

She nodded and turned toward the chair, automatically starting to close the door. The second guardsman spoke, a gravelly voice amplified by the helmet.

"No. Leave the door open."

She felt helpless to do anything other than what they demanded. She moved to the chair, drew her robe around her, and sat down. She pulled at the robe, covering her nightgown. Her mind was spinning.

Should I let someone know what's happening? She thought of Flek. She framed a message in her mind, then sub-vocalized it through her implant to the InfoNet. The Net responded that her communications were temporarily restricted by the Solity Guards. *I can't even tell anyone!*

The first guardsman stood in front of her. The second man moved behind her, where she couldn't see what he did. She felt like a child in school being chastised by the headmaster, except the threat here was much greater.

They started with innocuous questions about her work, her apartment, her presence in Timpi, her activities. The answers were easy and straightforward. She was the leader of the engineering team. She was here to work on the factory. Her apartment was Assigned to her for the duration. She jogged, ate out, had not found friends yet. The questions did nothing but increase her anxiety. *What is this about?*

The answer finally came as their questions zeroed in on the discussion group.

"You were there Friday night. What did you discuss?"

"We talked about Solity and how it works."

"What was the topic?"

Suddenly, she saw where they were heading. Her heart started pounding harder. "We had a presentation on the Justice department."

The guardsman asking the questions moved suddenly, violently slapping his palm against his thigh. A resounding crack sounded in the room.

He shouted, "Don't prevaricate with us. What was the topic?"

Alba nearly jumped out of the chair. "I didn't do anything. I just listened to the talk!"

The crack sounded again. "What was the topic?"

She was so frightened she almost couldn't get words out. "The presenter talked about the connection between Solity Guards and the Justice department, how sometimes people are arrested for doing nothing at all."

He stood and stared at her, or at least it seemed so through his mirror face.

A part of her rose in indignation. "Like this," she said. "I've done nothing at all, and here we are!"

A heavy gloved hand grasped her shoulder painfully. She had nearly forgotten about the second guardsman.

The one in front spoke again, "You haven't done *nothing*. You've chosen to take part in a subversive group seeking to overthrow Solity."

"What? No, no. It's just a group of people talking about issues. They're not doing anything subversive!"

The hand on her shoulder squeezed again. She winced, knowing there would be a large bruise there later. The gravelly voice came close to her ear, "That's how it starts, young woman. Our job is to make sure it goes no further."

The man in front said, "We are not here to arrest you today. We're gathering information about your...group. Action will come later."

He nodded, and the heavy hand lifted from her shoulder.

"You will hear more, Alba Castilan."

The two spun on their feet and left through the open door. Alba sat and shivered, looking out the door into the hall where one of her neighbors was peering wide-eyed around her own door frame. As their eyes met, the woman quickly closed her door.

I'll can't go to the meeting again.

But the answer didn't feel good. She hated giving in to the threat. She had met a few people there who could be friends. And what was Flek's connection to the group? That was particularly hard. She liked him. She was getting to know him. She had already considered applying for fraternization to date him. He was kind and strong, and it didn't hurt that he was good-looking, too. She shook her head in dismay, got up, and closed the door on the empty hallway.

She went to the factory that day, and again on Endday. No one else came, which made it difficult for her to test her new algorithm; the equipment was never meant to be operated by a single person. Nonetheless, she threw herself into fixing the problem. The limited tests she did seemed to work. Under the new algorithm, the fillets were more even.

Success helped. Her mind cleared while focusing on the work.

After lunch on Endday, she got a message from Flek, almost as if her thinking about him had caused it. She read the message through her implant.

We need to talk. Can you join us for dinner at the farm? We eat at dusk.

Every muscle in her body relaxed at once. The tension that had filled her ever since seeing the Society Police at her door fell away. She hadn't smiled in two days, and now the smile stretched her cheeks in joy. Her own reaction told her how important Flek was becoming to her. She nodded, even though he couldn't see it, and sent a response.

I need to talk, too. I'd love to join you. See you then.

Flek sent the address. The prospect of an evening at his farm allowed her to set aside her worry about the factory. She put away the current batch of fish, shut down the machines, and went home to prepare. The walk home felt light and easy in the bright sunlight.

❧ ✳ ☙

She was impressed when the autocar arrived at the farm. The cheery yellow house, surrounded by fields, had three sets of windows on either side of the door. Behind the house, a matching yellow barn held heavy equipment. She knew very little about farming, but her engineering instincts were curious about how it all worked.

Flek met her at the door with a big smile. He reached out to hold her hand gently in both of his. "I'm glad you were able to come," he said. "I've wanted to invite you here to meet my team and see what we do. But also … some things have happened we need to talk about."

Alba was surprised at the size of the dinner. Flek had eight people working and living at the farm, as well as two pre-school children being raised by the housekeeper and her husband. The

94

dining room held a huge table piled high with food. Unlike the refectories she was used to, the food was all fresh and delicious.

Flek introduced her to everyone, one by one, but the names skittered out of her memory even as he said them. It was rather overwhelming. She learned they all lived here in the farmhouse. Some of the men lived bunk-style in paired bedrooms, others had their own rooms. The housekeeper, who kept bustling in and out with more food, lived with her husband and children in a two-room suite.

Alba heard the leisure of their weekend in contrast to her own. They'd had three days of light tasks and games. They laughed and talked about the bean-bag toss games they'd played that afternoon, about who was best and about funny failures. From the talk, it was clear to her the work was constant and varied. Summer was nearing its end.

"What do you do this time of year on a farm?" she asked.

One of Flek's field hands answered, "It's weeding time. We take equipment out to the fields to prepare for the coming harvest."

Another laughed, "Yeah, but we also have to keep the equipment running."

It quickly became a joke, as everyone pointed to someone else as responsible for repairs. It was obviously not a popular task. These men would rather be out in the fields.

The dinner was like nothing Alba had ever known. Like everyone in Solity, she had moved to primary school at age four and only had vague memories of her early years and her parents. Her entire life had been institutionalized, living in barracks and apartments. As an adult, she had increasingly stressful Assignments appropriate to her engineering knowledge.

In this farm world, she found herself relaxing.

After dinner, Flek invited her to sit with him on the front porch. The sun was already down, but the western horizon still had a faint glow. Alba saw the familiar faces of both moons in the sky; their eldritch light and crossed shadows softened the contours of the fields and fences. The scent of the soil was stronger in the evening air. She marveled at how quiet it was.

"I know it's late already," he said, "but we still need to talk."

"I do, too. This weekend has been awful for me."

"You're not the only one. Several discussion group members were visited by Solity Guards yesterday."

Alba was shocked and relieved at the same time. "Me, too! They came into my apartment and threatened me."

He slumped in his chair. "I'm sorry. Apparently, the Guards have the idea that the group is rebellious, whatever that means."

She nodded. "I came to the conclusion that my only solution was to stop going."

He let loose a big breath. "I was afraid you might. I don't attend the group, but I've fostered its growth. It's important that people know more about Solity." He paused and looked in her eyes. "I've also enjoyed getting to know you. That's why I invited you here tonight."

The tension that had risen inside her at his news subsided. Alba smiled to him and took a sip of her drink.

"I'm glad you did," she said. "I've enjoyed getting to know you, too, and I'd like to keep on." She realized her heart was in her throat as she admitted it.

His smile broadened, his blue eyes sparkling. "In fact," he said, "I was thinking that we should clear our DNA for fraternization. We could get to know each other even better that way. We'd be able to spend time together." Then he looked embarrassed. "If you want to, I mean... I'm afraid I'm a bit awkward about this. I've never asked it of anyone before."

She shrugged, feeling warm but helpless. "I haven't, either. But I'd like that." She reached out to touch his hand on the arm of his chair, then discovered that her hand wanted to linger on his so she let it stay. He smiled more.

❧ ✳ ☙

After they made arrangement to do the DNA test tomorrow, Flek called for an autocar. She rode back to Timpi in a warm glow, watching the fields and scattered houses flow past in the light of the moons.

Until her implant gave her another official message.

Solity has determined that your participation in a dissident group is incompatible with your engineering leadership responsibilities.

Assignment as engineering leader is hereby revoked. Your related housing is also hereby revoked. You are required by tomorrow noon to turn over all engineering data to your assistant and to vacate the apartment. Further Assignment is under consideration.

She sat up in alarm. She could hardly believe it.

What? How can they do this? Give completion credit to someone else? And where am I supposed to go by noon tomorrow?

Her heart was pounding and she could hardly think. *What am I going to do?* Her mind raced in tiny, useless circles. As the car continued toward the city, she no longer saw her surroundings.

Then she thought of Flek. She had no idea what he could do, but at least she could share this disaster. She quickly sub-vocalized a message.

Flek, help! I've just been notified that my Assignment is cancelled and I must leave my apartment by tomorrow. What can I do?

The response came quickly. Instead of a message, he put in an audio implant call directly to her.

"That's terrible, Alba! Are you sure that's what they said?"

She was in tears. "It was very clear. I don't know what to do. I have to turn over the factory to my assistant and move out by noon. I have no idea where to go. They've not given me a new Assignment."

His warm voice was calming. "Go home and get your stuff together. Get a good night's sleep. Do what you have to at the factory. And then we'll make room for you here at the farm. We'll find a way."

Sobbing overtook her in relief, and she couldn't talk at first. "Thank...you," she finally managed to get out.

She slept very poorly on what was probably the worst night of her life.

❧ ❋ ☙

The entire factory team apparently knew by the time she arrived. Stepping into the facility and seeing the caution in their eyes, she felt heat in her face and couldn't meet anyone's eyes. She walked as quickly as she could across the floor and up the steps to her office. Her assistant was already there, in what was now his office.

The transfer went as fast as she could make it go. She showed him what she had done over the weekend; his eyebrows rose at her unusual extra work, but he said nothing about it. She gave him access to her computer and files. Then she left. She'd been in the building less than thirty minutes.

She walked back home—a strange word for a place she now had to vacate—through largely empty streets and gathered her things. All her success in past projects apparently counted for nothing today.

Alba traded messages with Flek. He was coming to get her, to do the DNA tests and then take her to the farm. She sat with her paltry bags on the stoop of the apartment house to wait for him. Fighting tears again, she had no idea what to do. She was homeless. No message had yet come about a new Assignment, and she was in a scary limbo, a sort of Labor purgatory. She kept her eyes down, trying to find some meaning in the cracks on the sidewalk. The street was empty. In Prime, no one just sat on a stoop. Everyone worked and did their part.

Bootsteps approached. She looked up and her heart froze; two Solity Guards. With their faceless helmets, she couldn't tell if it were the same two. She sat up straight on the steps, but a part of her wanted to crawl backwards up into the door. *Get away, get away.*

They stopped in front of her.

"Alba Castilan, we are notified that you have no Assignment. Be aware that Solity has laws against indolence. Everyone is expected to do their part. 'From each according to his ability—'"

She mouthed the standardized completion just as she had been taught in school, her mouth so dry, the words hardly came out. "'—to each according to his need.' But what am I supposed to do? I don't have a new Assignment yet."

"Assignments are not our responsibility. Talk with Labor Department about that. What is not acceptable is for you to do nothing."

Another voice spoke. "She's not doing nothing, sir." It was Flek. His car had arrived. "She's coming to my farm."

The relief that Alba felt was like a wash of clean, heavy rain rinsing a sewer. She jumped to her feet and wanted to hug

Flek—but stopped herself in time. Hugging a man without a fraternization permit, particularly in front of the Guards, was not a good idea.

The guardsman turned to Flek and regarded him for a moment. "Make sure she is gainfully employed, or we will have to visit again."

"I'll do that, sir. Thank you."

Alba wondered how Flek could thank the man so calmly, without even a hint of sarcasm. She didn't think she could accomplish that.

The two of them quickly loaded her bags and got into the autocar under the eyes of the Guards. Alba's heart was pounding the entire time.

❧ ✳ ☙

Things got worse when they completed the testing.

"Flekin Yamasubo, Alba Castilan, your DNA is not compatible for the needs of society." The woman technician was brusque and uncaring. Alba's heart sank. Without compatible DNA, they would not be allowed to fraternize.

Flek spoke quickly, before she could object. "Thank you, ma'am. We appreciate your work." He put a hand on Alba's shoulder to guide her out of the lobby. She kept looking back, trying somehow to change the woman's report. Her blood was boiling. First the integration problems against the Capital demand, then losing her Assignment, and now this.

"How can you be so calm about it?" she shouted when they reached the street.

"It's not the end of the world," he said. "We'll keep trying another way."

"Keep trying? It's DNA. It doesn't change"

"True. But we can get Solity to change." He hustled her back into the car, and they left for the farm. She had no idea what he meant. Solity didn't change.

Alba could never remember feeling so bleak in her entire life. She was without an Assignment, accused of sedition, homeless, and now she couldn't even associate with this one friend she'd found.

When they arrived, Flek took her into his office. "I've got something to show you," he said, and seated her at his desk.

He activated the holohaptic field above his desk. It flashed through several screens before settling on a database record. She gasped to see her own Solity record.

"What? How can you do this?" she asked.

"I have a few secrets I've developed through the years. It's why I don't attend the discussion group; I can't risk being targeted."

She peered at her record, then pointed her finger into the field to highlight the DNA test they'd just taken. Her jaw dropped. "We're incompatible because my mother had green eyes? How absurd."

His smile got broader as he shrugged. "I have blue eyes and you have a recessive gene for green. It's trivial, but Solity seems to believe that unusual eye color leads to bad traits."

"So, we won't be able to be together because my mother had green eyes?"

He ducked his head in a secret way. "Perhaps, or perhaps not."

She caught his drift and smiled wickedly. "Can we change this record?"

He waved a hand for her to try. She'd already selected the field, so she sub-vocalized an imp command to change it. Now it showed her mother had brown eyes, and the fraternization request changed to "approved."

Her breath caught at what she'd done. She found herself looking over her shoulder like a chikadent hearing the howls of a vulf pack. She looked up to see him grinning at her.

"How much of this can we do?" she asked.

He slid his head sideways, eyes narrowed. "We have to be careful. One of the great weaknesses of Solity is that people don't strive for quality. They never work extra to check things. So long as we don't trigger someone's concerns, we can do pretty much anything. It works best on the little things."

Her stomach was uneasy, but she felt a new freedom.

∾ ❋ ∿

By several days later, she still had no new Assignment. The farmhouse had an extra bedroom where she cached her belongings. During the day, she did what she could. She fixed a harvester that was not operating properly. It was good physical labor that also engaged her mind.

With fraternization approved, she and Flek spent much of their time together. She watched him do the farm planning and direct the team. It was more technical than she'd realized; fertilization schedules were tied intricately with weather, temperature, and soil sampling. He had a style of leadership that she admired, able to inspire his people to do more than the minimum.

Flek also joined her in the barn to see what she was doing. He knew the equipment but had not had time to do repairs yet. He praised what she did.

The two spent evenings on the porch watching the moons advance in the sky each night. They talked of her problems. At first, she wanted to rehash the difficulties of the factory, learning from him her mistakes in leadership. After two nights, however, the fish-packing plant seemed so remote it wasn't worth discussing.

Her life velocity was gradually slowing to match the pace of the farm, driven by seasons and weather rather than deadlines.

Four nights later, Flek had a new smile on his face.

"What?" she said. "Have you got another secret?"

He laughed. "You're quick, Alba. That's one of the things I like about you. Nothing much gets past you." Then he held her hands. "You're also intelligent and competent, and those are traits too good to waste. You need something good to do."

She nodded and smiled. "Yes, I do. But I'm still waiting for Assignment. I've been hoping that Labor will take into account our fraternization."

He chuckled. "They will."

"How could you possibly know?" She cocked her head at him in puzzlement.

Then an implant message came in, almost as if it were timed to arrive. It was accompanied by the special Assignment tone most people only heard a few times in their lives.

Solity has determined that your engineering skills can be used for repair, maintenance, and upgrade of equipment. You are hereby Assigned to the Yamasubo farm to support operations. Lodging will be provided by the farm.

Her eyes went wide. She spun her head to look at Flek, and he was laughing.

"There you go, Alba. No more worries. When I saw how good you were with the equipment, I put in a requisition and named you. And I can also engage your capabilities in some of our more...secret...activities." His eyes twinkled.

"What? How did you do that? This is wonderful."

"Approval happened almost by itself, because you're a good fit. I only had to do a minor tweak of the system," he held up a tiny pinch of fingers, "to push it over the edge. Just now, your notification was waiting for my release as farm leader. I gave it tonight, so I could watch your delightful reaction."

She laughed and jumped from her chair into his, wrapping her arms around his neck.

"Oh, you ..." She couldn't think of words to say, so she kissed him. And, oh my, but he kissed her back.

As she cuddled in his lap, she thought about her years of never finding peace through excellence in work. Solity controls always seemed to get in the way. Flek had shown her a different way, a path of freedom even within Solity. She was discovering the true meaning of peace.

Sixteen Hours of Love and Guns

Living in a pure democracy might not be as easy as many think. The political chaos of a lawmaking body spreads to the entire populace as advocates seek to influence the vote. Special-interest groups flourish, often with conflict that can easily spill over into violence. Public media outlets seek to influence the votes for and against multiple issues at once. Individuals live with a new set of problems.

9-32 of the sixteen-hour Verdant clock—early afternoon. When she saw the man, Yana Levin was laughing wildly and brandishing a needle gun. Her FAR group was marching to support private ownership of guns. The march was wild fun, like a street party. Yana hollered and hooted with the rest. The noise of their revelry echoed from the tall buildings on both side of the street. The sky above was blue and the air smelled fresh.

In the country of Tileus, she loved being young and involved. Full democracy with a popular vote on every topic led to lots of political groups. Everyone was passionate about something.

She'd progressed quickly to become the FAR Secretary, sitting on the Board of Directors. She treasured both the power and the excitement, a far cry from the staid life of her parents.

Then this man appeared. He stood on the street corner while her parade crowded past. She stopped laughing, and her heart lurched. She forgot herself enough to stop walking; her friend Thibault Leblanc ran into her from behind.

"Watch it, Yana," he laughed.

But she didn't respond. She was lost. The man's head rose above the sidewalk crowd with striking blond hair and sharp green eyes. His neat beard framed a look of amusement that curled his mouth. Muscular shoulders moved slightly when he shifted position, a red shirt with cut-off sleeves exposing his strength. Yana felt a physical jolt to her gut. She laughed louder, this time in the delight of possible connection.

He'd been watching the Freedom and Responsibility march, then his eyes stopped on her. He stood up straighter and cocked his head to one side. His smile broadened and his eyes raked her body just like hers had done his.

She knew she looked good, trim and curvy. His piercing gaze practically undressed her. She shivered in a frisson of delight. When he finished, he looked directly back into her eyes and tipped his fingers to his forehead in greeting.

For that moment, everything else in the street receded to background. She nodded back to him and nearly stumbled over her own feet.

How can I see him again? she thought, then quickly converted it to a subvocal command through her implant connection to the InfoNet: *Who is he?* She kept her eyes on him to focus the command.

The imp put red boxes in her vision, outlining several people in the sidewalk crowd, the boxes bouncing from person to person in imperfect programming. **Insufficient specification,** it responded in her aural channel. **Which individual?**

But the march moved on, and the crowd moved her along with it. She tried harder yet failed to focus her imp on the one man. In moments, he was lost to sight.

Desperately, Yana made her way through the moving group to the sidewalk. She was now half a block away. His head should be above the crowd back there at the last street corner, but she didn't see him. She looked all around at the streets and sidewalks to no avail. Torn between her duties to her group and this sudden incredible contact, she fretted on the sidewalk.

Then a passerby put a momentary steadying hand on her shoulder, and her heart flipped. She turned quickly in hope. It wasn't him.

With a disappointed sigh, she rejoined the FAR march. For the rest of the event, her mind whirled on how she could find that man again. She considered leaving the march now...but she had responsibilities, too.

❧ ✳ ❦

10-27—mid-afternoon. Rafe Cunha lingered on the street. He hardly believed the visceral reaction he'd had to that gorgeous woman in the gun march. Flowing blond hair, built like a curvy stack of pheromones, bold eyes that bored into his own. He shuddered when he pictured her once again. She might be part of FAR, an opposing group, but he still had to see her again.

Rafe was still getting used to Tileus. He'd fled over the mountains from the Rathas theocracy to escape its restrictive nature; coming here had been like jumping from a straitjacket into a skittering pinball game. Tileus was chaos, with every political voice shouting for attention. He wasn't yet sure Tileus was any better than Rathas.

He didn't know how to find that woman other than hoping she'd come back. He'd tried to capture her image in his implant, but it had all happened too fast. A spark had happened between them. He knew she'd felt it too—he chuckled to himself when he remembered watching her stumble. Her friend had almost run her down. *She's got to return.*

Disappointed, he was about to give up. He'd waited here for an hour. He let go a heavy sigh and turned to go.

And there she was, two stores away, as beautiful as he remembered. She was looking all around but hadn't seen him yet. He was so surprised he released a bark of laughter.

She whirled toward his laugh. Their eyes met again, and the spark rekindled. Suddenly, he found he couldn't say anything at all.

She broke the silence. "You're the man on the sidewalk. Uh. During the march."

His own tongue broke free, and he almost babbled, "I've been hanging around for the last hour, wondering if you'd come back. I'm glad you did." He stopped to regain some modicum of self-control. "My name's Rafael Cunha, Rafe." He was uneasy, uncertain whether to extend a hand for a handshake.

It took her two tries to get words out. "Uh...Yeah...I'm Yana." She looked flustered. "Yana Levin. I...uh...saw you." She blushed.

Rafe almost heard her telling herself to pull it together. Still uncomfortable with himself, he said, "Yeah. I saw you, too. And...something happened."

She suddenly relaxed. "Yeah, something did. I came back here because I wanted to find you again."

With that, Rafe also relaxed. *It's going to be okay.* "Right. And I stayed here in case you came back. Well, you found me. And I found you."

"Yeah, we did." The crowded street lit up with her grin.

"Maybe we should get to know each other," Rafe said. "Would you like to join me for an afternoon tea? There's a great place across the street."

She seemed startled. "Tea? Not coffee?" She laughed. "Tea's my favorite. I never thought I'd find someone else who liked it."

While they walked across the street, his mind was spinning like a supercharged carousel.

❦

10-53 – mid-afternoon. Yana sat at the table wondering if her glow was visible to everyone in the café. Rafe surprised her by ordering a "high tea." The service bot put a cone-shaped tier of trays on their table filled with delicate scones and sandwiches to go with the large pot of Freetown black tea.

"Where did you ever hear of this?" she asked.

"It's an afternoon custom from someplace on old Earth. I discovered this tea shop a few months ago." He slathered sweet creamed butter all over a powdered sugar scone, added a dollop of jelly, and handed it to her.

She bit into the scone. It filled her mouth with sweetness that expanded to fill her head. "This is delicious," she mumbled around the sticky cream.

"I thought you might like it." He selected a cucumber sandwich, then added, "So, what else do you do other than marching for guns?" He was smiling, but he seemed uncomfortable mentioning the guns.

"I'm training to be a manager at an implant factory. It's fascinating. And you?"

"I teach at Freedom College, classical literature. Shakespeare, Hemingway, Dingwaller—the strong English-language voices from old Earth before it died."

Yana was surprised and delighted. "How fascinating. I've read some of those old works. The language is obscure, but the emotional content is marvelous." *A man who appreciates literature! How interesting.*

"Now that's a contrast. You work in implant technology, but you like reading?"

She shrugged, grinning. "Yep. That's me. Full of contrast."

"I like contrast," he said, and Yana preened inside. "I've got some in my life, too, because I grew up in Rathas. I only came here two years ago."

"Wow. I'll bet that was a change." She leaned forward to listen, the delicious scones forgotten.

He nodded, his smile touching her heart. "Yes, it was. Life is calm over there, but really controlled. Here, life is wild and in constant turmoil. I'm still not sure which is better."

An angry voice intruded from over Yana's shoulder. "He's an active member of CARE."

Yana saw shock in Rafe's eyes, then spun around to see Thibault looming over the table. Her stomach dropped at his news, but she tried to ease his interruption. "Uh...Hi, Thibault." She sounded lame to herself. "Rafe, this is my friend."

"Yeah. I saw him in your march. Hi, Thibault." Rafe sounded belligerent and nervous at the same time, if that were possible.

Yana added, "Thibault and I are both in the FAR leadership. He's the Sergeant-at-Arms, and I'm the Secretary."

"Yeah," said Thibault to Rafe. "Don't 'hi' me. I'm the one who watches out for infiltrators. 'Citizens for Active Responsible Equality,' indeed. You people want to take away our guns and make us all sheep, don't you?"

"Well, what I believe has nothing to do with why I'm here with Yana."

"Yeah, right. Why *are* you here with our Yana? I've kicked a bunch of CARE people out of our meetings. You people keep shoving your way in to find out what we're doing, and then you publicize it in the worst ways."

"That's not me, Thibault. I'm just here to get to know her."

Yana laid a hand on Thibault's arm. "Please relax. We're just talking. This has nothing to do with FAR."

"It has everything to do with it!" shouted Thibault, shoving Rafe's shoulder. "CARE and FAR are at opposite ends of everything we believe in. You two together would be a scandal. You'd hurt our cause."

Rafe stood up to face Thibault, his palms out in peace. "We can disagree without—"

"No, we can't," barked Thibault, and he pushed Rafe's shoulder again, looking like a pit bull against a Doberman.

Yana jumped to her feet. "Knock it off, Thibault!"

Rafe stepped back further. His palms were still raised, but the fire of anger was rising in his eyes. He shook his head. "That's it. I don't have to take this abuse. I'm out of here."

He turned on his heels and walked away with feet pounding into the concrete.

"Wait," wailed Yana.

Rafe just kept going. By the time she got to the street, he was nowhere in sight. Her chest felt so tight she wondered how she was still breathing.

∾ ✽ ∾

11-52 – sunset. With a name and an image, Rafe was able to find Yana's public information. *Why do I have to find someone from the other side?* He paced outside her apartment building for fifteen minutes before he brought himself to ring the bell. Yana didn't answer, but another resident happened to come out.

"Excuse me, but do you know Yana Levin?"

The woman looked up at Rafe and smiled. "She's my neighbor, yes."

"Apparently, she's not home. I'm trying to find her."

She looked him up and down, still smiling. "I'd guess she'd want you to find her, too. You might try down by the lake. She likes to sit there."

"Thanks." Rafe saw a lake shining in the sun, down a grassy hill with trees. He walked down and found her on a secluded bench in the trees, looking at the water. He let out a long-held breath to see her.

"Is this a private lake, or can someone join you?"

She spun around and jumped to her feet. "Rafe! How did you find me?"

He shrugged. "I asked at your apartment. They said you often sit down here." He looked embarrassed as he continued, "I couldn't stay away from you."

"That's funny. I was just sitting here trying to decide if I should find your place."

He stepped closer and took both her hands. "No need. We're here, now." They sat together. He wondered if his smile looked as silly and confused as his mind felt. Giddy. That was the word.

He glanced up at the western horizon. The lowering sun laughed at them through layers of green clouds, the sky behind tinged with ochre and lavender. The sun's rays spread from cloud corners to create beams of bright orange. He thought it was perhaps the most amazing sunset he'd ever seen.

He looked back at her. "You know," he said, still holding her hands, "when I compare that sunset to you, I'm not at all sure which is more beautiful."

She blushed. "I'd always been told CARE people couldn't connect their thoughts, but I love the way you do it."

"Hey, I'm just doing what I do."

"But what can we do, Rafe?" She sounded desperate. "There's no way our friends in FAR and CARE are going to let us be together."

He shook his head in amazement. "This is all so strange to me. In Rathas, we didn't have all these...groups. The Church controlled everything. I immigrated here to get away from that kind of control." He thought for a moment. "Our friends can take care of themselves. Let's not allow them to dictate what we do."

He leaned down to kiss her, and felt her lean into him. All thought of words raced away. Her eyes closed and lips opened in the kiss, intimate breath intermingling. He gently put his arms around her smooth shoulders and pulled her closer to him. The kiss went on and on. Nothing existed but the sensations that swirled down to awaken every desire in his body. He never wanted it to stop.

She pressed harder against his mouth, her breath speeding. Her arms around him—*when did she put them there?*—pulled him in as tightly as he held her. Their lips were alive, clinging, imbibing the ecstasy of each other.

When she rose again for breath, she whispered, "My place is just around the block."

He nodded slightly and started another kiss. In the middle of the kiss, he lifted her to her feet and started walking that direction, barely letting their lips come apart.

∽＊∽

14-18 – late evening. Yana curled against Rafe's body. The tousled covers lay over their hips, letting the afterheat from their bodies radiate like glowing beacons into the bedroom. She was exhausted, but shimmered with joy.

"That was...wonderful," she breathed.

His chest rose and fell under her arm. "I agree. Even the third time. I don't think I've ever lasted three times."

She giggled. "Women do have an advantage, you know." She pulled herself closer to him. The strength in his chest and shoulders was like bedrock.

A sudden loud pounding on the door interrupted the afterglow.

"Yana," came a male voice. "Open up. We've got a problem."

"Thibault," she whispered to Rafe. "He's so hot-headed, everything's a problem. But he won't go away. Stay here. I'll be back"

She slipped out of the covers with a smile, pausing to drink in the carved curves of his body. Slipping on a robe, she closed the bedroom door while Thibault started pounding again on the front door.

"Yana! Wake up and—"

She interrupted his shouting by opening the door. "What the hell are you doing here at this time of night, Thibault? You're going to wake all the neighbors."

He pushed past her into the living room, hands waving.

"We've got a big problem, Yana. CARE found out about you meeting with that Rafe man. They've voted a censure against him, and they want FAR to do the same to you. The Executive Council met without you. You're the secretary. Didn't you get the notice?"

"What? Just because I met with one of their members?"

"More than just 'met,' Yana. I was there; you two were pretty deep in yourselves. CARE also had a couple of members in that silly tea house. After you left, they attacked me in the café."

Yana felt her heart pounding. *What would Thibault do if he knew Rafe was in her bed?*

"Well," she said, "what do you expect me to do about it?"

"You've got to face the music. Maybe if you accept a censure, the groups will calm down."

"She can't do that, Thibault." Rafe stepped in from the bedroom, and Yana's heart fell. *No. He can't do this here.* He'd pulled on his clothes, but the tousled hair, open shirt, muscled chest, and cooling sweat spoke volumes about what they'd been doing.

"You!" shouted Thibault. He looked back and forth from Yana to Rafe, his face going at light speed from concerned to angry. "You're here. Great gavels, this makes it all worse."

"No, it doesn't," said Rafe. "Tileus is a free country. You might not know what that means, but I do."

The conflict had Yana's heart pounding, but she took Rafe's arm. His male scent gave her strength. "Freedom," she said. "FAR and CARE are just going to have to deal with it."

"No, damn it. It's not right." Thibault, ever agitated, was working himself up to an explosion. "You can't link with these people, Yana. They're against everything we stand for.

Yana looked up at Rafe and felt his strength beside her. "I don't care what 'these people' may be for or against. But Rafe and I belong together, regardless of the groups we're part of."

Thibault pulled his needle gun out of its holster. "You don't know what you're talking about, Yana. These things," he waved the gun as an example, "are important. The nationwide vote is coming up on gun control. If our groups start squabbling in the streets, public sentiment will turn against us all. We'll lose the vote!" He was practically screaming.

"Maybe you *should* lose the vote," said Rafe. "Brandishing your gun over two people's love is exactly why guns are dangerous."

"You!" shouted Thibault, and he pointed the gun at Rafe. "Get out. Now. Leave."

"Wait a second," Yana shouted. "This is my apartment. You can't tell him to leave." She let go of Rafe's arm and stepped between them, her hands spread wide. "Calm down, Thibault. Put the gun down. This doesn't solve anything."

"Stay out of the way, Yana." Thibault swept his free arm to push Yana out of his line of fire. "I'm getting him out of here, now."

His pushing triggered her own anger. "No, you're not," she shouted. "This is my place. He's my guest."

She tried to block the line of fire again, but bumped into Rafe. Using Yana's distraction, Rafe reached over her shoulder and grabbed the barrel of the gun. He tilted it upward, and the gun went off. A flechette needle slammed into the ceiling.

"What are you—" Yana started to say.

Thibault slammed his free fist into Rafe's jaw. Then Thibault grabbed the gun with both hands, trying to wrest it from Rafe's grip. Rafe fought back, the gun wildly changing its aim while the men struggled. Rafe pounded a fist into Thibault's midriff.

Her heart pounding, Yana put both her hands on their separate shoulders, trying to pry them apart. "Stop it, you two! Someone's going to get—"

The gun went off again. Thibault went suddenly stiff, then collapsed onto the floor. There was a hole under his chin. Blood dribbled from the corner of his mouth.

"Oh, Earthfire!" exclaimed Yana. She dropped to her knees, hands fluttering to touch his chest, his face. She watched his eyes fade from glazed to a dead stare. Desperately, she felt for the pulse under his jaw, looked for the movement of his chest.

Nothing.

She spun to look up at Rafe. "You've killed him."

"Sweet Jaysus," Rafe whispered. His eyes were wide and round.

Yana looked back at Thibault, hoping against hope to see movement of any kind. When she looked up at Rafe again, he had backed up two steps. He was still holding the needle gun as if unaware of it.

"He started it," he muttered. "I never meant to—" Rafe turned and ran out the door.

"Rafe," she screamed. She jumped to the door, but he was already down the stairs and out the front.

Yana turned back into her apartment to see the dead body of her friend accusing the world. *I don't know what to do.*

ॐ ✳ ॐ

14-43 – late evening. Rafe burst from the apartment building and ran up the street. Around the next corner, he stopped in the dark of a shadowed doorway.

His mind raced. *I shot him. He attacked me, and I shot him. I didn't just turn the gun away from us, I turned it toward him. Jaysus help me, in that moment I wanted to.*

The gun felt like a two-hundred-pound weight. He stashed it in his belt under his shirt. *What do I do with it?* If he dumped it here, the police would find it with his fingerprints and DNA.

Rafe hurried away from the area. He had no place in mind. He just had to get away.

ॐ ✳ ॐ

00-03 – midnight. An hour and a half later, Yana sat in the back booth of an all-night easygo. She nursed a drink as a way to do something with her shaking hands while she thought. *I can't lose Rafe, but what can I do? He killed Thibault.* She hadn't tried to call him, because she didn't know what to say.

She'd fled her own apartment, leaving the door open and the body in place. *What will the police do when it's discovered? I didn't report it. I'm probably in as much trouble as Rafe now.* Her mind kept spinning and spinning, the webs getting tighter with every thought.

She considered turning herself in and taking the consequences. Would they arrest her? Take her to jail as an accomplice?

Or.

Perhaps she could hide. Change her identity. It would have to be a complete break with everyone she knew. She sucked in a frightened breath. *Very extreme thinking.*

Her mind went into darker realms. *Why did Thibault get so angry? What was he thinking, pulling out his gun?* Then she stiffened, realizing her own thoughts. She was blaming Thibault for his own death. How callous of her. She shifted to Rafe. *Men, fighting over everything. He didn't have to grab the gun.* The thoughts warred inside with her love for him.

In any case, she would leave FAR. Thinking about the philosophy of guns was one thing. Using one in anger made her shudder. She felt dirty, fouled by the event.

She tapped the table with a fingernail over and over. She watched her own finger, remembering from somewhere that repetitive motion indicated a stuck mind. She was certainly stuck.

Really, it's all my fault. Falling in love with a man from CARE.

An incoming call rang in her implant. Rafe.

She sat up straight. *Do I want to talk with him?* The answer jumped into her mind like a welcome pop-up: *Yes!* She accepted the call and subvocalized. "Where are you? Are you okay?"

"I'm okay, but I'm struggling. I can't believe it happened."

"What are you going to do?"

He paused a long time. "I don't know. The police don't know I was there yet, but they will when they do DNA tests."

"I can't deal with this, Rafe. I can't—"

"We have to, Yana. It's done, and it's real."

"I can't believe you killed Thibault. And it's all my fault."

"It's not your fault. He was the one who pulled the gun. And..." his voice shuddered "I was the one who pointed it at him."

"But I made it happen," she said, "by crossing the boundaries."

"Where are you? Let me come to —"

"No!" she said, the word ringing out loud in the easygo. She saw the bartender look up, and subvocalized again. "No. I can't deal with it. I can't deal with it at all." She ended the call and locked her information away from him.

01-23 – dark of night. The streets she wandered were as foreboding as her thoughts. She heard and saw no one else in the middle of the night. But Yana was coming to a crazy solution that might work, a way to get away from it all.

She'd kill herself.

No, not really. She was depressed about this whole thing and didn't want to face the consequences. But not so miserable she wanted to end everything. She'd been thinking it out while walking, and she thought it could work. She'd fake her own death in some way that left circumstantial evidence, and she'd have a friend hack her implant to a new identity.

Afterwards, she'd find Rafe and help him do the same. They could move together to another city or another country.

The question she pondered while she walked was "How?"

02-06 – Silver moon rise. Rafe still had the needle gun hidden under his shirt, and he didn't know what to do with it. He walked the streets desperately looking for Yana. Her imp refused any more calls and wouldn't give him her location. The streets were dark. The late crescent of the moon Silver gave little enough light to see his steps.

Every time he saw the lights of an open place, he checked for her.

03-35– early dawn. Yana left her suicide note displayed on the workbench of her parent's boathouse. She included a gift for her parents, her childhood journal. They'd probably read it long ago, but it would be a sweet reminder. Her stomach churned as she took each step toward revising her life. *Will I ever be able to see my parents again? But life with Rafe will be worth it. After I do this, I'll get together with him. We can move to Freetown or Uptown and start a new life.*

She accessed her bank accounts and made a huge donation to a charity. It would look like a last act of kindness, but the charity was run by her friend Frederica. She would go to Rica later for her help, and ask her to contact Rafe.

The boathouse was far enough behind their house that her parents wouldn't be awakened by lowering the boat. She activated the release and the speedboat dropped gently into the water. She left the boathouse doors open so her parents would see the missing boat first thing in the morning. The work of a moment was all it took to unmoor and back out. She didn't start the engine until she was well clear and kept it at idle until the boat was out in the channel.

Advancing the throttle, she headed for the open sea. She would cut her finger and leave a bloody knife on board, turn off her implant, then swim back while the boat continued outward.

Someone would find it.

❦ ✸ ❧

06-08 – mid-morning. Rafe had finally given in to sleep just before dawn, but he set an alarm for only two hours. He was frantic to find Yana.

The police knocked on his door while he was wolfing down a breakfast. They had DNA evidence that he'd been there, and they asked him what happened.

He told the truth—mostly—leaving out only the key fact that he had pointed the gun. When they asked what happened to the gun, he lied. He could tell his answers didn't satisfy them, but they left without arresting him—yet.

Afterwards, Rafe collapsed onto his couch and shuddered with fear. His thoughts filled with blackness. *I've shot a man, and I've lied to the police. I don't even like guns. What am I going to do?*

He tucked the gun again under his shirt. Its presence in his apartment was too incriminating. He'd been unable to think about anything else the whole time he talked with the officers. While he was out, he'd get rid of it somewhere after cleaning off his DNA and fingerprints as thoroughly as he could.

His real reason for going out, though, was to find Yana. This whole affair wouldn't be worth anything if they didn't end up together. He'd had little sleep, but he was awake now, so he could get on with his search.

Outside Yana's apartment, a clot of people milled around, with police officers controlling the scene. He stopped at the street corner. It was obvious she wasn't going to be there.

Then someone clapped him on the shoulder, and he nearly jumped out of his skin.

"Hey, Rafe."

Rafe turned to see one of his CARE friends. "Hey, Mercer," Rafe said, with his heart racing. "What's going on?"

Mercer shook his head. "I'm thinking you should be telling us. You were the one who got yourself entangled with the FAR girl, and now her friend's dead."

"Yeah, I know. And now I'm trying to find her. Does anyone know where she went?"

"You haven't heard?" Mercer looked nervous and glanced over at the crowd.

"Heard what?" Rafe's breath caught. His friend knew something.

"This morning..." Mercer paused, searching for words. "I don't know how to say this. If you really liked her..."

"Just tell me." His body was tight. It sounded like bad news coming.

"The rumor is she killed herself in the night."

"What? How?"

"Took a boat out into the ocean, slit her wrists, and jumped overboard. They found the boat and some blood, but no body."

Mercer might have punched Rafe in the stomach. He staggered back, shaking his head, then turned and ran.

06-42 – mid-morning. After being up most of the night, then swimming ashore, Yana was exhausted. Yet she still needed to do something about her implant. She changed into the dry clothes she'd stashed and went to Frederica's house. Her friend was a wizard with software, skating on the edge of the law.

When she opened the door, Rica's eyes went wide. She looked Yana up and down. "Ya look like hell, girl. What ya been doin'? Get yourself on in here." She flung the door open and pulled Yana in.

"Yeah, it's been a rough night."

"C'mon in. I'll get ya some coffee, and you can tell me 'bout it."

Telling her about it took only a few minutes. Getting the comfort she needed from a friend took more time. By half an hour later, Yana was wrapped in Rica's arms and crying. She let out all the fears, all the worries, and she shared her joy at the love she'd found.

"But I need your help for more than comfort, Rica"

"Anythin', girl. Just let me know."

"I need you to make contact with Rafe for me. It's not safe for me to do so."

"Sure. That's easy."

"I also need you to hack my imp, change who I am. I can't go back, and I need a new identity. And I'll need the same for Rafe. And there's also some money in your charity." Yana felt like she was babbling.

Rica made an amused snort. "Never thought *you'd* ask for somethin' like that. Straight-lace girl that ya are."

"Well, I am."

"Not a prob," Rica said with a nod. "Done it before, can do it again. Who do ya wanna be?"

Yana managed to fall asleep for an hour while Rica worked.

07-28 – late morning. Rafe was desperate. He still wandered the streets looking for her, without success. The gun was still in his belt. Every time he saw a place he might discard it, he thought of ways the police would find it. Guilt filled his soul.

He'd heard nothing from Yana, nothing from his friends. Only some crazy message from someone he didn't know: *Look for Naftali at the lake.* It made no sense, but it reminded him of meeting Yana. He made his way to the lake by her apartment, as miserable as any man could be.

He felt cut off from the world. How long would it be before he was arrested?

09-32 – early afternoon – exactly one 16-hour day after Yana and Rafe saw each other. She was now Yana Naftali instead of Yana Levin, having decided to keep her first name. Rica had not only changed her imp, but had also given her a rich new background she could use to find work wherever she went. Rica had made several "payments for services" from her charity through convoluted paths that ended with Yana's new identity, extracting her fee for the work.

She was ready to meet Rafe. She knew Rica had sent him a message. It wouldn't make sense to call him from her new identity until they'd met. The lake was risky, but would work. It was rather near to her old apartment, but she could approach the lake from another direction.

Yana walked under the trees along the lake, marveling at the shades of russet, contrasting with the bright green grass in the sun. A few puffy clouds lined the sky. Her heart was lighter.

She remembered her excitement of yesterday while in the gun march, shaking her head at her naivete. Guns or no guns, she'd discovered love was more important than any political issue. She'd lose her friends in FAR with this move, but she could live with that. Thibault's actions had shown her how fanatical they could be.

The bench was hidden behind the trees around the next bend. The InfoNet told her that's where he was. Her heart fluttered and she anticipated surprising him. She stepped quietly through the trees.

She heard his voice and stopped. *Is he meeting with someone?*

"It's no good. It's just no good," he said.

She stepped forward, staying hidden, and peered around a tree trunk. He was alone on the bench. He must be talking through his imp? Or to himself?

He continued talking, a bit disjoint. "I don't know. Yesterday was fantastic, until that firebrand busted in."

She saw his head lowered toward the water, and he had something in his lap.

"She was everything I've wanted. I never believed in love at first sight, but that's what it was."

Yana's heart swelled. He was talking about her. A huge smile creased her face.

"I can't believe she's gone. I no sooner find her than…" His voice paused, and he dropped his forehead into his left hand. His shoulders shook. "It's just not worth going back."

Yana started forward, tiptoeing through the grass toward him. She thought the smile on her face might brighten the whole area and give her away.

Then Rafe lifted the needle gun from his lap and put it to his head.

"No!" she screamed, and she lunged toward him, hands outstretched to stop him.

Rafe jumped. The gun wobbled in his hand and went off, just before Yana's hands grasped it.

"No!" she shrieked again. "I'm here, Rafe, I'm here!"

His hand pulled on hers, a reflex reaction, then he turned his face over his shoulder to see her. His eyebrows had risen practically into his hairline and a bloody streak striped his forehead where the needle had grazed him.

"Yana!" he shouted. He dropped the gun, jumped to his feet, and clambered over the bench to wrap her in his arms.

"It's okay, Rafe," she cried while she hugged him tightly to her. "We're going to be okay."

Rules Are for Those Who Follow

Religious oppression is one of the most insidious kinds of control. From the most ancient of times, religions have tried to influence people "for their own good." Often, masked behind the altruism is naked power that surfaces quickly when threatened.

"Praise Jaysus, son of Elláh," Thoret Speakeach's voice resounded from the raised pulpit, echoing across the carved stone walls. "He showed us how to live in the Four Goals using the Five Pillars. He died for our sins, so we might follow His way."

Thoret led this congregation of Elláh's church in the capital city of Praise. The respect he'd earned echoed in the city like his voice from the walls. He knew today's message would offend some of the Rathas national leaders, as had this entire series. It might even have repercussions for him personally. Yet his passion was to change the way his people thought about Elláh.

"More than two thousand years after Jaysus, our Church came together from the warring sects of Christianity, Islam, and Hinduism. For most of those years, Elláh's people fought against Elláh's people." He punctuated his message with broad gestures spreading his flowing scarlet robe in mesmerizing shapes. "Holy Wars were anything but holy. Each sect tried to win the souls of men away from the other sects. Yet each had only a limited view of what Elláh wanted. Only in the final hundred years of Earth did the people of Elláh come together to foment a rebellion of peace."

He shook his head sadly, and he filled his voice with anguish. "It was too little, too late. Earth destroyed itself, but the believers brought the Church away in the colony ships."

Thoret felt power rising in him, a lightness in his soul. He saw the empathic reaction in the congregation, tears springing from some eyes.

The national leaders in the front rows, however, were more guarded. Like the ancient priests, today's leaders wanted to codify Elláh's way into human-made rules they could administer in their worldly power. Thoret, in contrast, wanted people to follow Jaysus. Rules were helpful, but their rigor often made people as inflexible as the rules themselves.

"Jaysus spoke in His sermons of the Five Pillars, even though Islam had not yet been conceived. His message included surrender to Elláh, frequent prayer, concern for the needy, self-purification, and mission to others. He said, 'Blessed are the meek, for they shall inherit the earth.' He also included the Four Goals of dharma, artha, kama, and moksha in his teaching, though in his time they were only spoken in the Hindu tradition. Those who followed were slow to see how His message included it all."

The faces in front of him were rapt and he fed on that. In merging the thoughts from the three source religions of the Church, he knew he was tapping deep places in the souls of the congregation.

One of the key people he watched for reaction was Beltaret Leaderlist, a long-time friend. Beltaret radiated intelligence, dignity and power in all he did. He was the national Minister of Security, with influence at the highest levels of both nation and Church. So far, Beltaret was nodding in agreement with Thoret's message.

Thoret made eye contact with individuals. "And today, here on the planet Verdant, the battle for souls is not yet won. Most of the people of this planet have no faith. Conflicts are growing, wars are coming, and we face the same problems that condemned Earth in its last days. Our dharma is clear, the mission to spread the love and peace of Jaysus and thereby stop the growing clashes."

There were many nods in the huge congregation, and a few voices echoed "Amen" aloud.

He paused so the next words would ring. "Yet even here in Rathas, we... *do... not... do...* what Jaysus would have us do." Thoret pounded his fist on the pulpit, timing the words. He locked eyes for a moment with Namabruthi Shapserv, the congregational Eldress for Women's Studies. He and Nama had worked together to frame this sermon series, and he was now coming to the main point. She was smiling; he saw encouragement in her eyes.

"Jaysus spoke harshly to the leaders of his day. He said they preach but do not practice, tying up heavy burdens for others while loving the places of honor for themselves. He called them *whitewashed tombs,*" Thoret thundered, pointing to the cemetery outside, "*shutting* the *gates* of the Kingdom of Heaven." His hands clapped in a resounding crack to shut the gates, amplified by the sound system. "He decried the rules they laid down for the people."

At the back of the sanctuary, a grey-uniformed church proctor slipped out the main door. Another proctor was taking notes on a hand-held.

He watched Beltaret and other leaders' faces while he changed tack into the opposing wind of national rules. Heretics sometimes suffered arrest in Rathas; the church proctors watched for major errors in doctrine. Some later recanted their heresy in public, but others simply disappeared. Yet Thoret relied on his position as leader of this prominent congregation. What he taught was core doctrine, not heresy.

The faces of the national leaders had changed. They were now set with resistance against his words. Dark eyes and frowns filled the first several rows.

He started again in a voice so quiet it hissed. "What happens today in Rathas is *not,*" his hand slashed sideways, cutting the cord of reality, "what Jaysus wants of us. The peoples of Tileus and the other countries look at us with *disdain...*" He allowed a long pause to echo the enormous word in the chamber, then stepped down to the stage. He continued in the silence of a near-whisper. "...because we preach love and peace to them while living our lives with rules...and restrictions...and condemnation.

Instead of our brilliant light inviting them to join us, we bludgeon them with disapproval."

Now, Thoret extended both hands to the congregation in supplication. He was at center stage front, as close to the congregation as he could get. "Please, friends. Let us surrender to Jaysus and to Elláh. Let us each seek the spiritual grounding that brings us tranquility. Study the scriptures. Listen to Elláh in meditation. Set aside the rules that bind our lives, and instead seek to live the Five Pillars."

Music swelled in the background and Thoret stopped to let it take over the enormous space. He raised his hands from imploring the people to supplication toward heaven, showing by his posture the surrender he asked of them all. The Music Elder moved up to lead a song, and Thoret lowered his hands and head and retired to his high stone seat behind the pulpit.

๛ ✳ ๛

After the service, Thoret made himself available to those who wished to speak to him. Rather than blocking the door as some pastors did, he had a corner of the entry hall. Some people thanked him with fervor. Others were more cautious, concerned about flouting the church rules.

Namabruthi, his cohort in planning this message, stepped up to him with a cautious smile. "You've stirred up a stingernest, Thoret. Those were stronger words than we planned."

He nodded and smiled. "They were, Nama, but they have needed saying for a long time."

"I don't disagree. I only hope you haven't gone too far."

A deeper voice sounded. "I also hope the same, Thoret." Beltaret Leaderlist stepped up from one side. "Your words verged on sedition. I fear you may suffer some repercussions."

Thoret turned to Beltaret. "If we suffer for Jaysus, how can it be suffering?" He smiled again.

Nama quietly stepped away, leaving the two leaders to talk.

Beltaret shook his head. "I caution you, my friend. Suffering can be real no matter how spiritual you are. When you speak against the Church leadership, you cannot expect to continue without ramifications."

Both men radiated power and authority, and they respected each other. Thoret answered, "But what should we do, my friend, when the leadership guides us wrongly? You know what Jaysus did. He spoke against the priests."

"Jaysus was crucified for his honesty."

"Muhamet also spoke against the tribally fractured leaders of his time. He gathered his followers to mission against those who were on the wrong path."

Beltaret countered with the obvious third example. "Yes, and Matma Ganzhi was also outspoken—and was assassinated. Learn from them, Thoret. Our nation hangs by precarious threads against Tileus and Prime; we cannot also afford internal conflict."

Thoret paused and looked down in thought, then met Beltaret's eyes once again. "If we need internal conflict to bring us to the path of peace, then we must not avoid it."

Beltaret said nothing more, just watched Thoret's eyes for a moment. Then he bowed his head slightly in respect and stepped away. Thoret's heart was pounding. Conflict was never easy. Although they were friends, Beltaret as Minister of Security was a dangerous man to cross.

❧ ✳ ❧

By mid-afternoon, he was able to go home. An autocar dropped him at his door. Despite his prominent position, Thoret's pastel green house was small and unassuming. He kept flower gardens, one of his worldly delights. Unlike the story of Cain, who believed he himself grew the crops, Thoret gave Elláh all the credit for the beauty of his gardens. His part was to plant and tend; Elláh saw to the growth and wonder.

He had changed clothes to casual when a heavy knocking sounded at the door. He opened it to find five proctors on his porch. Their grey uniforms contrasted with the colors worn by normal people. Each wore a stylized peaked hat with a shiny visor, also of grey, and a red collar designating their position. Each one also had a needle gun in a holster. One of the five had a gold pip on his collar.

"Thoret Speakeach," said the leader with the gold pip, "come with us." Two of the others pushed through the door and forced themselves to either side of him, taking firm hold of his elbows.

Thoret held his ground. "What is this? Why should I go with you?"

The man glanced around at the empty street. "I am Captain Frinat Forsfear of the Heresy Angels, and you are under arrest for heresy. You will come with us."

Thoret knew this name. Forsfear was prominent in a recent campaign against heresy. Thoret reacted with alarm. He pulled against those holding his arms.

"Stop. This isn't right. I've spoken no heresy."

He pulled again. Their fingers dug into his arms. They forced his wrists together behind him. He pushed with his feet to put them off balance. Nothing worked. A third proctor shoved past him and wrapped a tangler cuff around his wrists.

He stopped the useless struggles. His heart pounded, and he felt flushed. "Heresy is a strong charge to place against the leader of a congregation, particularly a fellowship with so many national leaders."

"All the more reason to make the charge, if it is true. Yet the charge has indeed been made. Your guilt or innocence will be determined by fair trial." He waved a hand toward a black autovan at the curb. "Take him away."

The two holding his arms pushed him forward.

Thoret looked around at the street and houses, hoping someone would come out to witness this abduction. No one was there. Forsfear led the proctors—and Thoret—off the porch. The van waited with rear doors opened. They shoved him inside. The back of the van had no seats.

❧ ✳ ❧

Thoret laid on his side on the carpeted floor of the van during the short trip. He squirmed frequently to ease the pressure on his shoulders. He felt outrage, but he also knew he was powerless. He realized something he had never considered before: Rathas had no legal avenue to contest a charge of heresy other than the ensuing trial.

When the Heresy Angels opened the van door, he tried to slide over to sit up on the edge. Instead, the proctors pulled him roughly out of the van. He stumbled onto his feet and almost fell.

He tried to maintain dignity and said, "This really isn't necessary. You're treating me like a common criminal."

Forsfear sneered at him. "No, we're not. We're treating you like a heretic. Come along."

He looked up at the shiny Church administration building. He been here many times, but never as a captive. The six-story building had smooth marble facades, statues of prophets in alcoves, and gold trim shining in the blue-white sun. A gold statue of the archangel Michael blew his trumpet on the highest roof. The proctors hustled him down stairs to a side entrance, leaving behind the sweet scent of borgen flowers in the garden plantings around the entrance.

"Move along, Speakeach," the captain said as he held the door for Thoret and the two proctors holding him.

They entered a basement level with no windows. Neutral pale green walls gave it an austere institutional look. The floor was bare composite. The spartan surroundings contrasted with the well-decorated upstairs rooms Thoret had seen on other visits. Halfway down the hallway, Captain Forsfear unlocked an unusually heavy door on the left and led them in. When the door closed behind him, sound from the hallway cut off.

Behind the door, the next room made Thoret's heart stop in his throat. The area was spacious, filled with heavy equipment. It took only a moment for him to recognize torture equipment filling every space. They crossed the room to a door on the opposite side, but the few short steps were long enough to destroy what little ease was left in his soul. The devices loomed shiny and threatening around the space. He recognized a rack with motorized draw wheels, a pyramidical Judas cradle, a spiked iron maiden, a Spanish donkey to split the body from below, and more. Other devices were more obscure, some of them quite modern with computer controls, motorized actions, and obvious electrodes. A heretic's fork, choke pear, and other fiendish devices hung on the walls. Thoret hardly knew what most of them were for.

The devices around him filled him with horror, even more so because he had no idea Rathas possessed such things. A sick part of him had a morbid curiosity about those he did not recognize, wanting to know more. He was repelled by that reaction inside himself. The room smelled antiseptic, but a darker, foul scent lingered. Making it worse, none of the equipment looked like museum pieces from centuries before. All of it was shiny and new and obviously well-maintained.

Forsfear opened the far door, just as heavy and soundproof as the first, and led the way into a second room. With his mind in shock from the devices in the first room, Thoret tripped on the threshold. The two proctors held him from falling, their fingers digging into his arms.

Thoret wanted to ask about the torture equipment. He wanted to know why it was there, who it had been used on. However, words failed him and his mouth was suddenly dry.

He remembered seeing the public confessions of those arrested before him.

The second room was much smaller and contained nothing but two chairs and a table, a side door, and a large mirror on the wall. The proctors shoved Thoret into the first chair, facing the table and the mirror. They twisted his arms behind the chair back and fastened another cuff to hold his wrists to the chair. Then they stepped away.

"You get comfortable here," said Forsfear with a smirk. "We'll be back in a bit."

"Wait," Thoret managed to say, "How long—"

They ignored him. One of them closed the door they had entered. Then all three swept out through the side door, slamming it shut behind them.

"Hey," he shouted, before realizing it would do no good.

The room was now silent. After the torture chamber, this space had a clean, fresh scent. Thoret swallowed to moisten his mouth, but his saliva didn't work. He couldn't believe he was in this position. After all, he was a respected member of the Church clergy, and he had preached nothing but straightforward Church teaching. In the silence, air whispered in the ducts and his heart pounded. The pulse in his throat joined a painful lump to emphasize his helplessness. His cheeks flushed with embarrassment and fear. He squirmed his rump into a slightly better position.

Some details jumped out at him. The mirror was obviously one-way, and he suspected people behind it watched his every move. He had no desire to give them any satisfaction by pleading; he tried to stay still and expressionless. A video camera mounted in an upper corner of the room probably recorded everything. The walls wore the same pale green as the hallway and torture room. The metal side door featured nothing but a latch handle. He realized, for all his looking, the room had few details. It was likely designed that way.

Feeling as helpless and exposed as an animal in the zoo, Thoret settled in to wait. For a while, he watched his reflection. He noticed his shirt rode crooked on his shoulders, but nothing he tried straightened it. Looking at his reflection didn't help. Seeing his undignified position depressed him; it reminded him of the trouble he was in and made him think of the devices in the first room. To avoid the mirror, he focused on the table in front of him. As featureless as the room itself, the plastic surface showed a few scratches from use. He forced his mind on one scratch, emptying all else. Meditation, one of his spiritual strengths.

Thoret believed in Elláh, and he believed in the saving grace of Jaysus. He closed his eyes and centered his mind on silent prayer. This entire incident was an example of the Fourth Pillar, self-purification. Whatever happened here, he would be refined and purified. He would come out of this event with a new understanding of power in the Church. He alternated prayer with meditation, listening to Elláh for any guidance He might give. His heart was finding peace.

Little things began to be uncomfortable. He squirmed his rump again but couldn't do anything to gain comfort. After an indeterminate time, his left shoulder cramped. He twisted in the chair with eyes still closed, moving the shoulder. He found the cramp only eased for a moment before flaring again. He needed to move his arm, but movement was impossible. The cramp got worse and intruded on his praying and meditating. He hissed in air through his clenched teeth, now moving both shoulders to find some way to stretch the spasmed muscle.

The silence was oppressive. Off in the distance, he heard a door open and close, followed by footsteps receding. The possibilities swelled in the uncertainty. Would they question him first, and if so, about what? Would they drag his helpless body back into the torture room? He squirmed again. No position was comfortable.

How long had he been here? *Has it been one hour? Three?* He could only guess at how much longer it would be before something happened. Again, he was certain they were watching through the mirror, whoever "they" were.

A moan escaped him at the continued spasm in his shoulder. Almost as if in response to his sound, the side door suddenly opened.

Thoret gritted his teeth and kept his eyes shut for a moment, not wanting to be desperate in their eyes. He heard footsteps of at least two people. Then he took a deep, calming breath and looked up.

"You shouldn't be here, Thoret," said Beltaret Leaderlist. His friend was standing across the table with crossed arms, an irritated look on his face.

Thoret felt a sudden wash of relief at the voice. Almost as quick as the relief, however, came a sense of caution that made him question the man's friendship.

Beltaret spoke to the proctor who had entered with him, "Release his hands. There's no need for him to be bound. Then leave us alone."

The proctor did both, closing the door behind him. Thoret's breath shuddered in relief. When he stretched his arms, though, they came alive to worse pain. He felt more spasms trying to cramp while he eased the worst one. Moving his right arm set off a storm of electric nerve reaction. Eventually, he reached a point where he could move both arms, and the hard spasm in his left shoulder had subsided.

Beltaret sat in the chair across the table and waited for Thoret to settle his muscles. "I am most sorry the proctors reacted so strongly, my friend. Are you okay?"

"As good as I can be, after being hustled away from my home like a criminal."

Beltaret gave a single hard shake of his head. "You are a key congregation leader in the Church, Thoret. I'm part of your congregation because I respect your teaching. We've known each other a long time. Why have you now departed from the true path?"

Thoret was startled by the sudden question, because it clarified that Beltaret's friendship was precarious and with conditions. Thoret's answer might make the difference in what happened for the rest of his life. The room behind frightened him. It opened up possibilities he had never dreamed in his worst nightmares. He was also certain there were still proctors behind the mirror, regardless of Beltaret's statement to leave them alone. Thoret needed to walk a careful line between truth and what this national leader wanted to hear.

"It's not a departure from the true path, Beltaret. The true path includes the First Pillar of a deep religious life in surrender to Elláh. That's what I preached for people to do."

"According to dharma, the true path also includes the Fifth Pillar of mission. You said it yourself. The entire country of Rathas has a mission to bring Jaysus and the True Church to the people of Verdant. When you teach people to set aside the rules of the Church, to think and act individually rather than collectively, our mission is weakened. You cannot trade off one Pillar for another."

Had they been in a different circumstance, discussing these issues in casual friendship, Thoret would have pointed out how the rules were taking people away from Elláh, as had happened many times before—those following Buddha, the people of Israel in the time of Jaysus, the people of Islam, the Christians in the end days of Earth. But he could not speak of these in this threatening room with watchers behind the mirror. Thoret was learning extreme caution.

"You may be right, Beltaret. The dharma of mission is also important."

"We must act as one people, my friend. We must be strong. Anything less will have no impact on the other countries. Our love for Jaysus must come through in our consistency."

Thoret could not resist the burning question inside him. "And is it for consistency you have the devices in that room behind me?"

Beltaret answered with sadness, "You should never have seen that, Thoret."

But I did, and it was likely on purpose, Thoret thought. Aloud, he said, "And if I didn't know about that room, would its use be acceptable?"

"Its use is sometimes necessary for those who are intransigent. I pray it might never be used for someone like you."

The words hung in the air as a not-so-veiled threat. Thoret received the message loud and clear. Glancing at the mirror, he stopped the next question before it flowed. *How soon?*

Thoret was on the edge of a knife. The slightest movement in the wrong direction would cut—either slicing him from humanity into the torture room, or carving the heart out of his soul's personal mission. He knew Elláh wanted His people to follow only Him because rules made by humans often took people away from Elláh. He considered being bold enough to confront further the methods used by Beltaret and the proctors. However, doing so might cause him to disappear and no one would ever know.

Whatever he did must align with his faith. Pleading for his life would mean giving in to fear rather than faith. Engaging Beltaret intellectually, teaching him of his error as congregational teacher to congregant, would not work. Those were not the roles they had today in this room.

Here and now, Thoret had no power at all.

The only path consistent with his faith was to acknowledge in honesty the worldly power in this place, and to trust Elláh to see him safely through this. He chose to hang his head in contrition or what he hoped appeared so. The image of the evil devices in the room behind were at the forefront of his mind, but the immediate problem was to get out of this room in one piece. If

Thoret were not free, he could do nothing else. He took a deep breath and let himself slump in physical surrender.

Then he volunteered, "This entire incident is unnecessary, Beltaret. You're right. I've spoken wrongly. How can I correct my error?" The words tasted foul in his mouth like regurgitated bile.

Beltaret didn't answer at first. Thoret held his posture of abject surrender, waiting. After a long minute, he saw from the corner of his eye Beltaret's hand rise in a signal to those behind the mirror.

❧ ✳ ☙

A proctor escorted Thoret back to his home. The street was as quiet in the gloaming as it had been earlier in the bright sun, almost as if the world didn't care what had happened.

He'd spent the car ride pondering what to do next. People needed to change their relationship with Elláh, or Verdant would follow the same path as Earth. The urge within him was strong; he needed to act, to tell people the truth, to help them grow.

But on the other hand, the threat he saw this afternoon was real. If he continued openly, the next arrest would likely be the last. He would find himself again in that torture chamber. He might become one of those "reformed" heretics with haunted eyes, mouthing an apology to a Church that had broken him. Or he might never reappear. Either prospect filled him with fear.

He called Nama, and she arrived in less time than he expected. She took one look at his ashen face and reached out to lay a strengthening hand on his shoulder.

"What happened, Thoret? You look like a ghost."

He knew what to say next, and almost couldn't get the words out. He found himself waylaid by outrage and shame. "I was arrested this afternoon."

She gasped. "What? Arrested for what?"

He couldn't meet her eyes. "Heresy."

"No. That's not possible. Your teaching was straight out of Church doctrine."

"Yes, I know. And you know. But tell it to the Heresy Angels. I spent the afternoon in an interrogation room with them." He looked into her eyes. "They are more powerful than we knew.

They can treat as heresy anything they wish, including speaking against the rules."

Another thought struck him. "We think, here in Rathas, we have freedom. We think our nation protects us from the chaos in Tileus and the strict control in Prime. The leaders here hide their power well."

"Surely there is something we can do—"

"No," he interrupted, "our country has no court of appeals to bypass those who have power. That's what the rules enforce."

He could not do this alone. But second thoughts began to parade in his head. Should he involve her further? Was it fair to risk her, too? He needed to start with somebody.

He looked in her eyes, and he saw more than shock. He also saw outrage, determination, the core feelings she would need to take part.

He locked his eyes on hers and continued, "We're going to have to change our methods, Nama. Today, this evening...you and I are the beginnings of an underground movement to sap the strength of this misguided leadership. The Church is more than rules and structure crushing the spirit of its members. We need the Church to live in the collective spirit of its members."

He nodded at his own words. "First, we need to plan how to find and involve others. It will be dangerous."

"We'll do it together." Her voice was firm but shaky, matching the frightened—and determined—sense inside Thoret's own heart.

Duty to Society

Living in an oppressive situation is not as difficult as people think, because those in the situation get used to it. They don't know anything different, and they think what they have is normal. When slapped in the face with the reality, it's still often tough to accept. But what if the reality is that your work might destroy the world? How much can you avoid? And what might you be willing to do to change?

Jake felt his own pulse beating with hers as he pressed his fingers into Zofia's neck. The wound in his neck still oozed blood; the traumatized flesh throbbed with his pulse. His other hand held a sharp knife.

He stopped to take a shaky breath. Around them, the squalid litter of the Warrens stank in this blind alley.

"Don't stop, Jake. You've got to do this." Her voice quivered. "It's the only way to be free."

"I know, I know," he breathed. "But I've never done anything like this before."

"Neither had I."

He lifted the knife once again and pushed harder on her neck.

Had it really been only three weeks since he'd met her?

Three weeks earlier, Jake was in the antimatter lab. His Solity Assignment was to design and build an antimatter bomb, leading a team of three other engineers. He could think of much more useful things to do with his physics and engineering knowledge, but this was what Solity needed. Or so he was told. Jake was proud to be part of Solity; it gave him purpose.

Berndt Denmark was reviewing the work in Jake's cubicle, slightly larger than the others in the space. Large equipment and workbenches littered the other end of the room.

"So, Jacoby my boy, how's the progress?" The man had a perennially dangerous edge to his smile. "We've been bringing you along for two years now."

Denmark was the Director of General Defense. Jake felt honored one of the Verdant Prime country leaders mentored him and his work, but honor carried a harsh pressure. Denmark wasn't an easy man to satisfy; he wanted others to be as driven as he was.

"Slow and cautious, Director. We can contain the antimatter," Jake waved at the humming containment chamber, "but physics demands a large piece of equipment to hold it. It's still too big for a bomb."

Being with Denmark was a roller coaster ride, exhilarating one moment and threatening the next. The Director was much shorter than Jake, swarthy in complexion, with short-cropped dark hair and penetrating black eyes noticing everything. His persuasive presence called for Jake's best.

"So, what are you doing to make it smaller?"

Jake felt the needle of stress. One of Jake's assistants stepped over to tap the lab table and bring up a holo of test data, then returned to his work. Jake and his assistants wore pale green coveralls, the standard attire for Defense workers. Denmark was in Administration purple.

Jake used his comms implant to connect to the holo display, then manipulated his hand in the haptic sensor field to control the display. "Yesterday's data shows us the laser power needed." He pointed at a graph in the data. "It varies with temperature, so we're starting to pursue superconductors under extremely cold conditions. That might reduce the size."

Denmark walked over to the chamber and inspected it through the viewing port. The tiny, actinic dot in the center always hurt Jake's eyes.

"Time is short, Jake. Very short. I've given you good advancement, because I've trusted in you. We've rewarded you with a good living, a nice apartment and leadership, right?"

Jake nodded.

"Well, I have other irons in the fire. War is coming, and we need this bomb. I need you to work faster."

Without waiting for a response, Denmark swept out, his expensive scent lingering.

Jake let out a held breath and rubbed the mole on his chin. Conflict between countries on the planet Verdant was common, but he'd heard nothing about war, so he was surprised at the Director's words.

"Work faster," Jake muttered aloud when he turned back to his work. "Faster doesn't change physics."

∾ ✳ ∿

Jake worked late that evening to find designs for superconductor magnets. An hour later, he noticed his assistants were gone. *Time to let it go for now.* Jake decided to go to the local easygo for dinner; bar food was easy.

The easygo had a bar stretching down the right-hand wall with glass shelves and bottles surrounding a mirror. A few booths nestled against the opposite wall; the rest of the room had small tables and chairs. A large holo display in one corner played music holos, the beat filling the room with empty excitement. He didn't see any of his usual friends at the easygo, but an intriguing woman sat at the bar. She was tall and well-proportioned with long black hair. Her Maintenance yellow coverall fit tighter than usual, so he could appreciate the curves under it. Solity prohibited fraternization without DNA approval, but casual conversation was acceptable. She held what looked like a fizzy gin.

"Do you mind if I join you? The place is pretty empty tonight."

She looked up with dark eyes and a friendly smile. "Not at all. I was hoping for company." Her voice was feminine and a bit husky.

"There's always room for a new friend. I'm Jake." Jake knew he was good-looking, with even features, pale blue eyes and dark hair. He kept himself healthy by gym work and racquetball in the zero-G courts.

"Zofia," she said as she turned on the stool to face him. "I think I've seen you in here before." She flipped her hair out of her eyes with an intriguing shake of her head.

"It's possible. I come in here when I'm wanting to get away from things."

"And what are you getting away from tonight?"

He shrugged with a wry smile. "Life. Solity. Problems."

She laughed. "Sounds like normal in Verdant Prime."

"And what are you doing here?"

"Just relaxing after a hard day fixin' imp programming." She shrugged. "It's my Assignment."

"Interesting. I work in technology, too, but mostly I can't talk about it." Jake took a sip of his drink and smiled. Zofia looked relaxed and comfortable.

They ended up talking for over an hour. He learned Zofia Dobrunik lived a simpler life than his. As a technician, her duties changed little day to day. She carried an imp test set; she went where she was told and used the set to fix software problems in peoples' imps. She rarely had to think about her work.

"I spend my time thinking about life," she told him. "Have you ever wondered whether Solity really works best for us?"

Jake was taken aback by the question. "No, I haven't. Solity seems to work well. The other countries are the ones with problems."

"Think about it. We're told what work to do. We're told where to live. We don't have any choice." She laughed lightly. "We even have to get approval to date and to marry. Whatever happened to love?"

She continued to lead the conversation into similar paths. Jake found her philosophy fascinating and dangerous. Occasionally, when she said something particularly wild, he looked around to see if anyone was watching. He had a respect for the way Solity worked. She talked about the ways in which it might be better. She talked of people choosing their own work. Jake had never considered such things before. Solity frowned on people questioning its ways. It could lead to arrest for sedition.

Yet, when he walked home down the city street to his third-floor apartment, she kept playing in his mind. Strange ideas or not, he wanted to know more about her.

❧ ❈ ☙

The next day, Jake was still bothered by Denmark's injunction to work faster. He looked up at the containment chamber. Its threatening hum reminded him of the incredible forces held back by his engineering. If that tiny bit of antimatter escaped, its reaction with normal matter would destroy the lab, the building, and part of the city.

He turned back to his designs for superconducting magnets. He assigned a task to find suitable parts to one of his assistants and gave another the challenge to calculate field strengths.

Late in the day, the Director came in again. He was brisk and direct.

"Can we make it smaller yet?"

Jake was surprised at Denmark's attitude. He was used to encouragement and help from the man.

"We're working on it, sir. I think I have a design for a new magnet to reduce the size."

"You think?"

"It's only been a day, sir."

Denmark shook his head, a frown on his face. "We don't have many days left, my boy. When can you give me assurance?"

Jake winced. "I have the theory, but we can't know whether it works until we build a prototype. We'll have to get parts, build the new system, and then test it."

"I'm disappointed." The Director was still frowning. "Let me know of any obstacles, and I'll do what I can. But it's up to you to make it happen."

❧ ❈ ☙

He saw Zofia again in the evening. Meeting at the easygo, they both wanted a better meal, so they decided to go down the street to the Tangled Tackle. After the tension of the day, he felt himself relaxing and enjoying the evening. They had no trouble getting a table.

"Have you thought any further about how to make Solity better?" she asked while they waited for food.

"Well, you've got me thinking. I'd always assumed what we had was the best. But having mentioned it, I see things that could improve."

"Like what?"

He tilted his chin in thought. "Well, I notice my assistants don't seem to be as dedicated to work as I am. They put in their hours, but they don't do their best."

She nodded.

"And I see that all over, like the bar food at the easygo. It's just sustenance."

"Yeah," she said. "When I was in school, I had to create a distribution app for Capital. Turned out to be an impossible problem, just to figure out how much of a product should be sent to each commune."

He chuckled. "That would explain why we have shortages."

"That...and the lack of work ethic. When Capital sets a production goal, there's no guarantee Labor will meet it."

Over dinner, he became more fascinated with her thoughts about Solity. She told him facts he'd never known, in ways that enlightened him about the system under which he'd always lived.

Even more, though, he found himself fascinated by Zofia herself. She was vibrant and intelligent as well as gorgeous, a stirring combination.

He whistled happily walking home.

❧ ✳ ☙

Two days later, Jake and his team were assembling a new version of magnets. The Director had expedited parts procurement and given them first priority in manufacturing. He'd been in the lab to check on progress each day, with increasing irritation at the lack of assurance.

In mid-morning, Jake's imp buzzed. A nasal-sounding official voice spoke in his ear.

"Jacoby Palatin, report to the Assignment Office."

He sighed. Another interruption. The administrators kept order, but he sometimes wished they would ask instead of command. He left instructions to his team and hurried out. It didn't do to delay responding.

Slidewalks took him through the austere corridors of the huge five-story General Defense building. The Assignment Office was two floors down at the other end, a bare room with a few hard chairs and a clerk behind a battered desk. A sour smell infused the lobby. He looked around but could not identify the source.

The desk clerk pointed at a numbered door, so Jake went in. Behind the door was a tiny interview booth with another door at the opposite end. A built-in glass wall divided the room in half, clinically separating the administrator from the client. The lower part of the glass wall merged with a two-sided desk with a small opening. The plastic chair on his side faced a larger, more comfortable chair on the other side. Jake thought the booth looked like an aquarium, but he wasn't sure whether he was inside or outside the glass.

He sat in the hard plastic chair, his fears rising. Why was he called? A summons was rarely good.

After a few long minutes, the opposite door opened. The older woman who entered was so haggard Jake winced. Like the clerk, she wore the light blue coveralls required for Labor jobs, but it made her skin look sallow and sick. She had pinched eyes and pointed ears, with her mouth set in a permanent scowl. Her hair was in uneven, bedraggled curls.

"Jacoby Palatin." Her voice was flat and nasal.

"Jake," he responded with what he hoped was a friendly smile.

She stared at him for a long moment of petty power, then repeated. "Jacoby Palatin. You are an engineering leader for General Defense."

His irritation morphed into dark humor. "Yes, that's me." He pointed to his name on the coveralls.

She ignored his gesture. "Jacoby Palatin, Solity has determined your skill is providing less value than in the past.

Balancing the value with the benefit is essential to Solity. 'From each according to his ability...'"

Jake joined her saying the ages-old mantra in the approved fashion. "'...to each according to his need.'" This interview was going bad places, and he didn't like it.

"Therefore, Solity has decided your reduced value should be met with appropriate compensation. Your requisition allowance is now reduced by twelve point two percent for the common good, and you are being reassigned to a smaller apartment. You have five days to move your things. Here are your new parameters." She slid a holochip across the desk, stamped with "Solity Approved." While she touched the chip, the holo of his information momentarily appeared in the air above it.

Jake stiffened. His ears were ringing. Do the same work, yet receive less compensation? He had heard of this happening to others, but he thought Denmark had earmarked him for advancement instead of demotion. This had to be the director's doing, in punishment for not creating results faster. He ground his teeth, angry deep down inside, as he saw his hopes dashed. He knew this petty martinet couldn't change the situation, but he spoke anyway.

"Is there any avenue for appeal?"

She looked directly at him, her eyes crinkling in disgust. "Of course not. This is the decision of Solity. Jacoby Palatin, it is your responsibility to support it."

Worse still, Jake knew he had to return to his lab and continue his work for the afternoon. The sour smell in the lobby seemed stronger as he left.

❧ ✳ ☙

In the evening, still upset, he couldn't face packing up his apartment. He was angry at Denmark but also at himself for his inability to make progress. He was intelligent and capable; how did he get to this point of a demotion?

Then Zofia showed up, knocking on his door.

"Didn't see you at the easygo tonight. Thought I'd invite you for dinner."

Still with his hand on the open door, his shoulders slumped. "Can't. I have to move my stuff to another apartment. My allocation got changed today."

She quickly offered to help him move. After an hour of work—Jake discovered he had very little stuff that was his alone—Jake slumped onto the couch and looked around. The new walls weren't really closing in. He felt comforted with her presence. She flopped down beside him. His eyes met hers and he sighed.

"Okay. That's that," he said.

She looked around at the room. "This place is a lot smaller than you had. What'd you do to deserve this?"

He waved a hand helplessly. "Nothing. But they want...something. Results. My work is limited by science, but my director keeps pushing. He says it's important to the war effort."

"War effort? I didn't know we were at war."

"Oh, not yet. But he thinks a war with Tileus is imminent, and we have to take them down early." Jake shrugged. "He says they undermine our perfect society. As for me...I don't know."

She slid closer to him on the couch and put a hand on his knee. "Our society's not perfect, I know that. But I don't think a war is the answer to anything."

He felt his blood surge at the touch. She pushed the Solity boundaries in many ways. This one both excited and scared him. Excited at the possibilities, afraid of what Solity might do. He began to wonder how much his imp tracked.

"I don't, either."

"And yet you're working in a war effort?"

"It's my Assignment." Jake felt defensive. "I can't say I like it." He surprised himself by saying so; he realized it was true.

Jake enjoyed talking with Zofia. He enjoyed the way it felt when she pressed against him, and he wanted more. Mindful of the Solity rules against unauthorized fraternization, though, he kept his desires to himself even while she seemed to become bolder about touching him.

Two days later, Director Denmark came again to the antimatter lab. Jake's mind wasn't on his work. He was fiddling with minor changes to the magnet configuration without any real purpose.

The door burst open and Denmark strode in. "Okay, Palatin. Show me your progress."

Jake felt a flash of angry resentment; his demotion still burned. He jumped to his feet, feeling guilty for fiddling instead of working.

He suddenly noticed Denmark's purple coverall: better tailored than others, it had a smooth material and looked much more comfortable. He'd never noticed this before. If people were supposed to be equal, why did Denmark get better clothes? Zofia's conversations had changed his perceptions.

Flustered by his realization, he hoped Denmark hadn't noticed his pause. "Yes, Director. We're still assembling the superconducting magnets. But this morning, we got some new data from another test. It's good news. It shows we can increase the containment field ten percent by lowering the temperature of the fixed magnets—"

"Ten percent isn't enough, Palatin. You know that, don't you?"

"Yes, Director, I do. It's only an incremental improvement, but it shows—"

"We need you to be working harder, Palatin. We need breakthroughs, not 'incremental improvements.' Right?"

"Yes, Director."

"If we don't have your antimatter bomb working in time, then Verdant Prime will expend a lot of lives unnecessarily in correcting Tileus. Those *lives* would be your fault, the real effect of your...delays."

"Yes, Director." Jake felt his face burning.

"I would think, after your correction this week, you'd be spending every possible moment in the lab. Your new apartment can't be very comfortable, is it? What are your working hours this week?"

Jake knew Denmark likely tracked every minute. He blushed deeper. "We've been...uh...making progress."

"Progress." Berndt paused and glared at him while Jake became more nervous in the lie. "Right." Another long pause left Jake's hands shaking. "We are watching your progress closely, Palatin. Or lack of it. Overtime is expected, much overtime. Motivate your team. This work is critical to the war effort; you must not be doing anything else."

Jake could only nod as his throat closed up.

The director strode to the door, then paused again with his hand on the knob. He turned back and nailed Jake with his burning gaze. "Wasting time with a useless Maintenance wench is not helpful." He pulled the door open and left.

Jake sucked in a fiery breath that seared his soul. *They know.* They must be watching him away from work. But the more he thought about it, the more his fear turned to anger, to determination to do something new and different.

∾✱∿

"There's something we can do." Zofia said quietly. She was sitting close to Jake on the bench seat in a café booth.

They were choosing their lunch locations more carefully to avoid observation by the ever-present surveillance cams. This place was out of the normal ways in a back alley. The lighting was weak and the walls dark. Even so, nothing could stop their imps from reporting their location. Just being together was dangerous.

"About what?"

"About your work problem. About Solity."

Jake was surprised. All of their talk had been philosophical until now. He looked into Zofia's dark eyes and saw danger. But he liked the feel of her close to him.

"What can we do?" he asked.

She looked around to make sure they were private, then lowered her voice. "There is the Lazarite resistance movement. You've probably seen their posters."

Jake was shocked. "Lazarites? Do you mean...revolution against Solity?"

She shrugged helplessly. "What else can we do? You and I can't even date, the way things are. And you know how many things are wrong."

"But what about work? What about food? We can't hide from our imps, and sooner or later we'll be caught."

She nodded. "That's a problem I've been thinking about for a long time. There is a solution."

❦

Jake returned to his apartment after long hours in the lab. His work had taken his mind away from Zofia's suggestion. The closer he got to a solution for the size problem, the more it bothered him. He wanted to advance, but... *What am I doing? Building a bomb that's going to kill a lot of people.* Over the last few days, he'd realized he didn't want it to succeed. A thought occurred to him.

If I join the resistance, Prime won't have the antimatter bomb.

A hard knock at the door made him jump. When he opened the door, two Solity Guards were in the hall. Both wore black with gold identification and badges; their faces were hidden behind shielded helmets. The needle guns in their holsters loomed large in Jake's mind.

"Jacoby Palatin, we've had a disturbing report about your associations. Where were you at lunch today?"

Jake felt his blood pounding in his face while he thought fast. He had never before had any interaction with the Guard. He knew Solity could track his position at all times through his imp, so long as he was in range of receptors. He suspected they could also monitor his conversations. So, why would they be asking where he had been? Lies to the authorities were punished severely—but in this case, honesty would mean admitting to sedition. He decided a half-truth was best.

"Uh...I went with someone to a café in the Monument district."

"You were with Zofia Dobrunik, not just 'someone.' Correct?"

"Yes, that's true. We were just eating lunch."

"You and Dobrunik have been together frequently recently. Do you have authorization to fraternize?"

"No, sir. We're just friends." He felt slimy sweat popping out on his forehead.

"Has Dobrunik asked you about your General Defense work?"

"No, sir." At least this answer was true, but Jake's heart continued to race. He had heard Solity Guard had monitors for biometric functions, and he was afraid they would know he was telling half-truths.

"Are you aware Dobrunik is under suspicion?"

Under suspicion for what? "I had no idea. We were just talking."

The two Guards stood perfectly still for a long time, staring at him. For all he knew, they might have been conferring through imps with each other and with others in authority. He remained in place, frozen in fear.

"Jacoby Palatin, be careful. She is a dangerous person. Do not fall into the trap of becoming a risk to Solity. This is your one and only warning." They abruptly turned away down the hall.

Jake closed his door and slumped into a fit of shaking. *That was close ... too close. What can I do now?*

He opened a brew and sat on the couch thinking. Solity no longer felt like a protective umbrella. It felt more like a sharp lance aimed at his heart.

He was supposed to meet Zofia for breakfast. As much as he wanted to see her again, to feel her body next to his, the Guard had frightened him. She had knowledge of the imps through her work. She knew of areas in the city where the signal strength was too weak, and she'd suggested one of those areas—the Warrens—for breakfast.

How could he meet with her? She was under suspicion, and Solity was watching. He was afraid to be a traitor, but he knew Solity needed to change. The thoughts raced in his mind in tight little circles like whirlpools in a stream, going nowhere. He drew similar circles on the side table with his finger in the condensation from his drink, trying to make sense of his conflicting desires. Being with her made him feel excited and whole—but she was dangerous. She wanted him to change Prime, and yet this was his home, his work, his life.

Go with her? Or cut her off and go back to his life doing what he now hated? Was there another option, a third way? Some way which would be safe and allow him to see Zofia? He could see none.

His sleep was troubled. He kept waking from terrible dreams of fanged monsters, and he'd lie awake with his decisions as tousled as his sweat-soaked bedding.

The light of morning brought clarity. Meeting Zofia was dangerous, but he was ready to change his life. He filled a small backpack with a few food bars and water bottles. He included his pocket knife in a small act of defiance against Solity. He still hadn't decided what to do, but he would meet with Zofia and see what happened.

❧ ✳ ❧

"Solity Guard threatened me last night," Jake said.

The two were sitting side-by-side in an empty lot strewn with trash and debris. The Warrens were where Solity disposed of its dregs, both things and people. They had left breakfast and wandered for a while. He saw no surveillance cameras in this area, and his imp had no connection with the InfoNet. They found a battered old green couch complete with torn upholstery, sprung supports, and mildewed cushions. The couch was only slightly better than sitting on the ground.

She looked up quickly at his eyes and nodded. "They do that."

"I didn't like the feeling. And…I realized I have that feeling in small ways all the time. Solity always makes me feel threatened."

She shrugged. "Yes."

"I want to live without fear."

Her laugh was brittle. "I'm not sure that's ever possible. There's always fear of something."

"But Solity feeds on fear. I think I want to change. But how? What can we do? Can we escape to another country? Don't our imps tell them where we are and what we're doing?"

"Only if we're in range of a receptor. In most of the city, they always know. Where we are, what we do, what we say. Everything. The imp is our communications and gives us access to the InfoNet, but Solity also uses the imps." She looked sideways at him, as if there were an awkward secret withheld.

"So, what do we do then?"

She paused and looked at the ground, then bared the secret. "There's only one thing we can do. We need to get rid of our imps."

Tampering with an imp was a major criminal offense with severe punishment.

"Well, you're the imp tech. How do we get rid of them?"

She shrugged. "We can't disable them with anything we have. We have to cut them out. I'll cut out yours, and you'll cut out mine."

Jake sat up straight in surprise. "I thought removing the imp was life-threatening."

"No. That's an intimidating fiction from Solity. They're easy enough to cut out. It hurts, but it doesn't even bleed much."

It seemed to Jake as though every event led to something harder. Nonetheless, he kept pushing forward because this path was worth doing. Changing Solity was more important and more positive than building an antimatter bomb. He was gaining clarity. He felt at peace sitting with Zofia—even in this trash lot. In his well-equipped lab, he felt defeated whichever way he went. Going back to his old life, he would always be under suspicion.

Zofia nervously pulled a folding knife out of her sidepack. "Solity doesn't like us to carry knives; they consider them weapons. I've always thought of it instead as a useful tool. I keep it as sharp as I can, because a dull tool is worse than no tool." She was babbling.

When he looked at the knife in her hand, he thought of his own knife—just as suspect, just as useful. Both of them had chosen to bring one. Coincidence?

Their thoughts were the same. Perhaps they were meant to be together.

He made his decision.

Jake looked into her eyes, and he leaned over to kiss her lips. She sucked in a surprised breath and leaned into him. He had never kissed anyone before. He discovered a kiss was nicer than he had ever imagined.

❧ ✳ ❦

The Warren streets were narrow and dirty, twisting around each building as if the structures had been haphazardly dropped from orbit. They found a dead-end alley offering privacy. The narrow spaces blocked the sunlight, letting shadows grow to fill the space.

"This is as good a place as any. We're not going to find a doctor's office for our surgery." She gave him a deprecatory smile.

Her knife was sharper than his, but Jake was still nervous. "Do you know how to do this? Have you ever done it before?"

"No. I modify the software with the device in place. But I know where it is, and I know how it's connected."

He took a deep breath and agreed. "Okay. Let's get it over with. Let's start new lives. Let's change Solity."

She did his first, putting the point of the knife into the muscle at the right side of his neck.

"The imp's buried in the lower trapezius muscle. You can feel it with your fingers if you pinch. We need to open one vertical slit to expose it..."

While she spoke, he felt the knife slice into his neck. He gritted his teeth and clenched his fists against the sharp pain.

"...then cut across just below and just above it to sever its connections."

When she cut across the top, his mind exploded with a flash of visual brilliance, a loud bang, an explosion of acrid scent, and a tingling along every nerve in his body. His mouth watered acid. The reaction lasted only a split second but left him shaking and breathless.

"Wow." He exhaled the word; it was all he could say.

"Yeah. I'm told cutting the sensor paths is pretty intense." Her eyes were watching his with deep concern while he shook it off.

"That might be understating it."

She had a handkerchief in her hand and pressed on the cut to stop the minor bleeding. She held up a lozenge the length of his thumbnail. Shiny silver with his blood smeared on it, the imp looked like a large vitamin pill. Square-edged traces made designs on the surface, and one end had a bundle of cut fibers.

"This is it. You are now disconnected from the net."

He inspected the imp and touched it with his fingertip. "That's amazing."

Jake probed in his mind for the presence of the imp and found a disconcerting emptiness there. He couldn't contact the InfoNet. He couldn't think a message to Zofia, even though she was right beside him.

Yet he was free.

Zofia brought him back to reality. "The one thing to avoid is the carotid artery. It's right here." She put her finger further forward, under his jaw. "If you hit the carotid, I bleed to death. So, make sure you make a vertical cut on top of the imp."

He put his fingers on top of the handkerchief, pressing against his wound. The pressure eased the pain and stopped the ooze of blood.

"Okay. My turn," she said.

Jake's stomach lurched. The most surgery he had ever performed was removing a splinter. He didn't know whether he could do this.

And yet... "Okay."

He dabbed again at his own neck, removing some new drops of blood. Then she handed him the knife. He wiped it on the handkerchief as well as he could.

When she bared her neck to him, he thought about how precious she was becoming to him. What if he slipped? The image made him shudder.

With his left hand, he probed at the junction of her neck and shoulder. Her skin was smooth and soft to his touch. He was aware of her soft, flowery scent. His own pulse pounded in his wound, and with his finger he could feel her pulse in time with his. His fingers still buzzed with the sensory shock of his lost imp, so he shook his hand to clear the feeling.

He bracketed the hard lump of imp with his fingers, leaving a vertical space in which to cut. He took a shaky breath.

"Don't stop, Jake. You've got to do this." Her voice quivered. "It's the only way to be free."

"I know, I know," he breathed. "But I've never done anything like this before."

"Neither had I."

He didn't stop to think; doing so might have stopped him forever. The sharp knife went smoothly into her skin and muscle, and blood oozed out. He had to cut a second time to get deep enough to feel the imp. He cut below it with no problem, but when he cut above it, she jumped under his hand.

"Aaaah!" She voiced sudden agony, then froze in place.

She had only moved a centimeter, but it made the cut ragged and started a greater flow of blood.

"Hold still," he said. "I have to finish this."

He pressed the handkerchief against the flow. It seemed manageable, so he took it off again and used the tip of the knife to cut behind the imp and pry it out into his palm. He pressed the handkerchief to the cut again. He looked at the piece of cloth and thought, *Our blood is mingled.*

"Done. I've got it out. Are you okay?"

"Yeah, I think so...You're right. 'Intense' is understating it."

Bolder than he ever knew, he leaned in and kissed her again. She melted toward him, but he knew they couldn't indulge yet. They stayed in the alley for a few more minutes, cleaning up and letting their jangled nerves settle.

He wrapped his arms around her and looked down into her eyes. "Now, we need to find the Lazarites."

She nodded, and the two of them walked out of the alley into a new life.

The Consequences of Education

International conflict is never easy, but most of the time it's "out there," somewhere distant from individual lives. Some people are deeply involved in it: diplomats, war-fighters, intelligence agents, but the vast majority simply see it on the news. Until it comes home.

Marta Bloom and her younger brother Findie were doing some needed repairs on her boat, the *Pelagic Bloom*. They mended ropes and cranes and the repellor beam engine; the electronic technology they used was running fine.

The weak northern sun warmed the wood around them. She worked hard, confident in her abilities. She was the only woman captain in her tribe, and she'd earned that place after Father lost his foot to a huge tsifta fish. Her brother had been too young to take over, and Father had surprised the entire tribe by assigning her the captaincy. Since then, a grudging respect for her achievements had spread amongst the other fisherfolk, boosting her confidence and vindicating Father's unusual choice. She loved the scent of the ocean and the feel of the salty breeze in her face.

Findie broke into her reverie.

"Why do we always fish, Marta?" Findie's question felt like sudden rain from a clear sky, a strange query in a fishing family.

At fifteen now, Findie was in his last year of primary school. After the school year, he would join her on the boat and start to learn the trade. He and Marta shared intense, dark eyes as a family trait.

Marta narrowed her eyes in thought. "Because that's how we support ourselves, Findie. Or are you asking something else?"

"No, I'm not talking about just us Blooms. I'm talking about Winter, our whole country. There are lots of things we could be doing, but all we do is fish. And, I guess, things that support fishing."

Marta took the question seriously, as she always did when talking with Findie.

"We fish because it's productive. Look out there." She pointed beyond the harbor. "The sea is all around us. We can feed ourselves, sell product to other countries like Tileus and Rathas, and buy what else we need from them." She shrugged. "It works."

She wondered where that question came from. Fishing was their way; why would Findie suddenly question it? But Findie jumped to another topic.

"Marta, can you show me how to reeve these pulleys?"

Findie had a line in one hand and two blocks at his feet as he sat cross-legged on the aft deck. He was surrounded by equipment they had pulled out of the hold. The musty scent of below-decks storage filled the air.

Marta smiled. "That's important. You can magnify your own force by three times with those. All the tech on this boat automates our job, but lines still go through pulleys."

She took the line while Findie picked up the two blocks. Marta threaded the bitter end through one of the dual wheels, then the single pulley, then the other dual wheel.

"Now tie the end to one ring on the single block."

"Okay."

She watched as Findie tied an anchor hitch. "Good knot. You remember. Hang the rig onto that hook and coil the remaining line." She returned to sanding the bench. The salt scent of the ocean blew in on a slight breeze, mixed with the lip-curling smell of rotting seaweed and fish offal from the shore. Her mind went back to Findie's strange question, just as he continued the topic.

"But Marta, if everyone does the same business, then we never develop anything new. We don't have…diversity." He seemed tentative when he said the last word, as if he weren't really sure what it meant.

"Hmph. Diversity is over-rated. It leads to conflict."

"That's not what Mers. Sarah says. She says diversity is the basis of civilization." He paused in thought. "Aren't we civilized, Marta?"

Marta stopped sanding. "Of course, we're civilized. 'Civilized' means we work together; we cooperate so all can have good things. But our people moved to Winter to get away from the conflicts other countries have because of their diversity."

With the sanding block in her hand, she thought a moment longer about this new teacher and an icy hand gripped her heart. "What else does Mers. Sarah say?"

"She says we should choose what we want to do in life, and decisions should be made by all of us instead of just by the Elders."

Feeling even colder, Marta put down the sanding block and turned to face Findie.

"You realize that's not the way we do things in Winter?"

"Well...yes. But why not? It'd be nice to do what I want instead of having to fish."

"Is there something else you'd like to do, Findie?"

He shrugged. "No, not really. I don't want to end up like Father—fishing is good work... But she says we should have the choice."

Marta considered the teacher. She was from another country, another culture. The Indie Tribe had accepted an attractive offer to get a teacher under a Tileus program partially funding her. But Tileus was very different than Winter. Tileus had an arrogant pride about their total democracy. They used their implants through the InfoNet to vote on everything, with several votes every day. Laws changed daily. To Marta, it sounded like pure chaos, unlike the steadiness of their own tribal Elders.

"Findie, is Mers. Sarah still teaching you algebra? Or just these strange thoughts?"

He crossed his arms and looked defiant. "Yes, of course. We're still doing algebra. We just solved a problem today about how many people needed to vote to change a law."

Marta was stunned at the implications. In Winter, people only voted when the Elders needed to hear the voice of the community. The teacher infused her foreign values even into math problems. She got to her feet.

"I think we need to talk with Father about this. If Mers. Sarah is teaching strange ways, then we need to do something."

"Do we have to?"

"Yes, we do."

As she debarked, Marta touched the spirit icon on the rail and murmured a quiet blessing.

Findie still sat on the deck, his lip pushed out.

"Yes, Findie. Father needs to know what she's teaching."

"Okay, I guess." As he also touched the spirit icon in passing, he asked, "But what's wrong with voting?"

She and Findie started walking up toward the house.

"Nothing's wrong with voting. We vote in Winter. But the way Tileus votes is crazy."

Marta used her implant to tell Father they were coming in with a problem.

❞ ❄ ❟

As they walked up the steep path, Marta took a breath and looked at the mountains around their harbor. She smiled again, seeing the beauty of their land. The mountains reached a thousand meters in height, and they were covered with a summer mélange of russet, blue and dark green foliage. Some rock outcroppings thrust the trees aside, shouldering their way into the sun. As they got away from the harbor, the rich scent of forest loam filled the air.

Tengali Trude came down the path toward them. He was a neighbor, with his own boat, a seine fisher using nets to rake in feedfish. Seine fishing was hard work, but not as dangerous as the tsifta Marta caught.

"Have you heard?" he barked as he came close. "Tileus is trying to subvert us, and the Elders won't do anything."

Marta and Findie stopped to let him talk. Tengali was always on some issue, claiming conspiracies. Among the peaceful Indie Tribe, he was strange.

"What's going on, Tengali?"

"I'm organizing a meeting. That new teacher brought a horde of ideas we don't want in our kids. She's threatening our way of life! The Elders say to let it be, but screw that, we're taking matters into our own hands." He glanced down at Findie, dismissing him.

"I've heard some things I don't like, too." Marta was calm. "We're just going to talk with Father about them."

"I guess you could join us, too, if you want. Bring a weapon." Tengali's tone of voice dismissed Marta, too, as if she might be incapable of handling a harpoon. He was one of those who had never accepted her position. He still argued with her father for advancing Marta.

"A weapon? Do you think violence is needed?"

"You bet. We need to kick her out forcefully. Send a message."

"Well. We'll talk it over with Father."

"You'd better. I hope he does the right thing this time." Trude brushed past her and continued down the hill.

Marta shook her head as he left. Scary conflicts like this seemed to be increasing all over the planet.

Findie said as Trude walked away. "He's not very stable, is he?"

"Good observation. No, he's not. I can never tell what he's going to do. Let's go home."

The incident clouded the sunny day.

After telling Father what was going on, and on his advice, Marta visited Elder Cartook Greyling, a well-respected man who had been elected to Elder five years ago.

The Elder told them about hiring the teacher, that the Tileus managers agreed to the low cost of the contract because the teacher could use the curriculum she already had. They had specified basic Reading, Writing, Arithmetic, Technology, called RWAT. But the tribe problem was they would lose money if they defaulted. The Elders were considering what to do.

"Tengali Trude is advocating violence," Marta said. "I'd like to try a peaceful path. Why don't I go to school tomorrow and see what this Mers. Sarah is teaching?"

Elder Greyling liked the idea and asked her to report it to the Elders.

≫ ✳ ≪

The next morning, Marta walked to school with Findie. The smaller moon Silver was just past full, setting in the West opposite the morning sun.

It felt strange to be there again after years of working. The one-room school was smaller than she remembered. Colored cheerful yellow, it nestled into a copse of blue pindel trees whose needles carpeted the ground. Despite her concerns about what she would hear, she relished nostalgia of her own school days.

There were children flitting in the yard like the musical larkbirds in the trees. Findie joined some friends with a joyful shout. Marta watched him, her heart full.

As she approached the door, a huge man stepped out onto the stoop and blocked her way.

"The school is for children only." His voice was deep and dark with a foreign accent. The man's tunic and slacks were completely black, like a military uniform. His strong hands waited impatiently at his sides, seeming ready to do mayhem. His eyebrows dominated his face—yet a quick intelligence in his dark eyes spoke of competence.

Marta stopped, disconcerted. "And who are you, to stop me from entering our own community school?"

"My name is Krenz Hofsta, but my name hardly matters. Tileus sent me here to protect your teacher."

"From what? A student's sister who wants to talk with her?"

Another figure appeared in the door behind him. The woman was slim with symmetric features and a ready smile. She placed a soft hand on Hofsta's shoulder. "Easy, Krenz. These people are our hosts."

As Hofsta moved to one side, she moved past him down the stairs to Marta and held aloft her palm. "I'm Sarah Drogan. I see a family resemblance in the eyes. You must be Findie's sister?"

Marta raised her own palm. "Yes, I am. My name's Marta Bloom."

"Nice to meet you. To what do we owe the pleasure?"

Marta was not at all sure how to understand this bimodal greeting from the two. Krenz Hofsta stepped down the stairs; his stone wall façade was at complete odds with the woman, who seemed open and friendly. Her light brown hair was pulled back into a ponytail. She wore a long smock over tailored slacks, different from the heavy denim pants and work shirts worn by the Indie Tribe.

Despite her different attire, though, and a slight accent, Sarah Drogan didn't seem too unlike people of the tribe.

"I had hoped to sit in on part of your day today. We've heard about you from Findie, but I'd like to observe firsthand."

Sarah put her hand on Hofsta's shoulder again as the man started to move. "But of course, Marta. We'd be glad to have you." Hofsta turned and started to object, but Sarah's hand tightened to stop him. "Come on in. We have an extra seat in the back."

Sarah then turned to Hofsta. "It's time for the bell, Krenz. Please call the children." As Hofsta moved past them toward the bell pull, Marta saw a handheld needle gun tucked into a holster at his back. The gun seemed to grab her breath and hold it in shock.

❧ ✳ ❦

When the bell rang, twenty-six students filed into the room to take their seats. Marta watched the holos come alive above each desk as the students activated them. The teacher tapped her own desk to get attention, making her holo flash red repeatedly. The class quieted.

"This morning, we continue reading classic literature. Please open your holos to Robert Heinlein, chapter 2 of *Starship Troopers*." As she spoke, she strode to Marta's desk and quickly brought up the material on Marta's holo. All the holos around the room flickered until they showed similar images.

"You've had a chance to read the chapter. Let's explore some of the new words in this chapter. Who can tell me what the author meant by 'moral philosophy'?"

After a long pause, one boy tentatively raised his hand.

"Yes, Klutie?"

The boy stood beside his desk, but he paused before speaking. "I think...he means how we think about morals?" He quickly sat down again.

"Good, Klutie. Good start. Can anyone add something more to what he's said?"

One girl's hand shot up, and she stood up without being recognized. "He means some morals are good and some are bad, and we need to study to know which is which."

"Nice addition, Glera. But in the book, the class Mars. Dubois is teaching is called 'History and Moral Philosophy.' Why would history be combined with knowing which morals are good and bad?"

Marta saw Findie glance back at her for approval before raising his hand. He was self-conscious about her being in the room.

"Yes, Findie?"

"Because history shows us which morals have been good for people and which ones have been bad?"

Sarah nodded. "How does it show us morals?"

"When people use bad morals, like when only the leaders say what happens, then people get into wars. And when everyone has a say, then people are at peace."

Marta was stunned by her brother's answer. He was describing Winter's way as "bad morals" and the chaos of Tileus as "good morals." Immediately, Marta was seeing the problem: Sarah Drogan was teaching the children to hate the ways of Winter and revere the ways of Tileus. Marta set her jaw to stay quiet; she wanted to hear all the teacher taught.

The morning continued. Most of the lessons were straightforward, teaching the knowledge and skills the children needed to become adults. Every once in a while, though, the lesson would spin antithetical to the Winter culture, subtly teaching Tileus culture.

Two hours later, lessons transitioned to math.

"Turn to page 134. We've been studying word problems and how to set up the algebra; it's time to see how well you can handle them."

The students—and Marta—changed their holos with a rustle and flashes of light.

Sarah called out a student this time. "Brookie, please read problem number five."

Startled, the girl sat up straight and blushed. Her mind had obviously been wandering.

"Yes, ma'am." Brookie focused on the holo. "Number five. 'The village of Pilnet wants to send a technical helper to Winter for a year. The technical helper has an annual salary of fifty thousand credits. Travel and housing will cost another thirty thousand credits. If Pilnet has two thousand people, how much tax will each person have to contribute?'"

Brookie looked puzzled and hesitant. "But Mers. Sarah . . . does each person have to give the same amount?"

Marta waited for Sarah's answer with skepticism.

The teacher seemed surprised. "Of course, they'd pay the same amount, Brookie. That would only be fair."

Another hand popped in the air, and the student spoke before being recognized. "But Mers. Sarah, what if one family is really poor?"

Sarah waved a hand in the air to negate the question. "These questions are off the point. We're working math here. Please accept the problem as it is stated. Now, who can tell me how to set up an equation?"

❧ ✳ ❧

When lunch came, Marta had seen enough. Every subject was laced with cultural assumptions from Tileus, norms not accepted in Winter. She was ready to leave and carry a report back to the Elders.

As Sarah dismissed the students, however, she made a point of coming back to Marta.

"Marta, would you like to have lunch with Krenz and me? I'd like to meet you and have a chance to talk, and he probably would, too. We eat in the picnic area outside. It's a beautiful day."

Marta glanced at Krenz in the corner by the door and doubted he wanted to meet, but she nodded. "Okay. We could eat. I wasn't sure how long I'd be here, so I brought a lunch."

"Great." Sarah called to Krenz, "Would you please join us for lunch?"

The man nodded and stood like a panther sliding onto an overlooking branch. His eyes constantly scanned for danger. Or possibly for victims.

The two women walked outside together with Krenz behind. The pindel needles crunched under their shoes. About half of the students settled at some of the picnic tables. The others disappeared down the path, likely to their homes.

"What do you do for a living?" Sarah asked as the three took their places around a table.

Marta chuckled. "I fish. Of course. It's what most of us do."

"Yes, but not all. I've learned some people in Winter farm; some tend essential stores and services. But you do look like a fisher, with your tan and your strong build."

"When Findie finishes school, he'll join us on the boat. We can use the help."

"Doesn't he have any choice in the matter? He's a smart boy; he might want to go on to advanced school."

"If he showed aptitude for something else," Marta said, "then we'd certainly send him on to more school. But he seems ready to fish. He knows it's what supports the family."

Krenz's deep voice surprised Marta by cutting in, "He could train for security service. I've watched him. He's strong and he's quick."

In that moment, Marta had to re-evaluate the man. He had seemed disconnected and distant, but his words were right on point. Perhaps he was more than just obstructive muscle. She turned to him to answer.

"Yes, he's strong and quick . . . and smart," Marta nodded to Sarah, "but those traits are also valuable in the kind of fishing we do. It's dangerous work, and it's vital not just to support our family, but also to feed the planet. We ship fish products to Tileus and other countries."

Krenz agreed. "Well, that makes sense, too."

Sarah started to speak, paused, then said, "I'm glad you came today, and I'm glad you're having lunch with us. We want to ask your help."

It appeared she had something important to say. Marta waited quietly.

Sarah nodded and continued, "As we spend more time here, I learn more about what you do." Marta saw Krenz nod agreement as Sarah spoke. "I've come to admire it."

"We enjoy the life and freedom we have."

Krenz agreed. "It seems like a good life. And good freedom. Not what I expected."

"What did you expect?"

"We were told Winter was tightly controlled by a few Elders, and people had no say in their government."

Marta laughed lightly. "Not at all what happens here. The Elders provide leadership and make decisions for us, but we all have a say. And we're free to do whatever we want."

Sarah was still cautious, and her voice turned serious. "We've lost some students. Krenz and I have been talking it over. It appears there is some misunderstanding, and I'm afraid part of the problem is ours. I've been wanting to talk about it with someone. We were sent here as part of a Tileus program to teach Winter about freedom and democracy. Because you don't vote, we were told to expect a desperate need to understand what liberty and choice meant."

Marta started to respond, "A rather one-sided view—"

Sarah cut her off, "But I'm embarrassed to realize how wrong we were."

"Right," Krenz added. "My job was supposed to be security for the teacher, because the Tileus managers feared she might be in danger from these islanders...but we see peaceful people."

Marta remembered her meeting with Tengali Trude. "Well, our people are just people—"

"Instead of danger," Sarah hurried on, "we're seeing a nation with a different way of life, but it works for you. I find myself questioning our purpose. Our curriculum is embedded with many lessons about the Tileus way, like in the last math problem. They no longer seem appropriate. I've been trying to work out how to teach it differently, but I don't want to go against my directives, either."

Marta paused a long while, gathering her thoughts while her entire perceptions changed. Sarah and Krenz remained quiet to let her think.

"This is very interesting," she finally spoke. "I came here this morning not just for Findie, but also for the Elders. I will report back to them."

Sarah nodded. "I thought something like that might be happening."

"When we sat down to lunch," Marta continued, "I'd seen enough, and I was going to argue for your removal. Your teaching materials are filled with ideas that don't work here. You're teaching values to the children that have nothing to do with our basic RWAT curriculum. Values that can make them dissatisfied with what we have. I'm not alone. Indie Tribe people are angry about what you're teaching. I met one yesterday who was raging."

Marta stopped and shook her head in amazement. "Yet now, I hear you already realizing how wrong this is."

Both Sarah and Krenz nodded.

"So, what are we going to do with this?" Marta continued. "Can we change your curriculum?"

Before Sarah could answer, they were interrupted by a commotion on the path. A rousing rumble of angry voices came rapidly their way. One heavy voice stood out with heated questions. Other voices shouted irate responses. Krenz sprang up, as the two women turned to see what was happening.

A moment later, the clamor became a mass of furious men bursting into the schoolyard.

As soon as she saw the crowd, Sarah turned to the wide-eyed students. "Into the school, children. Now!"

The schoolchildren obeyed, grabbing their lunches and running inside. All except Findie, who moved to stand beside Marta.

Krenz Hofsta interposed himself between the teacher and the crowd. His right hand behind his back was on his pistol. Sarah and Marta quickly stood and stepped forward.

Marta was astonished; she'd never seen a mob in Winter before. These were all people she knew, but they were strangers today. Shouting and stomping, some held dangerous tools like fish pikes and hoes. A few carried loaded harpoon guns.

Tengali Trude led the group and egged them on. His voice rang over the crowd.

"Are we going to put up with this?"

The crowd shouted in response. "No!"

"What are we going to do?"

"Close it up."

"Scuttle it down."

"Kick them out."

At one side of the group, Marta saw Elder Cartook Greyling. He was trying to calm the men around him. Marta kept Findie close behind her.

Hofsta stepped forward again and spoke, holding his left palm out. "Stop right there."

The crowd didn't even pause. Trude tramped to within two meters of Hofsta, shouting the entire way.

"You don't have any authority here. This is our school, not yours. Get out of the way."

Further voices affirmed Trude's. "He's right."

"Move aside."

Trude continued, "We've had it up to here with your teaching. It stops here, today."

Sarah stepped to Hofsta's side. He adroitly kept a working distance for any action.

She spoke, "Please, people. We're not here to cause problems, only to teach."

"Right, teach," Tengali shouted, spittle spraying from his lips. "We don't want the fish guts you teach. Our kids are being brainwashed."

The mob surged forward. Wordless anger filled the yard with noise.

"We can change," Sarah said. "I was just talking about it with Marta." Her voice was only barely loud enough for Marta to hear her over the throng.

Marta stepped up, using her sea voice to be heard, "Neighbors. Friends. This isn't the way to change."

The Elder also spoke up, his voice ringing over the noise. "Calm, friends. We can work this out with calm." He was moving toward the front.

The crowd would not be appeased. The men secure in the middle of the pack pressed forward. A couple at the front were forced to stumble forward a step, waving their tools for balance.

Hofsta drew his weapon and pointed it at one who had come forward. "Stop! Stop now."

"Gun! He's got a gun."

An explosive crack sounded from the left side of the crowd. A harpoon shot forward, just missed Hofsta, and hit Sarah Drogan in the chest. Blood splattered from her back as the barbed shaft went through. She looked down in amazement at the shaft in her own breast.

Hofsta responded instantly. He fired twice into the crowd. His flechette needles were aimed at the source of the harpoon. The crowd went wild. Three more harpoon guns fired together. One hit the picnic table behind. Two impaled Hofsta, just as Sarah collapsed onto the grass.

Hofsta gritted his teeth at the pain and tried to stay on his feet. Then he, too, collapsed., first to his knees then onto his side, propped up by the harpoons through his body.

Marta heard Findie gasp behind her.

The anger of the mob disappeared into shock.

Marta saw these two people, whom she was just getting to like, lying on the ground with their lives pouring out. The blood in the pindel carpet under them accused the entire tribe.

"Oh, no," she breathed, and fell to her knees beside Sarah. She put her hands onto Sarah's chest, wanting to pull out the harpoon but afraid to do anything. Before she could decide, she watched Sarah's lungs slowly express their last breath like a wounded butterfly. She looked at Krenz and saw he also was gone.

Marta's hands were covered in blood.

"Oh, Spirit Lord," a voice sounded in the crowd. "Distal's shot."

People cleared a space around him. Distal was just a shopkeeper they all knew, dressed in slacks and a plaid shirt. Still standing, his face was pale and blood ran down his left arm from a needle wound in his shoulder. The entry wound was tiny, but the flechette had tumbled in his muscle and torn a large gouge out of the back of his shoulder.

All the wind had gone out of Trude's sails. He stood with an ashen face, unable to speak. His hands groped in the air.

In the silence, Elder Greyling stepped forward to take charge. He pointed to two of the men.

"Brandling, see what you can do to bandage Distal's arm. Practal, use your implant to call for medical help."

An aircar whooshed over the trees and came to a landing behind the crowd. Someone had apparently already called.

As two tribal warders climbed out, the Elder directed them. "Verstal and Grindie, please detain anyone who has a discharged harpoon gun."

He paused and took a heavy breath.

"Everyone else, go home. Please."

Greyling looked down at the carnage on the ground, at Findie's shocked look, at the kids watching from the door of the school...at the blood on Marta's hands.

"Are you okay, Marta?"

She nodded in tears. "We were just talking about changing the curriculum, Elder." She reached out to smooth Sarah's hair. "These were good people. They came here with good intentions. Wrong intentions, but good-—and they were willing to change. I can't believe our people would do this." She stopped speaking and hid her face with bloody hands.

Findie looked at his sister, his eyes wet.

He turned to Greyling, fear on his face. "Elder . . . is this how wars start?"

Too Much Good

People of faith have often found something that fills them with joy. Perhaps it is a relationship with a higher power, a way of thinking that changes their life, or perhaps it is nothing more than a philosophy useful to them. They wish to share what they've found with others, to help others find the same joy. For them, this sharing is an action of the greatest good. Unfortunately, there are times when it is too much good.

Morat Intelact grumbled while stumbling one careful foot in front of another. The mountain trail wound up steep hillsides and climbed over rocks, and hiking was never his favorite activity. He didn't have time for this. Instead, he needed to get ready for his Mission tomorrow. At age twenty-one, Mission was the final step in completing school in Rathas.

However, his classmate Penemanah Athletfor asked him to join her before he left. She said the climb would test and prepare him.

"Holy Elláh!" he said when he slipped on a rock, barely catching himself with his hand.

"Watch your language," chided Peni. "Don't take His name in vain." But she also smiled.

He dipped his head in faithful contrition. "It's this pack. It overbalances me."

She laughed. "I told you last night to keep it light. But you've got contingencies in there for every last thing that might happen. You insisted on packing your fears."

She chuckled at him while she reached up to adjust her wide-brimmed hat and brush back her chin-length black hair. She seemed to bear her backpack like a part of her.

"We're almost up to Magnum Gap, then we'll talk." Her tone had turned serious. "There are things I need to tell you about Mission over in Tileus."

"Okay. I can go a bit farther."

While they finished the climb, the glorious mountain forest expanded around him. Verdant was a beautiful world and humankind was fortunate to be here, though politics sometimes darkened its beauty. Through the understory, he saw tree boles standing uphill and downhill like soldiers of faith. The summer foliage was rich in the varied colors of different photosynthetic processes. The blue-white sun dappled and sparkled, so the forest shouted for joy. Morat heard the gentle sough of wind and distant twitter of birds. Most gratifying of all was the scent, the rich combination of growth and decay filling his nose like a fragrant prayer to Elláh and His Son Jaysus. Being here was a moksha, a release from the samsara cycle of life and death. He breathed a prayer of thanks, one of the Five Pillars, and it calmed his over-stressed heart.

Morat thought ahead to tomorrow. He hoped Peni had good advice for him. He wanted to share with people, to do good for others by bringing them to Jaysus.

Minutes later, they reached the pass. At this elevation, the air was thinner with glorious intoxication, and Morat felt the breeze that had been blocked in the forest. He chose a comfortable boulder to sit on. The rock was warm in the sun, with a soft layer of moss.

"Can we talk about your trip now?" he said. "I want to be sure I do all the good I can while I'm there."

She found another granite armchair, then looked down to gather her thoughts.

When she looked up, pain filled her eyes. She said, "It's very simple, Morat. I just got back from my Mission there, and I've got one plea to make to you."

She paused, then slumped. "Don't go. Please...just don't go."

Morat felt his body go rigid. "How can I not go, Peni? It's all scheduled. It's expected. Everyone goes on Mission, or they can't join the Church as a full member." He felt his heart pounding in dismay.

"I don't know how not to go. But it's much more dangerous than the elders have led us to believe."

She stood up and pointed, down the other side of the pass. "This is Magnum Gap. Right here, we're on the border. That way, to the east, is Tileus," she said. "That's part of why I brought you here, so you could see it from here."

"It doesn't look any different than Rathas."

"No, the trees and the rocks are the same on both sides. But the people aren't."

A silent chime sounded in his head from his imp. He saw Peni react to hers also.

He said, "It's time for noon prayers."

They each reached to unfasten a prayer rug from the outside of their packs. Morat struggled with the knots then found a place to lay it out, facing south toward the sun. He arranged his mat and stood at its foot, then he looked at Peni's mat beside him and smiled in dismay at his own unpreparedness for this hike. His heavy mat was the standard size; hers was of a lighter material and less than half the size. He was carrying this extra weight all day.

Centering his thoughts, Morat's mind went to history, marveling at how their faith came out of a time hundreds of years ago on old Earth when God, Allah, and Hindu had joined. Today, they saw the three-fold Elláh with the merits of all three prior faiths.

They intoned prayers together in slow reverent sequence. Standing, with head above heart, reminding them of the choice they made each day. Kneeling, in submission to Elláh, the essence of the choice. Prostrate, with heart above head, the spirit above the mind. To Morat, this Pillar brought him to peace three times each day, often in the midst of turmoil. After prayer, they busied themselves rolling up the mats and putting them away, their minds on the submission to Elláh they had just experienced.

He finished tying his mat onto the side of his pack before he spoke again. "How are the people different, Peni. They're just people."

She took a breath before answering. "Here in Rathas, we know what to expect from people. The elders guide us in the Way. In Tileus, everything is crazy."

"What do you mean, crazy?"

"People there are self-centered. Everyone does whatever they want. Some people are good. Some are violent. The rich are always grasping for more, while poor people can never get enough. No one thinks of service to others. They call it democracy and they vote on everything, but it seemed like chaos to me."

Morat said, "All the more reason for Mission, I would think. We can bring them the peace of Jaysus. I'm looking forward to that part."

"I know it's important. I know what I'm suggesting is contrary to our way. But we've been friends a long time, Morat, and I'm frightened for you."

He raised a surprised eyebrow as she paused before continuing.

"Some Tileus people accept why we're there, even if they don't agree. But there are fringe groups who get angry at being told how to live. They shouted at us to take our *good life* somewhere else. I had the sense our faith somehow threatened their vaunted democracy."

She shook her head in dismay. "No one wanted our message. Few would listen. They were too self-absorbed."

Morat always saw Peni with a strong, spiritually-grounded confidence. Today, she seemed nervous and uncertain, as if something had damaged her. He straightened a small red shoot bent in a crevice in the rock, in accordance with his reverence for life.

He asked, "How many accepted baptism during your trip?"

She shrugged helplessly. "None."

"None at all?"

"Our group of six was in Thad City for two weeks. We spoke to people every day except Endday, when we prayed among ourselves. Sometimes we spoke to arranged groups and sometimes on the streets. I gave my personal witness to about three hundred people."

She sighed.

"Not one. Not even one came to Jaysus."

"But you were fulfilling your dharma. The results are always up to Elláh."

"True." She paused like she was about to launch into dangerous territory. Her eyes were on the ground.

"But things were bad. Very bad. Someone spit on me while I was talking, right in my face. I dodged rocks and bricks. A man ran up and spilled a bucket of animal blood over my head. We were talking peace and harmony; our message somehow raised their anger."

She looked up into his eyes. "Morat, the evil of Saitan is strong in Tileus. You might be killed." Her voice sounded desperate, her own recent memories coming out in fear for him.

He was shocked and didn't know how to respond. He looked down to think.

After a pause, Morat looked up and said, "I have to ask. How did you handle the violence while you were in Tileus?"

She took a deep breath. "Twice, I had to run away. I mean, really run as hard as I could, twisting around corners to get away. I'm fast, but they almost caught me.

"I was terrified. In those moments, all my trust in Elláh faded away and I was frightened like a beaten dog. Afterwards, I prayed and prayed for forgiveness for my lack of trust. It has affected my soul, and I'm still working on it."

She paused again. "Don't go, Morat. Please don't go."

Silence extended for long moments, listening to the wind sigh in the upper trees. Morat thought hard about his upcoming trip. He remembered how unprepared he was for this simple day hike. Yet he would never have known how to prepare without actually being here and doing it. No amount of prior study would replace the experience. Finally, he shook his head in defeat.

"I have to go," he said. "It's what we do."

Three days later, in Tileus, Morat still fretted over his decision. His Mission group was in Uptown, in the eastern foothills of the same mountains he'd hiked with Peni. Somewhere near was the Tileus trailhead that led up to Magnum Gap.

The group stayed together in defense against the chaotic activity of the city streets. Tileans surrounded them in garish clothing of reds, greens, and purple—colors Morat normally never saw worn. They shouted greetings and imprecations with an exuberance never seen in Rathas.

"They're wild and crazy," he said to Failebaso Servdo while the six of them walked in a huddle behind Roloket, their group leader. "How can we possibly reach them with our message of peace?"

Peni was a long-term friend. Fai was more; she and Morat had dated several times. She delighted him and liked him. Morat had hopes he would grow closer to Fai on this trip. It thrilled him they could be together for the adventure.

Unlike his own worry, Fai's eyes sparkled with eagerness. "We'll find a way, Morat. Elláh will open doors." Her enthusiasm was infectious.

"I hope you're right. I try to keep my faith strong, but this place is a challenge."

She spun around and punched him on the shoulder. "So, buck up and meet the challenge. Elláh can do anything, including strengthening your faith in Him."

"Okay, okay," he said with a grin. "I know you're right. This will all be fine, and we'll grow from it."

"That's the attitude." She rose on her toes to put a quick kiss on his cheek, her hand lingering on his shoulder.

Fai not only excited him; she inspired him to reach higher.

"Hey, everyone," said the leader. Rolo was in his late twenties, somewhat older than the Mission members. This was his tenth time leading a Mission group. "Yesterday we spoke in an assembly hall. Structured witnessing. We didn't make any converts, but at least we had eighty people come by at various times. Today, we're going to work the streets."

"What, out here?" worried Gadet, the least adventurous of the group.

"Yes, out here. We've got a permit to speak on a specific corner about two blocks away. The rule is that we stay on our corner. We're not allowed to chase people. That's part of the law here in Tileus."

Morat spoke up. "They have laws about religious witness? They're not even religious."

"No, their laws apply to any group trying to send a message. Tileus has a problem with political groups fighting each other. They just include us in the same kind of group."

They continued walking while Rolo gave them more rules.

"And here we are, folks. This is our corner."

"It doesn't look any different than any other corner," Fai said with a bright laugh. She squeezed Morat's hand in encouragement.

It was a busy corner just like the last several they'd passed. Two streets crossed each other. A narrow center lane carried autocars, though not much traffic existed. Slidewalks on either side of the car lane were full of pedestrians. Buildings rose around them in different heights from three stories to as many as ten. Most of the ground floor spaces were filled with shops, with occasional doorways leading to upstairs. The noise of the crowds wasn't quite deafening.

Fai was the first to speak, her bold impetuosity coming into play. She let go of Morat's hand and held a copy of The Holiest high in the air.

"We have the Way, folks! You don't have to live your life in defeat and misery. Follow Jaysus in praise of Elláh, and you'll be uplifted into a joy you've never known." She glanced at Morat, her eyes twinkling.

Morat couldn't let Fai get ahead of him. His deeper voice joined hers as he held his own Holiest up. "Jaysus said, 'I am the Way, the Truth, and the Life.' We can show you the Five Pillars that keep you grounded in the Spirit."

His heart was in his throat. He'd never done anything like this before, but he knew what was expected. They had to reveal themselves to these strangers hurrying by, expose their own weaknesses so they could show what Elláh had done with them. So he kept shouting, conveying his understanding to the crowd. Maybe Elláh would work in someone.

The others joined Fai and Morat. Shortly, all six missionaries were striding back and forth on their corner, sometimes holding the book aloft and sometimes lowering it to read passages. They quoted their most meaningful verses.

Morat wondered how this message could reach the people. His job was to preach it; Elláh would move their hearts. He included personal revelations, times when he'd been astonished at how Elláh could act in his life.

No one stopped to listen. Most sped up to hurry past, their faces showing irritation.

He shifted tactics. "Your way of life leads only to dissolution and death, only to a useless end. You cannot find peace, because you think you must take charge of everything in your life. Let go, let Elláh. He can solve your problems as you cannot."

His heart lifted when he saw a group of five gather on the opposite street corner. They actually stood still and listened. Fai directed her words to them.

"Yes, you over there. Listen to us. You stop because you know there is something better than you have. Our Way is a way of spirituality, a way of togetherness, a way of surrender."

The group smiled at them, and Morat felt joy.

But then that group lifted signs they'd held.

"Down with Religion!"

"Stop the Missionaries!"

"Pass the Religious Restriction Law!"

The group walked in a circle on their corner, round and round, chanting, "No More God Talk, No More God Talk." They jostled their signs and stomped their feet in time with the chant. Some of them shook a free fist at the missionary group.

Morat was dumbfounded and silent for a moment. *They can protest against us? What kind of place is this?*

His ire rose, though, and he shouted all the louder. "Jaysus Saves the Lost." He shouted it over and over, giving it a rhythm, and the rest of the missionaries joined him.

Fai leaned in to tell him, "Great idea, Morat," before continuing the chant.

The missionaries stood together at the edge of the autocar lane facing the protesters, pumping their books in the air while they chanted.

Other passersby avoided the whole situation. Morat saw people swerving to stay well away from both groups. Some people turned around to go back the way they'd come.

The protesters escalated. In time with the missionaries' chant, they changed their own words to "Jaysus Sells a Book; Jaysus Sells a Book" The voices were ugly. The protesters kept walking in a circle, but their circle was now just across the roadway only four meters away.

Fai gave a scream at the blasphemy. She rushed across the car lane and put her Holiest in the face of one of the protesters. Morat's heart leaped at her boldness, and he jumped across the lane to keep her safe. The rest followed, shouting Holiest verses all the while.

Rolo grabbed at them as they crossed. "No, no, no. You're not allowed to cross the street. Come back, stay here." No one paid attention, so he crossed the lane to grab Gadet by the shoulder. He pulled him back to their side of the street, then came back for another.

The protesters kept circling with the missionaries in their faces, an irritating mixture of hostility and aloofness. Annoyed, Morat nudged one of them to get his attention. The reaction surprised Morat; the man he'd touched let go of his sign and swung a fist. He caught Morat squarely on his left cheek, knocking him to the ground.

"Don't touch me! You people talk about peace, but you don't even know what you can and can't do," the man shouted. He kicked Morat in the ribs.

The confrontation became a melee. Rolo tried to get his flock back across the street, but the protesters had turned themselves loose. Punching and gouging and grabbing, they pummeled the missionaries from every direction. On the ground, Morat heard grunts and screams. He'd lost his Holiest, and he crawled around to find it. Someone kicked him again just as he picked it up. Frantically, he jumped to his feet and retreated back across the street. His face ached and his ribs felt bruised. He had a sore spot on his hip where one of the kicks had landed hard.

Rolo pulled the last of the missionaries back into his group. They were all panting with exertion.

Morat counted heads. "Fai!" he shouted. "Where's Fai?"

They were down to five.

❧ ✳ ❧

"We're heading back to Rathas. An autobus will pick us up in an hour." Rolo spoke to the group in the hotel conference room. "Pack your things and return here. Your Mission is being cut short."

"Will it still count for Church membership?" asked Gadet.

"I can't believe you ask. What's important is whatever has happened to Fai," Morat snapped back.

Rolo palmed the air in a calming gesture. "We all need to stay calm. Elláh will work this out."

Morat took in a deep breath, let it out, and nodded. "Thank you, Rolo. But I'm very worried."

"So am I."

While Morat went to his room to get his bag, he continued to worry. His mind had been spinning widdershins since Fai had disappeared. First had been the horrible experience with the Tileus police. They'd treated the protesters gently and let them go quickly. The police blamed the missionaries for instigating the incident, saying the law required them to stay on their side of the street. *As if crossing the street could justify kidnapping!* They took names and detailed statements from each missionary, a permanent record of their transgression. The police didn't release them for two hours. Meanwhile, Rolo had used his implant to get advice from the Mission Ministry back in Rathas.

Now they were returning to Rathas. Without Fai.

❧ ✳ ❧

Back in his school dormitory late that night, Morat thrashed in his bed like branches in a wind, first too hot then too cold. All his covers found their way to the floor, then he'd chill and have to pick them up.

His eyes were red and bleary by the time the group met in the morning for a grilling by the school officials from the Mission Ministry. They'd taken over the dormitory study room for the day. InfoNet holostations lined the walls, but all were turned off for now. Morat saw other students pass by the door in obvious irritation at losing their space.

"What were you people thinking?" shouted the Mission Coordinator. "Or were you thinking at all? You can't win converts to peace by punching them out."

Morat kept his eyes on the floor, except when he looked up in shame at others in the group.

"We're going to interview you one by one, to get the most complete information we can. Wait in this room until we call your name, then return here afterward. We'll let you know when you can go."

The next hour was excruciating. Their imps were denied InfoNet access, so they had little to do but chat with each other. The general air was of disconsolate defeat. And Morat had still heard nothing about Fai. His anxiety reached a point of pain.

They'd interviewed everyone but him when the door opened once again. Expecting the call for him, he was surprised to see an older man enter. Tall and competent-looking, he carried himself with an assurance far in excess of what Morat expected in school official. Then he recognized the man. He stood up and nodded his head in deference, his heart in his throat.

"I know you, sir. I saw you on the news, speaking to the Bishopric Enclave about violence in Tileus. You're the Rathas national Minister of Security, aren't you?"

The man nodded. "Yes, I am. Beltaret Leaderlist. Are you Morat Intelact?"

"Yes, sir. But how would you know—"

"The others identified you as close to Failebaso Servdo. Is that right?"

Morat blushed. "Yes, I guess so. I like her a lot."

"I've come here to get you to help us." Beltaret's voice was charged with anger and dismay and determination all mixed together. "This whole thing is a horrible incident of international scope, because Servdo's father is one of our leading Bishops. A good friend of mine, he's devastated and broken. We need to find her.

"We also need to know what happened. People are no longer safe in Tileus. Our national leadership has been trying to plan what to do about it, everything from closing the borders to Holy War."

"How can I help, sir?"

"We've been working with Tileus authorities to find her, but they aren't very cooperative. Officially, they tell us our missionaries do their work in Tileus at their own risk, and the authorities are not responsible for keeping track of them. Unofficially, they tolerate violent groups. Yesterday afternoon, after your incident, the InfoNet got a location on her implant going up the trail from Tileus to Magnum Gap. Unfortunately, there's a large area around the pass with no connection to the InfoNet. She hasn't left that area of no signal…or her imp hasn't."

"So she's been up there all night?"

"We're organizing a search party. You'd be an asset, if you're willing to come. If and when we find her—"

"When, sir."

"Yes, *when* we find her, it would be good for her to see a friend."

∾ ✷ ∿

Morat was back on the same mountain he and Peni had hiked four days earlier. They took a different trail toward Magnum Gap, a more direct route. The trail traversed the side of the mountain with a moderately steep ascent. A dozen searchers were spread above and below the trail on the steep mountainside, paralleling each other while they climbed. Frequent shouts disturbed the quiet of the forest.

"Failebaso!"

"Speak up."

"Where are you?"

Morat asked Beltaret Leaderlist, "If we get close enough, our own imps can connect with hers, right?"

Beltaret nodded. "But someone has to get within about ten meters, which is the spacing we're using for the search line."

The group moved up the mountain, Morat and Beltaret on the trail and other searchers maintaining the line above and below. Everyone watched. Everyone listened, both with ears and with imps.

Despite the bright sun above the trees, the same mountainside that seemed so peaceful four days ago now loomed around Morat with dark threat. The ranks of trees were a threatening army now, and each rustle in the brush was a peril. He thought about Fai's condition after a night here on the mountain.

"I'm concerned, sir. What if she's hurt?"

Beltaret looked at him without stopping, then turned back to the trail with a dismissive answer. "You should be concerned. It's becoming dangerous to do good."

Morat shuddered.

Near the top, a gap in the forest revealed a precipitous field of huge boulders, one to three meters in size. The open rocks stretched hundreds of meters above and below. To Morat's shock, the trail disappeared in the rocks. A hundred meters away and thirty meters higher, he saw the trail resume where the trees started again.

"There's no trail, Minister. What do we do now?" he asked.

Beltaret gave a dry chuckle. "We scramble up the rocks, Morat. That's what hikers do."

Climbing the boulders took most of Morat's attention. He felt like a goat, jumping from one rock to another. His heart pounded with the exertion; fear was a large part. On his third jump, a patch of lichen slipped under his foot. He fell to the left and slammed his upper body into the solid wall beside him. The impact took his breath away and his eyes glazed. Fearful sweat suddenly suffused his body. For a moment, he stood there picturing himself slipping the other direction, careening down rock after rock like a twisted marionette, losing limbs along the way.

"Watch yourself, Morat. Be more careful."

Beltaret's advice seemed rather late and banal as he caught his breath. Morat crawled up the next few rocks, trying to be more careful. Unfortunately, he was falling behind. He stood up again and risked a few quick jumps to catch up—he even got ahead of the minister.

He stopped, sniffing the air.

"Do you smell something rotten, sir?" he asked.

"No, nothing," said Beltaret behind him.

Morat took another two steps forward. His imp pinged him with a notice about a new person.

He shouted, "I'm getting a signal!"

Beltaret had them hold the line while they advanced another few meters. Morat moved around one of the larger boulders and saw a shallow recess behind it. Inside the hollow…

"Oh, Elláh, I've found her." His voice rang out. The whole group converged on the spot one by one, working their way through the rocks.

Morat stepped into the recess. "Fai, we're here."

What he saw repulsed him. He felt nauseous. His girlfriend was stretched in a sitting position with her chin on her chest. Ropes tied to stakes pounded between the rocks held her arms high and wide. Her feet were tied together, stretched out in front of her. Hair straggled down past closed eyes toward her chest. Morat's arrival and the noise of others elicited no movement or response, though she was still breathing. Exposed for a night and most of a day with clothes partially ripped, her skin was burned by the sun. Bruises were black on her face, arms, and legs. Blood dried on her hands and face. Worst of all, her bare belly had been cut with the symbol of Elláh, a circle within a triangle. Blood had flowed around the shapes and hardened there; some blackened the ground at her hips. The wounds were still open and foul. Flies buzzed around her and landed on the blood. The smell was horrific, a mix of rotting blood and urine.

The scene was everything Morat feared after his failed Mission, and he was frozen in place.

"Sweet Jaysus," Beltaret breathed over his shoulder.

The words released Morat from torpor. He jumped to Fai's side, knelt, and touched her face with his palm. "My dear friend. What have they done to you?"

Morat pulled his hiking knife from its sheath and stepped forward to release Fai. She was completely limp, so he had to support her weight while he cut each rope. Her wrists were bloody and scarred with her efforts to pull free before she passed out. He had to wave away the persistent flies. Morat reached into his pack to get healing spray. It wouldn't solve the deep cuts in her belly, but it would help with the scrapes and abrasions.

His mouth filled with the sour spittle of anger. Whoever this Tileus fringe group was, they had beaten Fai, carried her up through Magnum Pass into Rathas, found a hidden place to stake her out, then cut the symbol of Elláh into her belly. All because they resented her sharing about peace. They hadn't cared whether Fai lived or died; their message worked either way. Even in his anger, Morat realized these people were sick and needed morality and spiritual grounding. He ground his teeth while he worked. He wanted to change them, to teach them better ways.

One of the searchers stepped forward with a canteen and moistened her lips. Fai moved her head to suck in the water. The man then wiped her forehead and eyes with the cool water. Another searcher carried a medkit and started scanning her for damage. The team was practiced and ready. She was alive. They would get her back safely.

Fai opened her eyes, encrusted with tears and sweat, and looked at him. Morat couldn't tell whether she was seeing anything.

"We're here, Fai. Back in Rathas. You'll be okay."

Fai nodded, wordless and weak. She closed her eyes again.

The team moved in with a stretcher.

Morat was free to step back and breathe clearer air. He was filled with anger, but also with new determination and confidence.

He looked at Fai and the cluster of people helping her, then turned to look across empty air toward Rathas and home. From this vantage, he saw the city in the valley below. Morat thought about how ineffective Mission had been.

His anger was turning to purpose. He wanted to do something greater than Mission, something that would change the way Tileus treated people. He had felt unready and uncertain, lacking any confidence. Now he knew he must set that aside.

He took a deep breath of decision.

Beltaret stood alone on another boulder and looked into distant space, his eyes seeing things most people didn't.

Morat stepped to him and said, "I don't want to just finish my Mission. I want to do something more than Mission."

Beltaret shook his head. "I don't think you need to worry about your Mission. There won't be any more."

A long pause ensued while Morat thought about no Missions. Not going back was a different solution to his fears, but now it didn't feel right. He wanted to help Tileus change. Not going felt like skipping out.

Beltaret continued, "I think it's time for Holy War against the infidels who can do something like this."

Morat's head snapped back. "Holy War, sir?"

"You've been schooled in its necessity, haven't you? You know we have the Khubar f'Elláh trained for it?"

"Yes, sir, but..."

Morat stopped to think. *He'd always thought of Holy War as something distant, not something here and now. Sometimes it's necessary, when infidels go too far and need Elláh's correction. Maybe this is one of those times.*

"But what, Morat?"

"But nothing, sir. You may be right."

"This problem with Tileus has been growing. They must learn to respect Elláh and His people."

These were huge thoughts, and Morat wanted to be part of it. "How would it happen?"

Beltaret treated the question seriously. "I'll have to take the idea back to the Service Ministry. It will take some convincing; some of the Ministry are pacifists."

Morat saw an opportunity. "I'd like a chance to speak to them, sir," he said, his heart in his throat at his own boldness. "I can tell them of our experience, of the godlessness we saw."

The minister cocked his head in interest. "That might be useful. I'll consider it. In the meantime, you can join the Khubar f'Elláh and train."

Morat nodded in new-found purpose. Righteous anger would be a powerful tool for good, and he would be part of it.

To Go or Not To Go

One of the most difficult things about cultural differences is that, in conflict, both sides believe themselves to be right. Viewed through different lenses, the same incident can be either good or evil, righteous or wrong. Assumptions make all the difference, and these assumptions color our entire lives. During international work, we must constantly question our assumptions. Or perhaps we can simply escape from them.

In the holo display, the missionaries marched across a street to shove their book—The Holiest, they called it—into the faces of Tileus passersby. They crowded around their innocent victims, trampling flowers along the sidewalk, and shouted their message of so-called "peace and love." They made no physical contact, but it was a clear violation of the Tileus laws on assault by partisan groups.

Lisa Westhof shook her head in disgust and tagged the video for her crimes portfolio. Going through surveillance camera records didn't feel like work for a diplomat, but these incidents had the countries of Tileus and Rathas close to war. The videos would be essential in the upcoming negotiations. When she felt generous, she told herself the Rathas missionaries simply didn't know Tilean laws. Most of the time, though, she didn't feel that generous.

If they're going to come into our country, they should know the laws.

Negotiations were not going well.

The next video wasn't missionaries but caught her attention anyway. Two political groups on opposing sidewalks were arguing some minor issue scheduled for nation-wide public vote tomorrow. Tempers rose, the groups fought with each other in the street, and she watched while police arrived to break it up.

And that's why we have the laws requiring groups to stay on their side of the street.

She returned her mind to work and called her boss, the number two person in the national Department of Outside Affairs.

"This is Susanna Nintuk," her boss answered, then caught herself. "Oh, it's Lisa. How is your search going?"

"I found another one, ma'am. I've now got a dozen of these videos. Each one shows the missionaries stepping way over the bounds."

"Good work. I knew you'd do well nationally. That's why I enticed you away from your city chancellor position. Let's get together this afternoon and plan for the meeting with the Rathas ambassador. I'll want you to take part."

"Yes, ma'am."

Lisa's heart pounded when she ended the call. It was heady to be working on international affairs.

After lunch, she joined Nintuk in the woman's office. She smiled when she saw the plaque beside the door: Susanna Nintuk, Secretary of Rathas Affairs. Lisa had never expected to have influence at this level. Stepping inside the office was like entering another world, a universe of rich appointments and luxury. Nintuk's workspace had a large desk, of course, but also two separate groupings of opulent furniture, wood-paneled walls, and fine art on display. Lisa's future looked bright, but she was nervous about her capability. She felt the pressure every day.

"Here are the videos I've assembled, Secretary. I've cut each one to show the essential crime along with what led up to it."

"Excellent, Lisa. Now, I'd like you to add something more to it. Please gather all you can about last week's kidnapping. Get the police records from Uptown, where it happened, and get anything you can from Rathas. Our police don't yet know who did it, but they suspect one of the extremist Tilean protest groups."

"We have some crazy people here."

"Yes, we do. Unfortunately, the kidnapped missionary was the daughter of one of the Rathas high bishops. They cut the poor woman with a knife and left her tied to rocks in the mountains in an area with no communications. Luckily, the Rathas people found her before she died, and she is recovering. This was one of the worst international incidents we've had, and it's why we're holding these negotiations."

"I've looked into it some already. I'll gather everything I can."

"Bring it all to me for review tomorrow morning. Ambassador Grufhand from Rathas is livid about the incident, as he should be."

"Yes, ma'am. I'll add it to the incident videos."

More work. Important stuff, but it's piling on.

☙ ❈ ❧

Lisa carried the frustration home. Her husband had made a good effort to clean up, but no effort was going to be good enough for her today. The kitchen was clean, the spacious apartment was neat, and the pillows were straight on the couch. Yet her attitudes colored the place in darkness. When she couldn't find the Shiraz, the work stress bubbled upward inside her. She poured a glass of whatever they had instead—a too-sweet Cabernet—and downed half the glass in one gulp.

Chris burst through the door.

"A starship's in port from Brightness," he shouted, "with a great offer!"

Lisa winced at his exuberance, though it was one of the things she loved the most about him.

With a slow smile, she said, "You don't have to be so loud. The neighbors don't need to hear it, too." Then she greeted him with a kiss, rising on her toes to reach him, holding her wine glass off to one side.

Chris wrapped her excitedly in his arms, pressing the kiss into a huge hug.

Lisa lost herself in the kiss, almost spilling her wine down his back. Chris was the most important person in her life. They'd been married for eight years, holding off on children, and their love was better than ever. She loved his physical strength, the way he wrapped her up in it. He made her own work problems fade away.

But he couldn't hold his news. When the kiss broke, it bubbled out of him. "Brightness—the whole planet—they've decided to build a colony ship and plant a new world. Someplace called Bluewater."

Lisa nodded, taken out of her own troubles by his excitement. "It's been a long time since people went to a new world."

"Yeah, three hundred years, and they're inviting us from Verdant to join them. It's a chance to start over, to get away from the disasters here."

"Hey, that's my job, dealing with those disasters," she said, pulling away. She would have softened the objection with a laugh, but the current situation with Rathas was too painful.

"Oh, I'm sorry. Bad joke." He shifted to concern. "How difficult are the disasters?" He sat on the grey leather couch and patted the place beside him.

She poured Chris a glass of wine and topped off her own, then joined him on the couch.

"They're pretty bad. All four countries on Verdant are at each other's throats over something. It's all differences in culture. Rathas keeps pushing their religion on everyone. Winter isolates and resents every contact. We in Tileus seem to alienate the others with our version of freedom, and Verdant Prime? Good grief, Prime still wants to bring everyone else back under their control."

"That's pretty bad." Chris frowned and reached to squeeze her hand.

"Yeah. I'm working on a problem with missionaries from Rathas that could easily spark a war. And it's not the only one. We've got wars brewing in every combination. It's all we can do to keep the negotiations civil."

Chris nodded. "Huh. We had some of those book-shouters across the street from our landscaping job today. They're obnoxious, shouting about their 'Elláh' all day. My guys got angry, and work suffered. I had to knock some heads to keep the guys on the job."

"You didn't really 'knock heads,' did you?"

"Not quite, but I did shove two of my workers back into the work area when they started to cross the street. You know my guys; they're all rough and tumble."

Lisa winced at the violence. "I guess you know what you're doing."

Then Chris paused with a twinkle in his eyes. "We could get away. The colonists are accepting applications now," he said, wiggling his wine glass as if dangling a temptation in front of her. "You and I would qualify."

She fingered the gold filigree necklace Chris had given her. "Qualify? Are you serious? That would be quite a decision, to leave Verdant for some new planet. We'd need lots of information. What world are they going to? How dangerous is it? How assured is the colony? How long is the trip? Are they inviting people from Verdant's other countries? What about culture conflicts among the colonists, country against country, Brightness versus Verdant—"

He patted the air as if to counsel patience. "We'll find out all of that," he said. "They wouldn't be doing it if they hadn't thought it all out. This is the most exciting opportunity in our lifetimes. It might even be dangerous, which adds to the excitement." His eagerness shoved aside her concerns, as it often did. She'd rather he shared her caution instead.

"So, you're serious. What about your landscaping business?" she continued. "You've spent years building it up, and you've got clients all over Tileus."

"No problem. I've already been thinking about moving on, and I've been bringing Sam Yilong up to run the business. He's tough enough to deal with the hard-nosed guys we hire. I'm leaving a good legacy behind, landscaping jobs that will beautify Tileus for decades. Me, I'm ready to do something new, something challenging, maybe something dangerous."

Why doesn't he understand? I feel like an elastic band tethering him to reality.

Chris's enthusiasm was why he'd done well as an entrepreneur. He approached each new job with excitement, then finished with gusto. His work was always high quality. Give him a new opportunity, and he'd be all over it. But the flip side of his enthusiasm was his willingness to jump to the next excitement without stopping to think. He didn't think ahead; instead, he dealt with problems when they happened. She preferred to prevent them in the first place.

"There's my work, too," she said. "I've just gotten the appointment at Outside Affairs a month ago. I'd have to give all that up. What work will there be for a barely seasoned diplomat in a new colony?"

"Tons," Chris said. He leaned forward; he had an answer for everything when he was excited. "Put ten thousand people together in a spaceship for months, then dump then onto a new world—there's bound to be conflicts. We'll probably have some of your Rathas crazies on board, and some of the Verdant Prime idiots. The colony will need your skills. It's a bigger opportunity than what you've got now. Damn, you could become the Governor of Outside Affairs for the whole colony."

He was so enthusiastic and his arguments made sense. She didn't want to rain on his parade.

"Lisa, this is a once-in-a-lifetime opportunity. Why am I having to persuade you?"

Because it means giving up all we've worked for. It means running away.

❧ ✳ ❧

The next morning, she and Secretary Nintuk went over the package Lisa had assembled for the meeting with the Rathas ambassador the following day.

"This is brutal, Secretary. Rathas gave us pictures of the kidnapped woman. She was left with her clothes torn and her belly carved in a Rathas religious symbol. By the time they found her, she was dehydrated, nearly dead. Blood was everywhere."

Nintuk shook her head, her lips compressed. "We do take pride in our free speech, but we have to make sure it stays at the level of words. Shouting across the street can be okay, but we can't allow invading someone's space. Otherwise, we'd have fights all the time. It'd be a disaster. And something like this kidnapping is completely unacceptable.

"Yet somehow, we have to heal our relations with Rathas."

Lisa responded, "Perhaps we can convince Ambassador Grufhand to have Rathas train their missionaries better."

"I'm not at all sure he's ready to listen. My boss, Governor Moller, tells me our military intel shows Rathas amassing military forces on their side of the Gortooth Mountains."

"Military forces? What can we do to stop them?"

"You and I can find a way to mollify the ambassador without breaking our own country's laws. It's up to us."

Lisa joined Chris that evening at an information session about the colonization. Her mind was still on the diplomatic problems, racing around possible ideas to soften the Rathas ambassador tomorrow.

The room filled with a thousand people. The group from Brightness held the event at the gaudy ballroom of the Eluxor Hotel, the largest room in Thad City. She'd been there for political rallies and had used this very room for her victory speech when she won the city chancellorship two years ago. Crystal chandeliers hung from the high ceiling with bright lights focused on them to scatter rainbows around the room.

Chris nudged her while they found seats near the front. "Look at the backdrop, Lisa. They've got pictures of the new world. And there were samples in the back of the room of plants I've never seen."

"Settle down, Chris," she chided. "You're a successful businessman. You don't have to see everything all at once. Take it easy and learn."

"I can't, Lisa. I'm hyped."

She shook her head in amusement, but underneath it all, her stomach was still tied in knots. She took a calming breath, then opened a holo above her handheld to do some work while she waited.

An older Brightness man with charismatic authority took the podium. Lisa put away her work. Everything about him was different. He spoke Standard with a distinct accent. The bold colors in his clothing clashed.

"Good even, all. I be Deniz Erdogan, and I be leader for the Bluewater colony. My confrères," he gestured to the six others on the stage, "be here to tell you of our marvelous plans. We hope many of you to us will join."

The large holo behind him showed the image of a blue-green world surrounded by distant stars. Overlays showed graphics and information: suitable for humanity; a larger world with heavier gravity; much slower rotation than Verdant; the year about the same length.

"Bluewater be our new world."

Over the next hour, Erdogan and his team told them about the colonization. Bluewater presented some challenges. Air and water were within human range. The important plants humanity used could grow there. Some of the native flora and fauna provided new possibilities as food sources. Although there were moderately large carnivores, there were no animals that would present any extraordinary problem. However, some native plants grew aggressively and produced airborne toxins that would require protective masks and clothing outdoors at all times.

The crowd murmured at the bad news.

Erdogan hastened to reassure them. "The search team did find some controls effective; they did clear a ten-kilometer area where they could go without protection. They be confident the same techniques will make large areas livable. Over decades, the toxic plants can be brought under control."

"Weeds," Chris whispered. "I know how to control weeds. I can kill that stuff."

"Shush," she laughed. "Watch the presentation."

The team showed videos of the planet, its scenery, vegetation, and animals. There were four major continents surrounded by vast areas of ocean. The largest continent had more land area than the entirety of the planet Verdant. The system sun was larger and had a reddish tint, creating unusual colors. They showed spectacular scenes of an untouched world with natural beauty. Several times, Lisa caught her breath at the splendor of what they showed. *It's beautiful, but how could we possibly leave what we have?*

After the presentation, Chris bulled his way to the front. Lisa followed less enthusiastically and arrived when Chris spoke.

"Coordinator Erdogan, my name is Chris Westhof, and you will definitely see my application."

Lisa's head snapped back in surprise at his statement, made without consulting her.

Erdogan smiled and shook Chris's hand. "This be why we be here, Paron Westhof. I well wish you in our selection process."

"Oh, I'm sure you'll want me. I've been working with plants all my life and have built a successful business with them. I'm excited to solve the challenges you describe with Bluewater's flora."

The coordinator perked up. "That be good. We need people for that. The plants be our biggest challenge. You and I, we will talk more later." A long line of people waited to talk, so Erdogan turned to the next after shaking Chris' hand again.

Lisa's surprise was transforming into anger while they walked out of the ballroom. "I can't believe you committed us without my agreement. I told you last night I wasn't ready to do this."

Chris stopped in surprise. "You're not ready? You only said we needed more information."

"Of course, I'm not ready. I told you last night. I'm still growing in my career. I can't believe you didn't listen."

Leaving Chris behind, Lisa walked away fuming.

❧ ✳ ☙

The next day, Lisa took part in international negotiations for the first time, in the meeting between Secretary Nintuk and Rathas Ambassador Grufhand. She looked forward to the meeting. They were prepared, and she had every expectation they would find a path to agreement.

After short, polite greetings, Grufhand, a rather pompous man, got right to the point.

"We do not understand your difficulties, Secretary Nintuk. Our missionaries come to Tileus to offer good news, so more people can live a better life under Elláh. You have freedom of speech here, yet you do not seem to control your people's actions."

"Ambassador, coupled with our freedom of speech is accountability for the consequences of what we say. Speech is one thing, actions are another. We have strict laws about physical contact; surely you understand it is a legal assault to intrude on someone's personal space?"

"Our missionaries only talk. They do not assault people."

"In our system," Secretary Nintuk told the Rathas ambassador, "organized groups must make their pitch from a defined space. Otherwise, we could have fights in the street. That is our law. The zeal of your missionaries often transgresses our laws. They don't seem to understand."

"All we ask," said Grufhand, "is that you control the protesters to keep our missionaries safe. Last week, your people kidnapped and brutally assaulted our bishop's daughter. They left her to die in the mountains!"

Secretary Nintuk replied quickly. "I beg your pardon? Do you know who did it? Do you have information we don't have?"

"It must have been Tileus people. Who else would do it?"

"Well, our police are still investigating, with help from your proctors. Ambassador, we don't condone kidnapping or attempted murder. But even in this extreme case, the instigating incident was done by your missionaries. Lisa, you have the data?"

"Yes, ma'am," Lisa said. She brought up a desktop holo and turned to the ambassador. "This is a street camera of the incident prior to the kidnapping. Your missionaries were shouting at the passersby, insulting people about not being part of your faith."

"We don't insult," said the ambassador with indignation. "We help people come to a better life."

"It may seem so to your people, sir, but there are cultural differences. The custom in Tileus is to let people make their own decisions. When your missionaries tell people they're wrong, that steps over the line in our country."

Grufhand jumped on Lisa's words. "And that justifies kidnapping and leaving someone to die?"

Nintuk stepped in. "No, sir, it does not. But it can lead to escalation."

"And that's not all they did," said Lisa. "Please keep watching, sir. While the protesters across the street marched peacefully back and forth, your missionaries crossed the street and pushed holy books in their faces. Got in their way. Even shoved them." Lisa tried hard to keep indignation out of her voice.

The secretary added, "In Tileus, such behavior is illegal. It is a form of assault. Your missionaries must abide by our laws. It's fine for them to speak their views. They can carry signs and their books. It's not acceptable for them to assault our citizens."

The ambassador thrust out his chest and his face got red. "You would equate offering a holy book to kidnapping? How absurd!"

"No, sir. Kidnapping is certainly a worse crime—but both are crimes. Perhaps, though, we can find areas where we agree and work from those."

Grufhand calmed down with some effort. "Yes, indeed. What you show me looks normal to me, but I do understand about your Tileus laws. Perhaps we can train our missionaries better."

"Perhaps we can help," said Nintuk. "Maybe we can jointly create an educational program to use before your people arrive."

Lisa's shoulders relaxed. This had been her idea. They seemed to be coming to an equitable solution, and she had fulfilled an important role in this negotiation.

The Secretary continued, "However, sir, there is another related issue. Over the last several months, Rathas has increased the number of missionaries, sending them in larger groups. Confrontations are frequent. Why have you been increasing the problem?"

"We simply want to help others to Elláh, Secretary." Something about the ambassador's words did not ring true. He twitched his head in such a way he seemed to be hiding something.

"Does it help others for you to increase your military presence on our border?"

"You worry about where we train our military? Pah! That is our business, not yours."

"When you 'train' your military close to our border, and also create clashes in our streets, we cannot help but be suspicious of your motives. Lisa, would you please show the special video we found?"

Lisa's shoulders tightened up again. Things seemed to be coming to agreement, and now the secretary had brought up more sensitive accusations. She keyed the video into the holo display. All three watched while a group of missionaries provoked some protestors. Shouting transformed to shoving. Then one protestor swung a fist at a missionary. The response by the missionary was astonishing, a practiced personal combat move that left the protestor flat on the ground gasping for breath. The other protestors backed away from the missionary in fear.

"Ambassador," said Lisa, "why is this missionary trained in military-style bodily mayhem? How does that 'help others' in a missionary group?"

"Help others? How can you ask? This man defended himself and simply left the attacker on the ground. Your people staked our daughter out to die in the mountains. How can you equate these actions?"

Nintuk stepped in. "Can we ask, at least, for you to select your missionaries with more care? To choose those who will be more peaceful?"

"Peaceful? What is peaceful about trying to punch a missionary?"

Nintuk's request became the final straw for Grufhand. He would not be appeased and rose to his feet.

"If you cannot protect our missionaries, and if you continue to blame us for the attacks by your people, we have little further to talk about." He shook an angry finger at Nintuk. "Our bishop's daughter will be avenged!"

He stalked out of the conference room.

Though the secretary assigned no blame, Lisa was devastated. She brooded on how she might have handled it differently.

➮✷➭

That evening, still reeling from the diplomatic failure, Lisa explored the eight-hundred-year history of colonization. She wanted to get her mind away from her work, and she needed more information to talk Chris out of his fantasy. What she found made her sit back from the holohaptic display in alarm.

This is what Chris wants to put us into? Forty percent of the ships never arrive, and when they do, over half of the ten thousand colonists might die?

While she kept reviewing the numbers in shock, Chris came home. He filled the apartment with his energy.

"Wow, Lisa! This whole colony thing gets better and better. I took time off this afternoon to meet with the colony leaders. You should see what—"

She spun in her chair. "You did what? You met with the colony leaders without me? I thought we were going to talk more about this."

"Yes, of course we are." Chris' head jerked back. "But we need information, hon, that's what you said. We can't talk about it in the dark. That's what I was doing. Getting information."

"So, you go traipsing off without me? What about partnership?" She knew she was being unfair. He really was just getting information. But today had already been too much. "We decided years ago we would make any major decisions together."

Chris sat in his easy chair, perched on the edge and facing her. He spread his hands in a conciliatory way.

"You're right," he said. "We did. But you're upset. What's going on, Lisa?"

She slumped. Tears stung the back of her eyes. "It's been a bad day. Our negotiations with Rathas broke down today. The ambassador walked out in anger, threatening vengeance."

"Oh, I'm so sorry. I know you've been counting on that to go well. This was over the missionaries, right? We still had those clowns bothering our work site today. Standing on the far side of the street waving their holy books at us. I wanted to punch them out, but we ignored them instead."

"Oh, please stay away from them. We don't need another incident."

"We're doing our work. It's up to them to stay away." He paused. "So, what happens next with your negotiations?"

"I don't know. The secretary doesn't know. It's as bad a situation as we've ever had. She can't understand why the ambassador doesn't acknowledge the cultural differences. It's almost like he's looking for excuses to fail. She says she's never before faced such a total breakdown and doesn't know what to do."

Chris rose from his chair and knelt beside her, wrapping her in a strong hug.

Oh, I do love this man. She let the tears fall on his shoulder.

They selected dinner together, the autocater producing two dishes of steaming goodness. She had a lemon-infused chicken quiche, while he chose a brolsteak and veggies. Over dinner, she told him more about the failed negotiations. She was relieved he simply listened and nodded in the right places. She knew he had more news about the colony effort. He kept his excitement under wraps, though, and let her talk.

When her stories of politics wound down, she turned him loose. "Thanks for being here for me, Chris. Now, tell me. What did you learn about the colony?"

His eyes lit up, and he sat straighter in his chair.

I love watching his passion. I just wish it were directed at something better for us.

"They already have a lot of information. The search team was on-planet for ten weeks. No one's ever done that before. Until now, the transit times were so long, colonizers only had pictures and probes. I actually got to meet some of those who were there. They say it's a beautiful place, and they can't wait to get back. They created a beach-head, and everyone on the team made it back safely.

"It's a huge challenge, but an exciting one that's right up my alley. Most of the problems have to do with plants, and that's what I've been doing all my life. I know, I've only been doing landscaping with Verdant plants, and I'm not a biologist. But they have scientists as part of their team. I can implement the strategies they design. We'll be terraforming the planet!"

Lisa waited her turn, giving him the same courtesy he'd given her. When he finally wound down from his excitement, she asked, "Have you looked into the history of colonization?"

"Not really. I know it's been done successfully as many as fifteen or twenty times."

She nodded. "I looked into it this afternoon."

"That's great. You're getting interested in this after all."

"Well..." she scrunched a shoulder. "I got some information. But what I found isn't good."

"In what way?"

"People have launched twenty-six colony ships since old Earth. Ten of them disappeared without a trace. Of the so-called successful colonies, sometimes over half the people died while getting the world started. Thousands of people. And no one has tried to do it for over three centuries." She looked into his eyes. "Chris, that's a huge level of risk. Are you willing to gamble our lives for this dream?"

He didn't answer. She watched him digest the news. His face showed shock at first, then he slumped and his lips got thin. He shook his head, eyes flashing with the anger she recognized all too well.

"You're trying to kill my dream, aren't you?" His voice was shaking. "Those statistics are centuries old, nothing like what we can do today. You just want to keep us from grabbing the opportunity."

This wasn't the reaction she expected. She extended a conciliatory hand. "That's not what I'm trying—"

He jumped to his feet and paced. "Technology has moved on in three hundred years. Then, the transit was years long. Now, it only takes six months to get to Bluewater. Those statistics are from a completely different situation." His voice was increasingly heated.

"I'm trying to look at it objectively." She backed off, wanting to reconcile. "We can figure it out together."

He shook his head angrily. "No. I came home all excited about what I'd found, and you're throwing foam on the fire. I can't deal with this." He swept out the door, not quite slamming it.

Lisa crumpled into herself.

❧ ✳ ☙

The next morning, she left early for work. Chris had come home late and slipped into bed without touching her. They hadn't spoken. In eight years, this was the first time they'd ever gone to bed angry.

Lisa and Secretary Nintuk strategized most of the morning, looking for something that might bring the ambassador back to the table. Lisa felt dead inside. It wasn't only the fight with Chris. She felt like a failure in every aspect of her life.

"Perhaps we can offer to control interactions with the missionaries, Secretary," she offered at one point.

Nintuk nodded. "We can try. I'll make the offer. Why don't you see what our police can do to track the missionaries and regulate who meets with them and where."

Over the next hour, Nintuk traded difficult messages with the ambassador, and Lisa followed up on her idea with the police. She reminded them of the international case of kidnapping and attempted murder, and they began to see the necessity when she talked about possible war with Rathas.

The idea was working. The police reluctantly agreed they could monitor and protect the missionaries. Ambassador Grufhand acknowledged it might be worthwhile to continue talking.

Late in the morning, a research assistant stepped into the room where the two were working. Lisa saw he carried bad news, and her heart sank.

"There's been another incident, Secretary."

Nintuk looked up and took a deep breath. "Tell us, Alcan."

"Missionaries intruded on a work site this morning and sparked a fight."

Nintuk let go her breath. "We can't seem to get a break, can we? How bad was it?"

"Two of the missionaries were hurt and are in the hospital. A landscaping team beat them off the site with shovels."

Lisa felt sudden alarm. "What landscaping team? Who did this?"

The assistant paused to check his InfoNet implant for details. "Westhof Landscape Wares. Oh, I'm sorry, ma'am. Your husband's company."

Lisa sagged, supporting her forehead with her palm. *I can't believe it. This just sucks. We're making progress, and now this.*

"Your husband, Lisa?" said her boss. "I just promised the ambassador you and I could manage the situation."

Lisa nodded into her hand, tears welling. "Yes, ma'am." She wiped her eyes and looked up. "How bad is the damage?"

"It's bad. The ambassador won't believe anything now. He'll likely report complete failure back to Rathas. I don't know what they'll do."

❧ ✳ ☙

"You don't understand, do you?" Lisa shouted at Chris on the street outside their favorite lunch place. "I had an idea that was bringing the ambassador back, and your little *incident* smashed it!"

"Those damned religious freaks walked all over our finished gardens!" he shouted back. "Yeah, they were trying to be peaceful, while shoving their stupid books in our faces. But they uprooted flowers we'd already planted."

"But did your people have to *beat* them with *shovels*?"

"They wouldn't leave! We told them to back up. To get off the gardens. A couple of the guys pushed them away with their shovels. They kept coming, and wouldn't stop. 'Read our book,' they shouted. 'Learn to love Elláh.' Senseless stuff. Yeah, my guys got hot under the collar when the freaks started pushing back. That was when pushing became swinging."

Lisa stopped shouting and held up a palm. She didn't want to fight, she wanted comfort. Her dreams were shattered. She went limp and stared at her own feet.

Her job was in crisis. The secretary had asked her to come up with another idea. She had nothing. Her head was spinning with shame and she couldn't think. She wanted to run away.

"I'm sorry, Chris." She shook her head sadly, still looking at the pavement.

"Ah, I'm sorry, too. Maybe I could have controlled the guys better."

"I need your help. Let's get lunch, sit down, and talk. Perhaps you can give me an idea."

"I can try. What do you need?"

They ordered food and took it to a sidewalk table. She picked at some greens with her fork without eating, then shoved it away.

"I have to go back after lunch with some new idea. Their culture is so different than ours. They think assaulting you with a book in your face is perfectly okay. How can we get some control?"

"We could just kick out the missionaries."

She gave him an irritated grump. "Not helpful. That's where we started."

"Perhaps require some training for their missionaries about our laws?"

She nodded. "Maybe. We talked about something like that. Anything else?"

Chris raised his hands in a helpless shrug. "I don't know."

Their implants interrupted the conversation with an internal alarm for important news. The café became quiet while everyone stopped to listen. The broadcast voice was filled with excitement and danger.

Tileus News Network, Breaking News! Rathas has declared war on Tileus. Before departing from Thad City, the Rathas ambassador delivered a declaration of war. Within minutes of the declaration, Khubar f'Elláh forces swept over the Gortooth Mountains to surround the city of Uptown. Fighting is intense in the foothills while Rathas soldiers are even now seizing key installations in Uptown.

The InfoNet exploded with activity. People in the street shouted at each other. The crowds moved quickly, casual individuals finding sudden purpose.

Lisa sat frozen in her chair. War. People fighting and dying. *How far will it go? Here in Thad City? How long?* Then a further thought struck her. *The Khubar f'Elláh forces were "training" on the border, ready to move. Did Rathas plan this all along?*

Their entire world had changed in a flash. Diplomacy now shifted to defense. Tileus would be calling people up for military service.

She saw no recovery for her in this. Everyone at Outside Affairs would remember the diplomat—and her husband—who precipitated a war while negotiating. A raw lump rose in her throat. Her breath wheezed and she couldn't seem to get enough air.

Her voice cracked when she spoke. "I'm ruined, Chris."

He seemed to be as shocked as she was.

"I'll never get another post," she said. "They'll blackball me from advancement. What do I do? Where can I go?"

Her mind raced. *Back to elected office? Practice private law? Perhaps slide into obscurity, trudging the road of destiny without a compass.*

Chris' eyes were alight with excitement, and a smile was spreading across his face.

Abruptly, she realized why he was excited—and his answer was her solution, too. She couldn't serve in Tileus, but the colony ship was a new opportunity ready and waiting. Her shoulders relaxed. Chris was right. She could use her experience to grow in the colony.

All Fall Down

Finally, we return again to the islands of Winter and the stories of Elder Narnit Concordi, the "peaceful man who wasn't." The world of Verdant has moved on. War was narrowly averted between Prime and Tileus, but resentments continue. Now Rathas has attacked Tileus, and a colony effort hopes to spawn a new world that can start over. Meanwhile, Narnit continues his lifelong mission to teach spiritual peace to the children, hoping to affect the world.

The conflict mentioned herein between Verdant Prime and Tileus, and how it was solved with the transpath, is the subject of my novel Not Like Us, the first book in the Empathic Humanity series.

"Sotal, take turns," yells the teacher, Mers. Klestra, to a ten-year-old boy on the swings. Sotal seems big for his age, with a permanent sneer on his face. She turns to me. "Elder Concordi, that is one child desperately in need of your lessons."

"I'm watching him," I say. "Perhaps I can help him."

I teach spiritual peace to the children of Winter. Today, I am at Haven Tribe, watching them play during recess, a small school with thirty-five children ranging in age from six to fifteen. It's good to be in Haven, where we meet annually for Conclave. Winter doesn't have anything resembling a capitol, but this tribe is closest.

Sotal scowls at the teacher. He lets a girl take one of the swings. When she is seated, he pushes her too hard, too suddenly, harder each time she swings past. She screams in fear when the swing carries her higher than she wants.

Klestra moves in and shouts, "Stop, Sotal. Get away."

He heaves the girl one more time. Losing her grip, she flies through the air to land on the hard sand, skinning her knees and hands. Her screams change from fear to pain, and she lies crumpled on the ground, holding her knees and crying. Klestra steps in to comfort the girl.

The boy clenches his fists. He glares at the teacher as if to say he can bully her, too, if she interferes with him.

Why does every class have a bully? I've been teaching harmony for over twenty years and still don't understand why they are so prevalent. Is it endemic to human nature? Maybe we will never escape it. At times, the inevitability overwhelms me.

Then I think of what I've accomplished—how many children's lives I've changed, how the country of Winter has been affected—and I believe my life worthwhile.

I can change this Sotal, as I have done others. He is already watching me, likely wondering what I will do about him. I am a large and powerful-looking man, which make my peacefulness all the more a contrast. People tell me I present an air of controlled strength. Sotal may be ready to battle me as he does Mers. Klestra, so I take a different approach than one of power. I catch his eye and cock my head with a raised eyebrow. He sets his jaw at me, yet I can also see his uncertainty. He's heard my lesson but doesn't yet know what to make of me. I gesture an invitation for him to join me on the bench. Amid the crying of the girl and his ignoring the teacher's admonishments, he is curious enough to come.

"Good morning, Sotal," I say, my voice calm yet strong.

"What's good about it?"

I nod, acknowledging his viewpoint, and indicate the bench beside me.

"Why would I want to sit with you?"

"Because standing in front of me feels like me judging you. Sitting beside me makes us equal, and we can talk as friends."

His face shows distrust, but he decides to sit.

I chat as if with a friend. "Before recess, I talked about how I used to boss my classmates around. I felt powerful, Sotal. I felt better than them. I liked those feelings."

He watches me with cautious eyes, his fists clenched but uncertain where my words are going.

"I had a few followers in that time. Do you have some followers?"

Sotal juts out his jaw and jerks a curt nod. He points to three boys who stand apart from the rest, watching us.

I look at them and see sycophants—and next year's bullies.

Turning back to him with a gentle nod, I say, "So, you have followers. Now, can you show me your friends? There is a difference, you know. Or are you as lonely as I was?"

His eyes are a dark gate into a murky inner world. I can see, through that gate, he knows these feelings. True to form, however, he cannot acknowledge the truth even to himself.

"I'm not lonely," he scoffs. "I can have all the friends I want. And you can leave me alone." He jumps up with a glare, hocks a gob and spits it at my feet, and runs back into the playground.

I hardly expected more at this point. From my experience, he'll be a tough case, yet I have laid a first foundation.

How many times have I done this? I smile to myself. Yet I want to do more, to affect more people than one child at a time. These days, I seek a larger challenge.

A long-range aircar interrupts our recess, passing low overhead with an intermittent whine. Such cars are unusual in the islands of Winter, and their repellor drive is usually smooth. It flies toward the communal hall. I know why it is here: to change the world.

I catch my breath, because the car has deep burn marks scarring its side. Seeing them, I hear the ragged rhythm of its drive differently: it is damaged; someone has fired on the car.

I jump to my feet. As an Elder, I must do what I can. I ask Mers. Klestra to resume her normal lessons, and I run toward the meeting hall. My breath is quick and my heart pounds—not just from the unaccustomed exercise, but from fear of what this battered aircar might mean to Winter.

❧ ✻ ☙

I am down to a fast walk by the time I get to the town square. Ahead is the national meeting hall. The aircar sits in the middle of the square, smoke rising from the burns in its side. I crinkle my nose at the acrid scent of burned insulation and hot metal. An agitated clot of people has gathered around the car. Most of the Haven Elders are there, along with others I do not know, some in unusually bright clothing.

My friend Elder Anton Radu is there, and I hurry to him. "Anton, what has happened?"

He turns in surprise. "Narnit. I thought you were teaching today."

"I saw the aircar go by, and I left the class to the teacher." I gesture to the damaged car. "Who did this?"

"We're just finding out. Let me introduce you." He turns to an older man who wears clashing bright pink and orange. "Coordinator Erdogan, this is Elder Narnit Concordi who may be able to help."

The man smiles and holds up his palm in greeting. "Good to meet you, Elder Concordi. Please, be calling me Deniz."

"And I am Narnit," I say, raising my own palm.

Everything about this man is different. I know he comes from the world of Brightness, a trip of three months, with an offer to work together with Verdant to colonize a new world. His clothes are like a surreal painting. He speaks Standard with a heavy accent and strange syntax. Yet there is an authority to him that draws me.

"What happened to your ship, Deniz? Here in Winter, we practice peace."

He shudders. Apparently, he is still rattled by the incident.

"We did come here directly from the city of Praise, in Rathas. They did do this as we did leave." He waves his hand at the aircar. "Our message be one of hope for all humans. Those people not want hope."

Anton places a hand on my shoulder. "I introduced you two because Narnit has been teaching spiritual peace to our children. His work has had an effect."

I smile and nod. "I have changed some young bullies, yes. My teaching helps Winter stay at peace. We have many adults now who follow a spiritual path to keep our tribes centered on the things of life that matter."

Deniz gives a bitter chuckle. "That will not fix my aircar, I be sure." He thinks further. "But we may share some goals. We also seek a way of peace for our new world to be replacing the violence we be knowing."

"History says it's important. Humanity has destroyed so many worlds in our never-ending cycle of war, and there are only three left."

"Yes. Our world of Brightness be very far along that cycle. Our end seems near. I must hope we launch our colony before we end our world."

"I believe Brightness and Verdant were founded near the same time," I say, "and we are also in great danger. Last year, our countries of Prime and Tileus were within a brol's eyelash of throwing world-wrecking weapons across the Channel at each other. This year, Rathas has sent its religious Khubar f'Elláh troops across the mountains into Tileus. People are fighting and killing each other as we speak. I'm not surprised Rathas fired on you. They've become very warlike."

I touch Anton's arm. "And it's getting worse, as my friend can tell you. Even here in Winter, we retaliate politically by withholding shipments of fish. I want to expand my mission beyond our country. I want to teach peace to the nations."

Anton nods with a serious look. "It is worse. There was a riot at Indie Tribe last year that killed two people. Right here in Haven Tribe, we have someone we've not been able to find doing disruptions. Graffiti on the walls, torn-up gardens, stalking in the night."

I raise a hand as if to say, *See? Here we are.*

Deniz looks back at his aircar. "Be you have someone who can fix our car?"

Anton says, "We do. We'll have a mechanic here shortly. In the meantime, we have a place for you and your team to refresh yourselves."

Deniz turns back to me. "Will be you coming to our presentation this evening? Regardless of this setback, we still wish to invite the people of Winter."

"I wouldn't miss it for the world." I chuckle. "For all three worlds. Starting another planet for humanity? It would be a new beginning. A chance to do things differently. Perhaps we could indeed build a world of peace, if only we could avoid taking our conflicts with us."

"Ah, but be you know of the technology we found right here on Verdant? They tell us this be the technology that stopped the war between Prime and Tileus."

"I heard there was something—"

"Tileus developed it. They call it the transpath, and we will demonstrate it later this evening, after our presentation about colonizing the new world. It be an empathy field that lets people feel each other's emotions. Under the transpath, it be impossible to lie and difficult to justify destructive behavior."

My eyes go to the hills and forests surrounding Haven, trying to imagine such a thing. If true, it offers a possibility. *Only a truly broken person could hate others with such a perception.* I think how poorly we humans communicate with each other. If such a device is real, what magic might it perform?

And yet... "Why didn't it stop the war with Rathas?"

Anton answered with an acerbic tone. "Because the religious Rathas people refused to subject themselves to it. They'd rather fight a violent holy war."

Human nature, again. The thing I battle in every tribe. Yet I do win skirmishes in my own way toward changing humanity.

I ask of Deniz, "Are you planning to take this transpath with you to the new world?"

"That be the plan. We did want to colonize a new start, but did have little idea how to prevent the destructive cycle. Then we did find this transpath in Tileus. It seems to be a beam of hope."

❧ ✳ ☙

That evening, I weave my way through a crowd on the steps of the meeting hall, listening to snippets of conversation as I pass. Most are excited about the colony ship. Some are interested in the transpath. I touch the spirit icon on the doorframe as I enter, silently praying for guidance. Inside the meeting hall, I go to the reserved seating at the front for Elders. Anton is seated on the dais as a host.

Over the next two hours, Deniz Erdogan and his company dazzle my dreams. The Brightness people have developed their plans into near-reality. The colony ship is already under construction in orbit around their world. They will carry fifteen thousand colonists from all three of the remaining worlds. A survey crew has already been to the new world—Bluewater, they call it with enthusiasm—and returned with more complete information than any colony ship has ever had. Challenges exist, as always, but the colony people have ways to meet them.

The offer intrigues me.

No, it more than intrigues; it entices. My lifelong mission to spread peace in Winter has filled me with joy. I've left behind a legacy of adults and children who look at life through a broad spyglass of harmony. Others are also now teaching my message. Perhaps this is the new challenge I've been seeking. *Can I help a new world start with a better beginning?* I think, tapping my fingers on the arm of my seat. *That would be a legacy.*

Nearing the end of the presentation, Deniz changes tack.

"We will be here for the next several days to answer questions and take applications. Before we end this meeting, however, we will give you a demonstration of a new technology that was developed here on Verdant. We will take it to Bluewater. This 'transpath' gives me hope, as leader of the colony, that we can end the destructive cycle humanity did be practicing on every world."

The crowd murmurs in anticipation. This is a boon added to the excitement of the colonization. Some are here just for this demonstration, because they'd heard of the device.

"Be preparing yourselves," Deniz continues, "for a new experience. It may seem intrusive at first, but you will quickly find it astonishing." He signals an associate at the side of the stage. "You can control the effects as they happen by choosing where to look. If they seem too overwhelming, be closing your eyes to cut them off."

I am watching the presenter as they turn on the transpath. Gradually, I sense emotions that are not mine: enthusiasm, determination, hopefulness. I share some of these, but what I sense has the character of a different person. They come from the speaker in an empathic connection. I feel what he feels. My eyebrows rise at the intensity of it. It is obvious the man truly believes in his mission, in the eventual success of the colony, and in the positive effect this transpath will have.

I look at my friend Anton seated on the dais. The empathic connection shifts, and now I feel Anton's astonishment and amazement. His eyes dart around the room, sampling person after person, and I sense his desire to learn more about the transpath, to experience more. Anton looks at me and our connection doubles. I perceive he feels my own excitement about this prospect, and I experience his compassion for others.

I become aware of the possibilities in this room. Understand each other's emotions? Communicate with a deeper level of empathy? *How astonishing.* Anton said it was nearly impossible to lie, and he might be right. Only a true psychopath could conceal duplicity when their emotions are on display like this. I look eagerly around the room, sampling the excitement, the amazement, the wonder in individuals, knowing beyond any doubt that what I feel from them is true. We could create a completely new kind of colony, based on this level of understanding.

Can it be possible to change humanity?

After twenty years of teaching harmony to children, I feel a new purpose. This is the challenge I have sought.

I want to be part of creating this new world that offers such a connection.

∽﹡∽

The next morning, Anton walks to school with me. The air seems fresher, the sun brighter. Trees on the surrounding hillsides laugh in the fresh breeze, flashing their multicolored leaves with the sheer joy of life.

"I took an application last night, Anton. I may join this colony."

"What?" he says, stumbling. "You would leave your mission in Winter?"

"The training here in Winter continues, my friend, and others are carrying it on. I want to work on something larger. Starting a new world with the promise of the transpath would be a purpose of great value."

"At your age? What can you offer the colony that would be useful to them? And what about the long trip?"

"I can survive six months of transit. I'm only forty-seven—not that old. And I can teach. Not just peace, but I can teach the basic subjects that all children need to learn."

"And you think that's more important than your work here? Those others who follow your footsteps are not as good. You are unique, my friend. No one else can do what you do here. Your mission is important to Winter and to our world."

His argument gives me a moment of doubt, but I set it aside with a light chuckle.

"I'm sure they'll do fine. Here, I teach the children for two days at a time. There, I can teach an entire world as it grows."

"But your children grow to affect all of us. You already teach this entire world, Narnit."

I snort. "No. I only teach within this one country, and it's too slow."

He apparently doesn't know what to say to that; I'd closed a door. We walk the rest of the way in companionable silence, two old friends mulling separate thoughts. When we near the school yard, I open a window to him.

"It will be some months before we part, Anton. I'll continue to teach peace as much as I can until then."

He smiles sadly and nods. "We'll see each other in these months. Teach well today." We raise palms and go our own ways.

The morning moves swiftly. Each school gives me two days to teach "history," my messages of spiritual harmony infusing it. It is a time of rest for the usual teacher; Mers. Klestra sits at the back of the room. On this second morning, I teach the students the history of humankind among the stars—the exhilarating story of how we left Earth and founded colonies, how those colonies sometimes founded further colonies, and how our planet of Verdant was seeded from One Hope. I teach about the cycle each world goes through, spreading around the planet and fractionating (yes, I even teach this word to the children) into different cultures. I describe how the four countries here on Verdant came to be and how they differ.

Then my lesson turns darker.

"As the cultures separate," I say, "they begin to mistrust each other. We humans are gregarious; we gather with people who are like us. But we are also tribal, which means we are wary of those who are different. Suspicion leads to conflict, and wars happen. That was always true on old Earth. With our advanced technology, though, it has reached a point where wars destroy our planets."

The import of the lesson never ceases to take my breath away. I pause before continuing.

"We humans have destroyed fourteen worlds. Only three remain. We are close to destroying this one we live on. Just like Branch...and One Hope...and Earth...and eleven others."

My holo track at their desks shows images of the destruction of worlds. I see the shock on their faces. Klestra has heard it before. I glance at her and see sadness like my own.

"It doesn't have to be this way, class," I say. "You hold the future in your hands, and you can change it. Yesterday, I told you my personal story, how I used to be a terrible bully, and how I became a peaceful man through spiritual growth—"

My lesson is disrupted when a disheveled young man, well past school age, bursts into the classroom. He rushes to an open space, recklessly slashing a sword back and forth.

For a moment, I think *What sort of playacting is this? And where did he get such an antique?*

Then I realize his eyes are wild, his motions jerky, his hair long and unkempt. Spittle hangs from his lip. A stench of unwashed clothing accompanies him. This is no playacting, and a man with a sword can kill. I gasp.

"School!" he screams. "Bad school. Teaches us to hate each other. Fills us with knowledge about how to build weapons."

Children jump to their feet screaming.

He shouts again. "Sit down! Shut up and listen." The sword flashes through the air near the students, a silver snake ready to strike. The children flop into their seats; several start crying.

He rushes to the teacher in the back of the room. "Teachers. Mongers of hate. Imbuing young minds with destruction to come." He puts the tip of the sword against Klestra's chest.

She turns pale and shrinks back.

Then he spins and waves the sword in my direction. "Two teachers in one room. Double-teaming the poor kids with your messages." Before Klestra can move, he has the sword tip back at her breast. "Once, just once, we can do something about this."

My mind races. At first, I don't know what to do. The children are helpless. Klestra is frozen in fear. It seems to be up to me. My teeth grind, hating this tangible symbol of my sometimes failure. Anger rises in me. I want to charge across the room and strip the weapon out of his hands. I want to beat him to the floor with my bare hands.

I want to run away to the colonizers and get off this terrible world, away from people like this. I want things to be peaceful as I have taught.

First, I want help. I use my implant to send an emergency comms call.

It will be some minutes before they arrive. What will this deranged man do in the meantime? My pulse pounds in my ears at this violent interruption to my lesson.

This man may have been one of the students to whom I taught spiritual peace some years before. Obviously, it didn't take. I glance at Sotal, the boy's future flashing before me. He leans forward eagerly to see what this man will do.

Sotal's reaction triggers me. I jump to my feet, about to rush at the sword-wielding man, anger filling me.

The man spins to face me, the point of his sword wavering in my direction. "Don't you dare," he shouts, and he lurches in my direction.

I stop. The students are transfixed.

This is not the man you are, Elder Narnit Concordi.

I am right to chide myself. This is not what Elder Pacaem taught me. I take a deep breath and lower my eyes to center myself, heedless of what the man may do. *Thank you, spirits, for the opportunity to teach.* When I raise my eyes again, I am at peace.

The man stops his rush, apparently sensing something different in me. "Who are you?" he demands, yet he seems uncertain. The tip of the sword is now only a meter from my own skin.

"I am Narnit Concordi, the peaceful man who wasn't." My heart pounds. At peace or not, it is still a dangerous situation and anything could happen.

He squints at me. Slow recognition colors his eyes. "I remember you. Years ago, in High Glade Tribe. You taught at my school when I was nine."

I smile at him, hoping my smile doesn't seem as forced as it feels. "Do you remember what I taught?"

Confusion seems to fill him. His shoulders slump and the sword tip droops. His eyes dart around the room, unfocused. He shakes his head. "A story. About a bully who stopped being a bully."

"Me," I whisper.

He gathers himself again, stepping forward to put the sword at my chest. "I'm not a bully," he screams.

"And neither am I," I say, standing my ground. "Not anymore. And yet..." I wave my hand toward the children frozen in fear, some crying. "...someone has bullied these children."

He looks at the class and his sword tip falls again.

He looks back at me, cocking his head in puzzlement. "And you still teach?"

"I do." Another deep breath, sadness filling me. "And sometimes I fail."

Two tribal warders rush into the room. They cover the distance to this troubled man in a moment. He raises the sword, alarm in his eyes, but they are too quick for him. It's over in an instant. The sword clatters to the floor as they force his arms behind his back.

"Thank you," I say to them. "Please take him outside. Mers. Klestra can tell you what happened while I speak to the children."

They agree and bustle him out. Klestra goes with them. I see her hands shaking as she passes me. I reach out to touch her shoulder.

"I'll release the children," I say.

She nods with a shuddered breath and goes.

My heart slows. An after-reaction of adrenaline washes through me and I am dizzy for a moment. Then I carefully pick up the sword by one end.

The students' eyes are on me as I dangle the killing weapon from thumb and forefinger. I look to the ceiling, gathering my thoughts.

"It's a sword, class. Though it's older, it's very much like a needle gun or a blaster or a harpoon. It's also akin to a spaceship filled with deadly, world-wrecking bombs. All of these are devices designed for one purpose: to kill. It would be healthier for us all if humans never had any of them.

I drop the sword. It clatters to the floor, then is silent. I study it, then turn back to the class.

"And yet...look at it, lying there. Impotent. It does nothing on its own." I pause and lock eyes with several students in turn. "None of the weapons we use do anything on their own. We are the ones who use them. It is the hate in our hearts that kills. It is the anger, the resentment, the jealousy, the fear. Yesterday, I told you my story. Each of you must create your own stories for the future. We can continue to destroy our human worlds, or we can learn a spiritual life."

I stop again, thinking what else to say. They hang on my silence. The youngest have stopped whimpering. The older ones listen with interest.

"You...can learn to live a spiritual life." My words are for all the class, yet my eyes are on Sotal as I say it. He looks cautious, bothered in some deep way.

I nod to myself, pick up the sword, and walk to the door. "Class dismissed."

„ ✷ ‟

Outside, Mers. Klestra and I talk with the warders. I give them the sword. They know this man. They have suspected him of the violence plaguing Haven Tribe, but had not yet gathered enough evidence. He is a sad case, a man with problems that have overwhelmed him.

The children stream by with curious looks, some still frightened and others thoughtful. Casually, two by three, they leave the school yard until only one is left sitting in the picnic area.

The warders take the man away. Klestra goes back into the classroom, still shaking but apparently calm enough to prepare for the next day.

With a quiet smile and a bit of hope, I step to the picnic table where the one boy still sits.

"Hello, Sotal. Are you waiting for me?" I sit beside him.

His attitude is still belligerent, cocky, but with a tinge of uncertainty. He tilts his face up to me. "How did you do that, Elder?"

"Do what, Sotal?"

"I saw you. Your jaw was clenched. Your fists were tight. You were angry, ready to fight. But then you stood up...and it went away."

I nod. "That's right."

"You got peace again." He looks down. "I can't do that. When I'm angry, I have to beat someone. I would have run him through with that sword."

His words had become strident, but he pauses before continuing in a quieter voice. "You were right, yesterday. I'm not always happy with what I do. It just makes me feel powerful."

Warmth suffuses my body. My breath catches. As I release it, my shoulders relax.

He looks up again at me. "I want to know how to do what you did." He juts his chin. "You can show me."

The boy is still filled with aggression. It will take time and effort, just as it did with me. Yet I know that I have touched another child, that he is on a path to becoming a good man.

And his request—almost a demand—renews my hope in what I do.

I could go with the transpath to create a new world. I could, but I won't. The transpath is here on Verdant already. With it, I can expand my mission to more than this one country. I can use it to fix this world.

Acknowledgements

These stories started over two years ago with the vision I described in the Introduction. I foresaw a bleak future for humanity and I wanted to illuminate life with disaster looming—and yet do so from the human viewpoint. That vision has not changed. I wrote eight of these stories, including the keystone "The Peaceful Man Who Wasn't," but then "Duty to Society" came along. The totalitarian society of Verdant Prime had so many interesting themes that the story grew to over ten thousand words, rather long for a short story. Phil Walker, the leader of my local writing group (*The Scroll* and seventeen other books), suggested it deserved to be a novel. So the short stories went on the back burner while I wrote *Not Like Us*. The remaining six stories came after the novel.

Even though writing is a solitary task, we do not write alone. Every one of these stories has been reviewed and helped in detail by Phil's group, the Working Writers' Workshop. We use a powerful process of both written critiques (and changes) and reading aloud for further critiques (and changes). The process has had a marvelous impact on my writing as a whole. The members included Keith Abbott (*Lights Out*), Susan DeLay, Paul Eberz (the acclaimed *Smoke* series), Rich Friedman, Shelley Jones, Jack O'Brien (*The Roundabout Way*), and Carey Winters. I thank them all for their many insights.

Most of these stories also got critiques from the online Other Worlds Writers' Workshop run by Michele Combs and including

Jason Andress, Wendy Edsall-Kerwin, Irene Fields, Meaghan Haughian, Jessica Hawkins, Emily Renk Hawthorne, EJ Heijnis, Gregg Jansen, and Harry Whomersley. Of all the OWWW friends, however, my special thanks go to Clark Sodersten, who somehow manages to critique every posted story within days of its post.

Mark Newhouse (the award-winning *Devil's Bookkeepers* trilogy) gave amazingly significant help on "Fishing Hands," raising it to award-winning level.

But as always, my greatest gratitude goes to my wife Beth, who supports me and puts up with all those hours when I am buried in the laptop.

About the Author

Iconoclast, polymath, and author, Doc Honour has been a US Navy pilot, an international leader in systems engineering, and a successful entrepreneur. He is the author of *Not Like Us*, the first book in the Empathic Humanity series. He holds a PhD from the University of South Australia in systems engineering. Doc has led teams of up to 50 people to build complex systems; some of the technologies in this book reflect his real-life experience. He has taught nearly 500 short courses to help others learn to do what he has done. Doc Honour's short story Fishing Hands won a top (Gold) award in the 2022 Royal Palm Literary Awards of the Florida Writers Association. Born on Guam, he's lived in 34 different places. These days, he lives in Florida with his wife and a willful Australian Shepherd named Chip.